THE FACE OF MY

FROM SEA AND SKYE BOOK ONE
JORDAN VICTORIA

THE FACE OF MY KILLER

JORDAN VICTORIA

Book Cover and Interior Formatting: Katie Jaspersen @ K. Jaspersen Designs
Cover Art: Lea Digitartz
Editor: Kevin Barnes
Proof Reader: Kat F
Publisher: Jordan Victoria Press
Sensitivity Reader: Aaron Hunt

ISBN: 978-1-0676688-1-5 (Paperback)

For those who needed to be set free
before they could see the truth.

CONTENT WARNINGS

- Explicit sexual content for mature audiences only (18+)
- Undiagnosed PTSD
- Diagnosed cPTSD
- Flashbacks/nightmares
- Depression
- Panic attacks
- Anxiety
- Blackouts
- Gaslighting
- Situational Mutism
- Self-harm (hot teaspoon to skin and knife pricking finger)
- Kidnapping
- Murder (on page detailed)
- Physical violence (a couple of incidents between the MCs)
- Rage Incidents caused by emotional dysregulation (both MCs)
- Physical abuse (detailed on page, **not** between MCs)
- Sexual abuse (lead-up is detailed, but will fade to black, **not** between MCs)
- Grooming (does not go into detail)
- Emotional abuse (**not** between MCs)
- Psychological manipulation (**not** between MCs)
- Arson
- Dead animals (details of rotting carcasses)
- Death of a parent (on page memory in detail)

This book is set in the United Kingdom and is written in British English.

ONE

THEO

I sit bolt upright in a cold sweat, gasping for air, digging my nails into the puckered scars that circle my ankles. I squeeze my eyes tightly shut, waiting for my heart to stop trying to punch its way out of my chest. The room is dark, and I already know without having to look that I'm up way too early. I wipe tears from my face with the back of my hand and reach for my phone. Squinting, I read a text from my cousin.

ISLA

> Theo, remember Richard's family are coming up for the wedding, and you promised they could stay at yours.

I groan, pulling the duvet back, and roll out of bed. I had, in fact, *not* remembered agreeing to let her fiancé's family stay in my house. It's hard enough trying to remember what day it is, let alone keep track of Isla's wedding guests. I slide my suitcase out from the top of the wardrobe and shove as much as I can into it. When I try to zip it up, my hands shake and my vision doubles as brain fog sets in. I fumble the zip, and kick the suitcase with my bare foot.

"Shit!" Pain shoots through my toe and up to my ankle.

Fuck, that was stupid.

I collapse back onto the bed, toe throbbing. The world spins for a moment, and I wait for it to pass before rolling to the side and dragging my body off the bed for the second time this morning. I grab the zipper and try again, tugging it roughly until it closes, then head to the harbour.

The day has barely started and I've already had enough.

"THERE'S THE BOSS MAN!" Harry shouts as I get out of my car. I grab my sunglasses and give an awkward wave as I walk across the harbour to her.

"Ready to go?" I ask.

She flashes me a grin. "Yep."

We walk along the gangway and onto the boat, where I mutter "good morning" to the crew. Harry is chatting away excitedly next to me, saying something about a date in Portree tonight, but I can't focus. My head is gone. The nightmare lingers, and I feel ropes tightening around my ankles with every step I take.

The boat slowly drifts away from the dock, and we grab our diving gear from the lockers. Harry nudges me with her elbow as she finishes putting her arms into her drysuit. "All good?"

I hum in agreement, hoping that will be the end of it, but there's concern in her eyes. I put my hands on her shoulders and spin her around, checking that her fastenings are secure and the dry suit is fully zipped. "Yeah, I'm all good."

We sit on the edge of the boat while waiting to arrive at the diving grounds, and I take a moment to push all the anxiety that's been building up inside of me down. *Way* down. I check my umbilical cord, fix my mask and pick up my net before the skipper yells out our approach. The boat crawls to a stop and I give Harry a nod. Together we roll backwards into the frigid water.

My body calms as the pressure of the drysuit tightens against my calves and thighs. I click on the torch and kick my feet harder, pushing myself down to the seabed until I find the scallops. Reaching out, I grab one, placing it in my bag, pausing as bubbles drift past my mask. I float in the darkness, feeling it press in on me, hating that I feel safer here than in my own home.

Nothing can reach me here, not even my nightmares.

Heat washes over me as the old wooden door to the pub swings open. I tilt my head to avoid bumping it on the low beams. Once inside, I scan the room.

"Theo!" a deep voice bellows.

My head snaps towards my best friend, who's waving at me a little too enthusiastically from a corner booth. I quickly make my way over to him, nodding to the locals as I pass by. I can feel my cheeks burning under their collective gaze.

"Did you have to do that? It's not like I wouldn't have seen you."

Robbie grins, pulling a hairband off his wrist and placing it between his teeth as he gathers his dark hair up. "How's diving been this week? Rain's finally staying away."

"Good enough. I'm bloody knackered; we've gone out

every day this week. Harry's going to be showing me up in no time."

He fixes the band around his unruly curls into a bun, exposing braids running along the sides of his head. "How's she getting on?"

"Fine," I say as he drains his lager then wipes the foam from his mouth with the back of his hand. I screw up my nose when he licks it off. "She's got more energy than the two of us. Said something about going on a date tonight."

"I have plenty of energy, thanks. I'm only thirty-two, basically in my prime," Robbie says, sitting up straighter.

He's right; somehow he has the energy of a five-year-old who snorted sherbert.

"She called me an old man earlier," I say, "because I didn't know what some new game was. Like I have time to keep up with that these days."

"What was the game—? Wait. What the hell does she mean *old man?*" Robbie splutters. "Do twenty-year-olds think we're old?"

"Why do you care what a twenty-year-old thinks?"

He sulks, running his finger along the rim of his pint glass. "I found some grey in my hair today, Theo ..." he whispers as though it were a secret.

"They've been there a while, buddy." I tap my beard. "Here too."

His eyes widen and he opens his mouth to argue.

"How's it going, lads?" My cousin cuts in as she walks towards us. The light-blue knitted jumper she's wearing makes her bright copper hair stand out more than usual against her fair complexion.

I look down at the dark hair on my tanned arm, grateful I got my dad's genes. No way I'd be able to survive working on the boats if I were that pale.

Robbie scrambles out of his seat and pulls Isla into a bear hug, kissing her cheek. "Drink?" he asks her.

"Excuse me? You didn't offer me a drink," I say.

"I didn't take you for the jealous type, Theo," he says, hopping onto my lap before I can stop him. He slips his arms around my neck and pecks my cheek. "Would you like a drink, sweetheart?"

"Get off." I push the heavy bastard until he's back on his feet. "IPA, please," I mutter, wiping the kiss off my cheek.

He winks at me then turns to Isla.

"Whatever cider they have on tap, please, Robbo," she tells him, and then slips into the booth as he heads off to the bar.

"So?" she asks.

"So what?"

She pokes my arm. "How'd the date with Rachel go?"

"It was … okay, I guess."

"And a second date?"

"No, I—"

"More excuses, Theo? Bloody hell. There's always something wrong with them," she sighs, and starts counting on her fingers. "One talked too much, one talked too little. One giggled too much, one was too serious. One chewed with her mouth open, and one refused to eat seafood." She looks at me pointedly. "I could go on …"

"Please don't."

She cocks an eyebrow. "I don't want to say you're fussy, but—"

"What are we talking about?" Robbie interrupts, carefully putting down three pint glasses.

"Goldilocks over here, and his total lack of motivation to date," Isla says, pulling the glass of cider to her lips.

Robbie points at me. "You need to get out more."

Great, two against one, just like it's been since we were

kids. "I don't want to. There hasn't been enough time for me to get to know anyone past a first date," I lie.

"Just take them on a second date!" Isla splutters. "Surely it's easier to take the same woman on a second date than it is to find a new woman to go on a first date?"

"You at least need to get laid more; maybe you wouldn't be so grumpy." Robbie smirks behind his pint.

"I don't care about that." Unlike him, I don't enjoy one night stands; can't even remember the last time I tried. It's never worked anyway. It takes me too long to get to a point where I can see myself taking things further with someone. I'm not willing to let someone get close enough to learn about my past, and I don't want someone sleeping over and finding out about my nightmares or hearing how I cry out in the middle of the night.

There's so much I haven't told them; I can see why it looks like I'm just refusing to settle down. They don't even know I'm bisexual because I refuse to date another man since—

"Can we move on?" I growl.

"I just want you to find—" Isla starts, but I cut her off with a glare.

"Subject's done, Isla. Leave it."

They finally take the hint and change the subject, discussing the wedding as I sit there quietly, losing track of my pints.

A couple of hours later, I step outside into the cold. The alcohol shoots straight to my head, and my knees buckle.

Robbie catches me before I topple over. "You've not drunk for a while, huh?" he chuckles.

"M'fine," I mumble, pushing Robbie's bear paw off my arm.

Isla leads the way as we follow her down the country lane. "Come on, Grumpy, we'll get you home and Robbo can tuck you into bed."

I grunt something in response to that, but for the life of me, I don't know what's coming out of my mouth.

The walk back to the farm feels like it takes hours as we stumble along the gravel path. Eventually we get to the farm, and I point to my cottage, but Robbie drags me in the opposite direction.

"But ... I live over there!" I shout.

"Shh. Not for the next month, you don't. Richard's family came today, remember?" Isla tells me.

Oh. I look back at my small cottage longingly, and movement catches my eye in the bedroom. There's a blurry silhouette of a man in the window. The light switches on, highlighting blonde hair brushing the tops of broad shoulders. It reminds me of *him*, and my blood turns to ice. I shake the feeling off. It's impossible. I've definitely had way too much to drink.

TWO

THEO

THERE'S NOTHING LIKE WAKING UP WITH A pounding headache and a dry mouth to remind me I'm too old for this shit. I pull back the duvet and rub my face roughly to wake up. The smell of bacon in the air promises some kind of relief, so I quickly take a shower and get dressed before making my way downstairs.

"Morning, wee lammie. Take a seat, won't be a minute," Gran says as she shakes the sizzling pan of bacon over the hob.

"Morning, Gran."

I walk over to the kettle and pour myself a coffee, then settle at the breakfast bar. The backdoor swings open and Gramps walk in, slipping his wellies off and banging them on the wall outside. He grins at me. "Morning, Grumpy. Sleep the alcohol off?"

I frown at him. "Who are you calling Grumpy?" Pieces of last night start coming back to me, and I roll my eyes. "You spoke to Isla?"

"Yep." He walks over to a plate of square sausages Gran has just stacked up. I eye him as he tries to be discreet, walking his fingers along the counter until he's within reach before picking one up.

"Malcolm!" Gran shouts. She pulls a tea towel off her shoulder and whips him on the arse, making him yelp as he drops the sausage. "Wait until it's served, you heathen," she scolds, heaping bacon, sausage and eggs onto a plate before pushing it towards me.

"Thanks, Gran." I smile.

She pats my cheek. "You're a good boy, Theo."

As soon as her back is turned, I grin at Granda then start shovelling the food into my mouth. He scowls back at me and takes a seat, waiting patiently for his breakfast.

As I'm finishing the last of my eggs, vibrations run through my feet and a steady thudding beat rattles my chest. I tilt my head to the side. "Where's the music coming from?"

"Renovations on the barn for the wedding. Richard's family arrived last night so they could start working on it early this morning. Did Isla not tell you?" Granda answers.

"She told me to get out of my house. I don't remember her saying they'd arrived."

"Well I doubt you remember much, the state you were in. Robbie carried you like a bride to your bed last night."

"He didn't." I scrunch my nose up picturing it.

"He did. Whether you needed it or not, I couldn't say," he says, smirking.

Note to self: stop getting drunk around Robbie.

"Still doesn't explain why the music is so damn loud at this time in the morning," I grumble, feeling my temples throb with every pulse of the bass.

"Well, I can't hear it," Granda mutters.

"Of course you can't." I stand up and slap him on the back. "I'm going to tell them to turn it down." After slipping on my boots, I head out to the barn. The music becomes clearer, and as a new song begins, I swear whoever is inside turns the volume *up*. As if it wasn't loud enough already.

The doors to the barn are wide open, with a tractor parked in the entryway. I squeeze through a gap and immediately see the source of my headache: a cylindrical speaker sits wedged between two wooden beams blasting out music. I step towards it, but my eyes are drawn like magnets to a man who has his back to me, stabbing a hay bale with a pitchfork. His blonde hair's been pulled up into a messy bun with some curls spilling free, and my skin crawls as I recall seeing someone in my bedroom window last night. How much they looked like—

The man turns around, and I'm suddenly looking into ice-blue eyes. My knees threaten to give out as the walls close in on me.

"Bailey?" My voice trickles out in a hoarse whisper as I stand mere feet away from the man I've only seen in my nightmares for the past twelve years. He's older, and his face has sharper angles than when we were boys, but that's definitely my ex-boyfriend staring back at me.

Bailey's eyes widen in recognition, lips curving up into a smile. He pulls his phone out and stops the music. All I can hear is my thumping heartbeat as he takes a step towards me.

The flames lick up the walls and along the floor. Too close. Too hot. Black smoke starts to settle, making it hard to draw in air.

Tiny pinpricks tingle on my palms and spread up my neck to the top of my head. *Why the hell is he still smiling at me?*

I see red. Clenching my right fist, I punch him hard in the jaw, and he lets out a grunt, stumbling back.

"What the fuck?" he yells.

"Get out," I grit out through clenched teeth, shaking my throbbing hand.

He stares back at me then lets out a hollow laugh, rubbing his jaw. "You've got some fucking nerve, Teddy."

Me? Why the hell is he even here?

I grab him by the bicep, pulling him towards me until we're nose to nose. "I said, get out."

He sucks in a breath as I start dragging him towards the barn door, but then he starts fighting against it, and I lose my grip on him. He shoves me, and I slip on some hay. We move at the same time; his fist connects with my chin, and we fall into a heap on the floor. He kicks and punches wildly, trying to get away from me. One of his punches catches me on the cheek, but I shake it off, pinning his arms down before straddling him. My hands lunge for his neck and squeeze.

"Teddy, stop!" he gasps.

I startle when I feel arms around my chest, hauling me up. Muffled voices break through the sound of my ragged breathing. I recognise Robbie's deep, rumbling timbre in my ear, but I can't register what he's saying. He drags me out of the barn as I fight the confines of his arms, and I see my uncle Liam bend down towards Bailey.

"Hey! What the hell has got into you?" Robbie shouts, spinning me around and gripping my shoulders tightly.

I have no words for him. He doesn't know my history with Bailey, and I don't want him or anyone else to ever find out. I want to go back to pretending those two years of my life never happened.

"Theo, look at me." He shakes me until I look at him. "This isn't like you; what did he do?"

"Nothing," I say, clenching my jaw tight. After all these years I'm not even sure how much of it was real, or whether my nightmares have tainted the memories. I shake free of Robbie's hold. His touch is too much; my skin feels as though it's on fire.

Robbie lets out a frustrated huff, putting his hands on his hips. "Go cool off." He motions for me to leave.

I try not to run as I head off down the shingle path, over the stone wall, and across the fields.

"Fuck," I rasp. *He shouldn't be here ... he has no reason to be here!*

I can't think clearly. My ears are ringing and I'm so hot I can feel sweat running down the small of my back.

I make it across two fields before I get the courage to check that no one's following me. The stone wall bordering the next field is warm to the touch as I swing myself over. I spot two familiar mounds of ginger fur lying under some trees and make my way towards them, boots squelching through the mud.

"Hey, lassies." The highland cows lift their giant heads, huffing in acknowledgement. A cold, wet nose presses into my palm. "Sorry, I didn't bring any treats for you," I say as I scratch behind Rosie's ears.

It's silent except for the sound of the girls' soft chuffing noises. I place my hand on Rosie's side and close my eyes, feeling the strong beat of her heart under the thick coat of fur. It isn't enough to calm me this time. My skin crawls when I picture Bailey's face. Why the fuck was he smiling? I try to place the man I saw today with the boy I met when I was sixteen—beauty still disguising the evil within.

I felt sorry for him when we first met, protective even, yet it wasn't him who needed protecting.

THREE

THEO - SIXTEEN YEARS OLD

"Pass!" I yell out to the field.

I'm standing in goal, getting more and more frustrated by my teammates' stupidity. I'm too far away to do anything other than shout. "Pass the fucking ball!"

I can't even remember most of their names. Since moving to Surrey and starting sixth form, no one's really bothered to talk to me—until now, and that's only because they were short on players.

There's a dude wide open to the left of the field, yet the one with the ball still isn't passing. I come off the goal line to get a better view. He finally passes, but not to the dude who's open. Nope, he passes to Bailey—one of the two names I actually remember—who is currently being marked.

I made sure to remember which of the Townsend twins was which when I was introduced to them so I'd know who was on my team. Bailey has a blue T-shirt, while his brother Shane is in white, but other than that they're fully identical. Same height, same ice-blue eyes, even the same shade of blonde hair.

Bailey dribbles away from the person marking him before

some fancy footwork takes him around two more, only to get slammed into by his brother. I suck in a breath, watching as Shane jabs his elbow into Bailey's ribs, stealing the ball out from under him. Bailey's quick; turning on his heel, he tackles Shane from behind. The ball is under Bailey's foot, and he drags it backwards almost free. I look up just in time to see Shane rear his head back—straight into Bailey's nose.

It feels like a bucket of cold water is tipped over my head when I see Bailey collapse to the ground. Everyone goes quiet as we wait for him to get up.

Bailey doesn't move.

I run to him, abandoning the goal. He's awake, but a little stunned, I think. There's blood gushing from his nose and Shane's bending over him, whispering something and holding a hand out to help him up, but Bailey flinches away.

"Hey, back off," I growl, shoving Shane's chest.

"It was a little tap; he's fine," he says, pushing me back.

"Fuck off. I watched you headbutt him."

"It was an accident; he got too close. I barely got him; he's just a dramatic bleeder."

I look down at Bailey as he wipes his bloody nose with a shaking hand. He looks at Shane with a scowl, then looks at me, and I see his eyes are wet with tears. I hold my hand out. He stares at it for a moment before grabbing hold, letting me pull him up. "You okay?" I ask.

Bailey looks between Shane and me, frowns, then turns and runs to the tree line before disappearing into the woods.

"Hey! The game isn't finished, Bailey," Shane shouts.

"Yes it is, leave him alone," I say, grabbing his arm. He shakes me off and walks towards the woods.

I know I shouldn't be putting myself between brothers, but I shove Shane in the back anyway. "Something wrong with your hearing?"

He rights himself and slowly turns towards me, nose flaring, jaw clenched tight. "Why the fuck are you getting involved?" He steps forward, bumping his chest against mine. I refuse to move. We're almost nose to nose; a wicked grin plays on his lips. "What's it to you, anyway?" He grabs my shirt. "Do you like him?"

Warmth spreads to my cheeks, and he chuckles.

"Is that what all of this is about? What about me, Theo? Do I make you har—"

I don't let him finish his sentence. I throw my head forward, but he moves at the last second. A sharp pain shoots through my head as I catch him in the mouth.

"Fuck!" he growls, releasing my shirt.

I run before he can grab me again, my legs carrying me into the woods as fast as they can. Eventually, the path splits off into different directions. I have no idea which way Bailey went. I look behind me and hold my breath, trying to hear if anyone is chasing after me, but it's completely silent.

Picking a random path, I start running again, the cold October air burning my lungs and prickling the tips of my ears. The smell of damp leaves and musty soil permeates the air, growing stronger the deeper I get into the woods.

I slow down and take stock of my surroundings. The trickling sound of water draws my attention to a stream running through the trees, lined with large moss-covered rocks. The ground's muddier and the trees denser, blocking out the last of the setting sun.

I walk towards the water, feet slipping as I go. I can't shake the feeling that someone's watching me. Goosebumps rise on the back of my neck and I turn around to check I'm definitely alone. Something wet drips down my face and I wipe it away. When I look at my hand, I realise I'm bleeding, and groan to myself—I'm never going to be able to hide this from my parents. I kneel by the stream, pulling my phone from my pocket, opening the front camera and inspecting the bloody mess I've made of my face. There's a cut on my forehead where I must have caught Shane's tooth.

The water is freezing as I scoop it up to wash my face. I doubt the water is sanitary, so I try to avoid the cut and just wash the blood dripping down my nose.

A twig breaks and my head snaps up, heart racing as I frantically search the trees. Quickly standing, I use my T-shirt to dry my face, then turn on my phone's torch.

"Fuck off Shane, I have nothing left to say to you!" I shout.

Another twig cracks as something moves closer.

"I told you, I—" My torch illuminates a blue T-shirt. "Bailey?" I say quietly.

He takes a small step towards me, squinting against the light. *Jesus*—his face is even more messed up than mine, with a swollen nose and mouth stained red with blood.

I ease forward, my hands having a mind of their own as they reach up to pinch his chin. I turn his head left, then right, checking whether his nose is broken. He flinches, and heat rushes to my cheeks. I don't even know him and I'm cradling his face like I have the right to. I drop my hands as though I've touched an open flame. "Sorry," I mutter. His arms wrap around his middle, silently staring off to the side. I frown at him, confused why he's not talking. "Are you okay?"

He swallows before opening his mouth to speak, but nothing comes out. I look around, unsure what to do with him. I can't just leave him alone in the woods. "Do you want help cleaning up?" I ask. He sways a little, and I watch him carefully, worried he's close to fainting. A crease forms in his brow, then he finally looks at me, giving a small nod.

Okay then ... I pull his arm from around his middle and guide him to the water. "Sit here," I say, nodding to one of the rocks. "Lean over a bit." He sits, following my directions, leaning over and resting his elbows on his knees. With nothing to clean him up, I take off my T-shirt and plunge it into the water, wring it out, then gently press it to his nose. He closes his eyes, lets out a little sigh, and relaxes his shoulders. I wipe away the blood that's crusted over his mouth while staring at his face. He's so determined to avoid looking at me that I have time to get a proper look. A breeze blows his blonde hair, a few strands sticking to his wet cheeks. Without thinking, I lean forward and brush the strands away, revealing a dusting of freckles. He sucks in a breath and his eyes dart up, locking onto mine. I stare into the rings of gold surrounding his pupils, watching how they blend into the blue. I'm held captive by them as they glisten in the torchlight.

I cough, and drag my eyes away from his. "You're alright," I say. "It's not broken, but it'll bruise like a bitch."

Turning away from him, I wash the shirt out in the stream. "Um, the water ... I'm not sure how clean it is, but if you want, you can come back to mine, and I can look in my ma's first aid kit," I say, standing and dusting off my trousers. "I need to clean myself up too, so we can help each other." I point to the cut on my forehead that's thankfully stopped bleeding.

He climbs off the rock slowly, and comes to stand next to me. I give him a lopsided grin. "I'm Theo, by the way."

FOUR

THEO

"Theo!"

I jump at the sound of Isla shouting across the field.

"WHAT THE FUCK HAVE YOU DONE!"

Shit.

I stand between the cows, barely breathing, wondering if she can see me or if she's just guessing that I'm out here.

"Theodore MacLeod, you better get your arse up here right now. Don't make me come and get you."

With a growl, I step out from my cow-cover. "Another reason why I don't date, can you imagine if I ended up with someone like that?" I mutter.

Heather lets out an indignant huff.

"Of course you'd side with her."

As I trudge back across the muddy field towards my cousin, I can see her face is pure rage. There's no time to gather my thoughts before she unleashes on me.

"Your bloody face! Jesus Christ, what the hell is wrong with you? Did you hit one of my guests?"

Guest? I keep the stone wall between us as a barrier, almost certain she'd grab me if I were closer. "I could tell you that," I say, "but I think you know it would be a lie, or you wouldn't be here in the first place."

"Okay, smart arse. Now tell me *why*?"

I open my mouth to answer but find I have no excuse—at least not one I'm willing to give. Telling her my history with Bailey would mean dragging my nightmare into the light when all I want is to keep it in the dark.

"Robbie told me that you had a fight in the barn. I laughed at him, Theo, thinking he was joking, but then he said that he had to pull you off Bailey while you were choking him out!" Her voice rises at the end, and she runs her hand through her copper hair, getting visibly more frustrated as the wind whips it back into her face. "Then, Granda said you were annoyed with the music being too loud, and that you went off in a huff."

I frown, wondering what that has to do with anything.

"So, please tell me you didn't thump a poor boy just because you were hungover."

The truth claws at my throat. I could open my mouth and tell her about him—what he did to me. But I know the first thing she would do is call the police. I can't talk about that. Not now. Instead, I say, "Things escalated quickly. I didn't realise what was happening until Robbie pulled me off him."

When I peek up, her eyes have gone comically wide. She looks over her shoulder towards the barn, then back to me, her blue eyes sharp like daggers. "I suggest you go back up there and apologise to him. I have to now explain to Richard why his friend got fucked up by my cousin."

Like fuck.

"I'm not apologising, Isla. I'll stay away from him, but I'm not doing that."

"I've known Bailey for twelve years, Theo. It's not like either of you to get into a brawl like that," she huffs. "I'm going to go check on him, make sure he doesn't report you for being a twat." She storms away from me, shouting back, "Bloody sort it out. The wedding's in a month and he's going to be here the whole time."

Reality slams into me. A whole month … I can't avoid him for a whole fucking month. He's going to be here—on my farm, in my *house*. I blow out a deep breath and try to think. If there were the slightest possibility that Bailey was a danger to anyone in my family, I wouldn't even pause for a breath before calling the police myself. But what he'd done to me was personal, fueled by emotion and fear that, to this day, I cannot even begin to understand. He was so desperate to get me out of his life, it wouldn't make sense for him to have come looking for me.

After somewhat convincing myself that him being here is just a coincidence, and not some grand plan to fuck with me again, I make my way back to the farmhouse. It's silent as I fill the kettle, maybe I'll get lucky and make it upstairs before anyone else tries to—

"You going to explain what went on in the barn yet?"

I groan, tipping my head up to the ceiling and slamming the milk down on the counter. *No. I'm not going to explain anything.* "Can you not just leave it, Rob? It's over. I won't go near him again."

Robbie slides his large frame next to me and grabs a cup from the draining board. "You don't fight, Theo," he says simply, holding the cup out to me. I look at it, then up at him.

"Would you like a coffee, Rob?"

"Tea."

I raise an eyebrow.

He rolls his eyes at me. "Tea, please."

I take the cup from him. "I just lost my patience; sometimes I can't control it."

He hums in agreement. "There's losing your patience, then there's punching a stranger and trying to choke him out for playing music too loud. I thought you were getting better with all that?"

I was. When I came back to Skye twelve years ago I was an angry little shit—snapping at anyone who tried to talk to me, hiding away in my room, losing myself in the sea when I went to work. It took years of patience from Rob and my family until I came out the other side. The anger never really left me, but I'm sure it'd been getting better. Now with Bailey here dredging up everything that I've worked hard to bury, I feel unmoored. "I don't drink much anymore; maybe I had one too many," I mumble, handing Rob his tea.

Isla blows in through the back door, face like thunder. "He's fine, by the way. A little shocked, but he won't be reporting it to the police, so happy days for you." She pushes Robbie out the way, picks up a cup, and holds it out to me.

"Want to know something interesting?" she asks when I take it from her.

I look to Rob for help, but he shakes his head. "Don't look at me. I don't know what she's on about."

Isla taps his chest with the back of her hand and shushes him. "Bailey said you used to go to school together in England. That you were best friends."

Of course he did. My stomach twists, and icy fingers stroke down my spine as I wonder just how much he told her. "Right, we did—"

"And you didn't think that was an important detail to tell me earlier?"

"Last I checked, I don't answer to you, Isla," I snap.

That was the wrong thing to say. Her eyes widen slightly, and I can almost see the flames of hell flare to life within them. "He is my guest here, Theo. Anything you do is a reflection on me. So when you punch my guest in the face, everyone looks at me as if it's my fault."

"That's ridiculous, you weren't even there."

She huffs. "I can't make you apologise to him, and Bailey said there's no hard feelings—which is more than you deserve, by the way. So let's just forget it happened and move on."

"Kind of hard to ignore the giant black eye coming," Robbie says, poking me in the face. I flinch and slap his hand away, realising how much my cheek is throbbing now. My blood boils, but I keep my mouth shut. I remind myself that I haven't told Isla about my past with Bailey, so all I can do is glare at her. I turn to Robbie. "Can I stay with you until the wedding?"

"You don't need to leave the farm, Theo—" Isla starts, her voice softer than it had been a moment ago.

"It's fine. I just need some time to cool off." I raise my brow, waiting for Robbie's answer.

"Sure, you can stay," he says.

I make excuses that I need to pack my bags—for the second time in two days—and disappear upstairs.

We get to Robbie's house a couple of hours later. I kick off my shoes and make a quick escape up the stairs to the spare room, hoping to be left alone. But then, of course, there's a knock on the door.

"You want to talk about Bailey?" Robbie asks, as he leans against the doorframe.

"No." I run my hand through my curls, ignoring the slight tremor in my fingers. "It's just a lot to process."

"Fair enough. ... Fish supper?" I look up, and he's all smiles.

"Sure," I say. He nods and jogs back downstairs, the front door banging as he leaves the house. I blow out a breath, grateful that Robbie isn't half as nosey as Isla.

By the time he's back, I'm set up on the sofa, leaning against the armrest, legs stretched out, with the football on. Robbie hands me one of the paper packages before lifting my feet and slipping himself onto the seat beneath them. As we watch the game, he devours his food while I pick at mine. Thankfully he doesn't stop talking, and the deep timbre of his voice is enough to distract me from my thoughts.

The evening slips away too fast, and eventually I make my way upstairs where the darkness calls for my dreams. I picture Bailey's face as soon as my head hits the pillow. I see him at sixteen with blood over his nose and tears running down his cheeks. Then at eighteen, crying, telling me he has no other choice. And now ... older, with a smile that—for a moment—was blinding.

I don't understand why the hell was he smiling at me. Not after the way things had ended between us. A pounding headache builds as I toss and turn, both wanting to sleep and dreading the moment I do.

FIVE

THEO

I MANAGED TO GO A WHOLE WEEK AVOIDING THE farm, but now it's Sunday and I'm out of excuses for why I can't go to dinner. I look through my suitcase for something to wear, groaning as I pull out my last pair of boxers. I must have forgotten to pack everything in my rush to leave the farm last week.

"Ready to go?"

"What the hell, Rob, get out!" I shout, grabbing the towel I'd just dropped to cover my dick, keeping my back to him.

"Interesting," he chuckles behind me. "I can get you an appointment with my aesthetician if you want?"

"What's that?" I ask, scowling at him over my shoulder.

He looks pointedly at my bare arse. "You're like a hairy wee bear."

I grab my comb and throw it at his head, but Robbie quickly ducks out of the room before it hits him. *No way in hell am I waxing my arse.*

An hour later we're at the farmhouse, following the sound of voices through to the dining room.

Isla blocks my way. "Can I have a word with you, please, in private?"

My stomach drops, knowing this isn't going to be good. I step back, letting her lead the way to the living room, where she closes the door behind us. "There's something you need to know."

"What?"

"Okay, so since you've been MIA, Richard's family have been eating pretty much every meal here—on Gran's insistence—and, well, Bailey is a part of his family. Just so you know ... he's here." She nods towards the door.

I frown at her. Bailey never mentioned having family outside of Surrey. Now I come to think of it, the amount of times Isla used to go down to Cumbria to visit Richard, she never once mentioned him.

"How?" I ask through clenched teeth.

"How what?"

"How is he family? You never mentioned him before, nor has Richard."

"Well, I didn't mention Noah much either, to be fair, and Richard isn't as close to Bailey as Noah is," she says a little defensively. "Anyway, as far as I'm aware, Richard's uncle Jake kinda took Bailey under his wing when he was fresh out of school. He moved in with them just as Richard was leaving for uni."

What was Bailey doing in Cumbria? He'd told me he wanted to get away from his family, but the plan had always been to come to Skye together. Not that that matters now, he made it perfectly clear that's *not* what he wanted.

"I can go," I say, stepping around her.

Isla grabs my arm. "I don't want you to go. Just tell me what happened between you two?"

"It was nothing ... we just fell out, Isla. People fall out all the time."

She squints. "You're lying to me. I can't help you if you don't talk to me, Theo."

"I never asked for your help," I snap. "Look, I'll stay for dinner, but then I'm going straight back to Robbie's."

"Fine." She releases my arm and opens the door for me.

If I leave now then everyone will think I have a problem. They'll poke and prod until the wound that barely scabbed over is ripped open again, and I can't do it. I need it all to stay in my head because if I say any of it out loud then it's suddenly real. I'll be that eighteen-year-old boy again, scared shitless because he didn't listen when his boyfriend told him he wanted to end things.

It's just one meal; I can do this. I don't even have to speak to him.

By the time I get back to the dining room, everyone is already seated. I settle next to Robbie, hoping he'll be a buffer if anyone tries to talk to me.

Different conversations ping around the table and I try to keep my eyes on my empty plate, all too aware that Bailey is sitting opposite me. I can hear him talking, and it's been so long since I saw him that his voice feels wrong. It's softer than I remember, and my eyes betray me when he chuckles, flicking up to peek at him. He has his head bent towards Richard's little brother, Noah, grinning like an idiot. Long blonde waves brush his freckle-scattered cheeks.

"Well look who decided to show his face."

My head snaps to Gran as she comes in with bowls of steaming roast potatoes. She places them down either end of the table without breaking eye contact, and I shrink under her withering gaze.

"How nice of you to grace us with your presence, Theo," she says coolly.

My eyes dart back to Bailey and I notice his chin is sporting some yellow bruising.

Facing Gran again, I force a smile. "Couldn't miss out on your roast again, Gran."

"Don't disappear after dinner. You and I are going to have a chat."

Robbie elbows me in the ribs after she's gone, grinning. "What?"

"You're in trouble," he sings.

"Piss off, Rob." So much for him being a buffer.

Granda comes in next with roast beef on a serving plate. When he locks eyes with me, he shakes his head. I underestimated just how much trouble I would be in by showing my face here. I should have avoided everyone for a couple more weeks until the wedding.

I look at Bailey again, like I can't help myself, to find him already staring at me. His gaze slams into mine and I'm anchored, unable to pull away. A little frown creases his forehead, and I'm taken back to that night again. His tear-stained face close to mine as he tells me everything is my fault. I suddenly get lost in the ocean of his blue eyes, and I'm dragged deeper and deeper until I'm drowning.

I can't breathe.

"You okay?" Robbie asks, looking at Bailey, then back to me, concern written all over his face.

I nod a few times, looking away from his questioning stare, wiping my sweaty palms on my jeans while trying desperately to suck in air without drawing any more attention.

"Dig in, kids," Granda says as he and Gran take their seats at either end of the table.

I'm not hungry but I routinely help myself to the food. Skipping the gravy, I squirt ketchup on the side of my plate. Robbie makes a gagging noise, but I ignore him, not in the mood for his shit.

"So, Noah, what do you do for work, dear?" Gran asks.

Noah peeks at Gran through his black curls, light grey

eyes wide as though he's surprised the attention is suddenly on him. "I, um, work for Jake's landscaping company, in the back office." He points to his uncle at the other end of the table, who's deep in conversation with Granda. "Basically admin."

Bailey laughs softly and I fight the urge to look at him. "He goes to clients' houses to discuss what they'd like done, and takes measurements and photos. Then comes *back* to the office and books them in," Bailey tells Gran. "You can tell he loves it."

Noah rolls his eyes and goes back to his food.

"And you, Bailey, what do you do?" she asks, smiling kindly at him.

"I'm the grounds manager for Jake …"

I tune out the rest of the conversation. Everything about him sets me on edge—his voice, his smile, the way he seems more confident than he used to be. I seem to have forgotten so much about him—except for how he was in those final moments we'd spent together. Wild. Scared. Out of control. It had been like the two years before that night just dissolved before my eyes.

Robbie asks me a question, dragging me from my memories, and I'm grateful for the mundane conversation to help me get through the rest of the meal.

An hour later I'm at the kitchen sink, scrubbing the roasting tin as I wait for Gran to find me for our little "chat". The sound of a shoe scuffing on stone tiles comes from behind me and my shoulders tense in anticipation.

"I'll be done in a minute, Gran."

There's a moment's silence.

"Um, it's me …" a quiet voice says.

No, no, no.

I can't talk to him right now, not when my head's a fucking mess. My throat tightens. "Go away," I say, scrubbing the pan harder than before, determined to get all the burnt fat off.

"We need to talk."

"I don't need to do anything. You don't get to demand anything from me anymore."

"I've never demanded anything from you," he huffs, voice getting louder.

I keep my back to him.

"I don't know why you're acting like this, Teddy. Would you just look at me while I'm talking to you?"

My shoulders are so tense that pain shoots across them. I throw the tin into the sink with a clatter and grab the kitchen towel. "What?" I ask, turning to face him, pushing down the nausea when I look into his eyes. "What do you want to talk about, Bailey? You said you never wanted to see me again and made sure the message got through. What could you possibly want?"

His face crumples, and I could almost fool myself into thinking he looks hurt. But I'm not falling for it again. I move around him towards the kitchen door, when a tug on my jumper stops me in my tracks. I look down to find him clinging to me.

"Wait, Teddy, I never meant that, I—"

I smack his hand off and growl, "Don't fucking touch me."

He pulls his hands to his chest, wringing them together.

"You made it clear you wanted nothing to do with me." I loom over him, getting as close as I can manage, testing myself to see if I can stand up to him without my chest collapsing in on itself. "Stay away from me," I order, shoving him backwards. He doesn't say a word as I wrench the kitchen door open and walk through the house to the front. "I'm going!" I don't wait for anyone to respond before I'm out the door and in my car, heading back to Robbie's house alone.

SIX

THEO - SIXTEEN YEARS OLD

WALKING THROUGH THE CORRIDOR TOWARDS THE science block, a familiar blonde head bobs through the crowd ahead of me. I push through them so I can get close enough to see whether it's Shane or Bailey.

I haven't seen Bailey properly since that night in the woods, not for lack of trying. I've spent weeks looking out for him in school. Whenever I spot him, he takes off in the opposite direction. Normally I wouldn't bother. I'm not the best at making friends or picking up on social cues, but in those brief moments when I do see him, he's always already looking at *me*.

"Hey!" I catch up to him at his locker.

He jumps, stepping away from me, gripping his workbook to his chest.

"Your nose looks good," I say, trying and failing to start a conversation.

Frowning, he runs a finger down the slope of it.

"Uh ... I mean, it wasn't broken after all. That's good." I stumble over my words, losing my train of thought. Bailey shifts his backpack then points his thumb over his shoulder as though he means to leave, but I pull on his sleeve to stop him. "Would you like—"

"Bailey," a voice says behind me.

I turn, coming face to face with Shane. His eyes narrow as he looks me up and down.

"Dean's waiting for us; don't want to keep him waiting," he says, never taking his eyes off of me.

I turn to face Bailey, watching as he blanches. He shakes my hand off his sleeve and walks away without a word.

"Theo," Shane says, nodding. "Any reason you're stalking my brother?"

"I'm not stalking him; I just wanted to make sure he was alright."

"Why wouldn't he be alright?" he asks, cocking a brow.

A hollow laugh escapes me. "Oh, I'm not sure. Maybe the fact his brother fucked his face up, and I'm the one who had to clean him up."

Shane hums. "Should have known he'd have found someone to feel sorry for him. He doesn't need you to protect him."

"I'm not—"

"Bailey likes to play games. Just be careful, yeah?"

I search his face, not believing a word coming out of his mouth. His ice-blue eyes hold my gaze, cold and unblinking, lips curling up into a grin.

"See you around," he says, turning to follow Bailey out of the building.

As soon as he's out of sight, I pull out my notebook. Ignoring everything Shane said, I write my number down with a simple message to meet me in the woods tomorrow and slip it into Bailey's locker.

It's four in the afternoon, and Bailey hasn't texted me, even though school finished half an hour ago. I shift my numb arse on the moss-covered rock, looking at the trees surrounding me. There's no sign of him either.

I'll give it another hour but I can't wait all night for him; Ma will flip out if I miss tea. I pull my phone out to check my messages. Maybe I can wait a couple more hours.

I'm picking at little bits of moss and throwing them into the water when a rustle comes from behind me. I turn around, jumping when I see Bailey closer than I expected. "I didn't think you'd come."

He nods and shuffles his feet, taking a step back as though he realised he was standing too close. He avoids looking at me, just like before, so I stand up and take a step towards him. "I've been in Surrey a while now and haven't really made any friends ..." I say awkwardly. He finally makes eye contact but remains silent. "I thought, if you wanted to, we could meet up after school and just, um, hang out?" Christ, this is worse than asking someone on a date.

After an excruciatingly long pause, Bailey nods, and relief washes over me.

"Do you game?" I ask, sitting back down on the rock.

He edges towards me, reaching out to stroke the soft green moss, shaking his head.

"Oh. Don't you have a console?"

He shakes his head again.

"That's okay, if you want to check it out, I got a game for my birthday that has a huge open world with dragons in it. You could come over on the weekend?"

He looks like he's going to shake his head again, but nods instead, shoulders drawing up.

This isn't really getting us anywhere. "Can we swap numbers?" I hold my hand out, and he passes his phone over for me. "You have unlimited texts?" I ask, putting my number in his contacts, texting myself so that I have his too. He makes a small sound of confirmation, and I hand the phone back.

ME

Hey

He looks down when his phone dings, then up at me, brows creased with confusion.

"I don't have an issue with you not talking to me, but can you text?"

Looking down at his phone again, his thumbs start to move.

UNKNOWN

Yes, I can text

I can't control the grin that spreads across my face. "Cool. I'll talk, and you can text—or I can text you back, if you prefer the silence?" *I hadn't thought about that.*

UNKNOWN

No, keep talking

A ruby blush spreads along his freckled cheeks and down his neck. Shaking my head, I try to not get distracted by how cute it makes him look.

"Okay, I can do that."

My phone dings, and I quickly change his contact details to 'Bailey'.

BAILEY

You have an accent

Chuckling, I say, "I'm Scottish." His eyebrows raise, but he doesn't text me anything else. "So, gaming night Saturday?"

He pulls his bottom lip between his teeth briefly as he types another message

BAILEY

Okay

THERE'S a knock on the front door, and I jump off the sofa, running to open it. "I got it!"

Bailey's standing on the doorstep, grinning at me, and my stomach flutters. It's been months since he started coming over, yet I'm still shocked whenever he smiles. He's so different from the timid boy I found in the woods.

My phone dings.

BAILEY

Move

I quickly move out of the entryway then start jogging up the stairs to my bedroom. "Come on. Homework first?" I ask, looking over my shoulder. He screws his nose up. "Nope, okay, no homework."

The hours pass by quickly. When I look out of the window, I realise it's pitch black, and Bailey's fallen asleep on the beanbag with a pizza box on his lap—empty, except for the crusts he left behind. I pick it up and head downstairs to throw it away.

"Bailey's still here?" Da asks, making me jump as he comes into the kitchen.

"He fell asleep," I say, fiddling with my sleeve. "Um, can he just stay the night?"

"Sure he can, if he tells his parents."

Bailey's never slept over before, so I'm surprised when Da agrees so quickly. "Thanks!" I yell, racing to the stairs, taking two at a time. Excitement ripples through me when I realise we can stay up all night watching shitty horror films.

By the time I get back to my room, I realise there's no chance of that. Bailey is still on the beanbag, but now he's curled up on his side, like he's trying to make himself as small as possible. One arm covers his head, and his knees are tucked in tight to his stomach. I hate to wake him, but he can't stay like that. Looking at the bed, then back at Bailey, I decide it'll be fine to share. It's a double, so there's plenty of room, and I can't be bothered to find the air mattress Da keeps in the shit cupboard.

"Bay," I whisper, poking him gently.

He stirs a little, and his phone falls from his pocket onto the floor. I pick it up and see it's unlocked, showing our text thread. He's listed me as 'Teddy' in his contacts. I look at him and frown. He's never called me that before, and it's not a nickname I go by. Everyone calls me Theo.

Bailey makes a soft noise and I quickly put his phone on the bedside table. He bolts upright, looking around the room a little frantically, until his eyes land on mine. His shoulders relax, and he puffs out a breath.

"Da said you can stay the night, seeing as it's pretty late," I say.

He blinks a few times, then stands up, stretching his arms to the ceiling.

"We can just share the bed, if you don't mind?" I strip off my top and trousers until I'm down to my boxers. When I look up, Bailey quickly turns away from me.

"I can wear joggers and a T-shirt if you want? I'm just used to sleeping in my boxers."

Bailey shakes his head, turning back around. He starts to shimmy out of his trousers and grabs the hem of his top, pausing for a moment. My eyes drop and get caught on the bulge in his briefs. I feel my stomach tighten in a way it's never done before. My mind is going a mile a minute, trying to work out what the hell is happening.

All those years my friend Rob had gone on about what he'd want to do with a girl he liked—or a boy, depending on who he was into at the time—I thought something was wrong with me, because I'd never felt like that with anyone. It's not that I don't find people attractive—I do. Bailey's beautiful. I've thought so since I first saw him, but it was more in appreciation than anything.

Over the past few months though, he's rooted himself so deeply inside of me that he's the first thing I think of when I wake up, and the last thing I think about when I go to sleep. But it's never gone this far; I've never had a physical reaction.

I drag my gaze away from his boxers and back to his face. His lip is trapped between his teeth again, and I wonder what it would feel like if it were my lip there instead; whether it would bring pleasure or pain. There's a pull, deep in my stomach, and my boxers stretch tight over my rock hard erection.

Fuck.

Clearly there's nothing wrong with me, but now I have a bigger problem—the only person my dick's shown an interest in is my best friend. I move my hands to cover myself and dive under the covers.

Bailey finally takes off the T-shirt and turns to throw it on the beanbag.

"What's that on your hip?" I ask.

Just above the waistband of his briefs, there's a small cluster of pink circles that looks like a rash. Bailey grabs his phone from the bedside table and climbs under the covers, typing away. I grab my phone just as it vibrates.

BAILEY

It was chicken pox

"Oh? Are you contagious? I mean ... I think I had it already when I was a kid—" My phone vibrates again.

BAILEY

Old scars

He puts his phone back down, and we settle down lower in the bed. Bailey rolls onto his side so we're face to face, just inches apart.

"I picked your phone up earlier, and it was unlocked ..." I say, searching his face for any sign that he might be uncomfortable lying this close to me. His eyes are closed, cheek smooshed against the pillow, with one arm underneath. My chest squeezes tight seeing him like this—like he belongs here, next to me.

"You put me in your contacts as Teddy." I grin as his eyes open wide and he quickly fumbles for his phone.

BAILEY

I can change it back to Theo

"No, leave it," I say as I close my hand over his. "Why'd you put it as Teddy?"

He rolls onto his back, staring at the ceiling for a moment before typing again.

BAILEY

Everyone calls you Theo. I wanted
something just for me

Little explosions go off in my chest, and I'm realising what

I've been feeling for a while now isn't just friendship. Something else has been growing right alongside it this whole time.

"I like Teddy," I say, a smile playing on my lips. I close my eyes and roll over, punching my pillow into shape. "Night, Bay."

"Night, Teddy," he whispers.

My eyes fly open. His voice is faint in the darkness, but I hear it.

SEVEN

BAILEY

I startle as Noah grabs my arm, so deep in my thoughts that I hadn't noticed the dust cloud, or how aggressively I'd been sweeping. My lungs burn like they're on fire, and I cough uncontrollably as I'm dragged out into the fresh air.

"Are you stupid?" Noah scolds. "Were you trying to give yourself an asthma attack for fuck's sake?"

"I don't have … asthma," I wheeze out. "I didn't realise it had got that bad," I look back at the barn and see a plume of dust drifting out the open door.

My head's been a mess since yesterday. I'm still no closer to finding out why Teddy hates me so much—hate might not be a strong enough word. His eyes had been like shards of black ice when he told me not to touch him, revulsion dripping from his words. I know I'm missing something important, but I have no idea what.

"I think the dust has settled. Ready to go back in?" Noah asks after a few minutes.

Looking back at the barn, the huge cloud I made has

finally dissipated. "Sure, are you going to actually help this time?"

Noah scoffs and leads the way, grabbing a broom as he goes. "Are you going to tell me why Theo punched you in the face yet?" he asks.

I keep my eyes down. "It was just an argument, I told you. We went to school together and it didn't end well." I shrug as though it were nothing, as if the memory of a grinning eighteen-year-old Teddy doesn't feel like a knife to the heart.

"That's a half-arsed answer."

"I'm not ready to talk about it." I stop to look at him so he knows I'm serious.

"You'd tell me if you were in trouble, right?"

My jaw clenches, and I go back to sweeping. There's so much I haven't told him, haven't even told my therapist. So many secrets stacked up inside of me, ready to collapse at the slightest breeze. I don't know if I'll ever be ready to tell Noah about my past. What would he think? If I saw disgust and horror in his eyes, it would destroy me.

"Yes, I'd tell you." I force the lie out.

After a couple of hours sweeping and washing the wooden floor the barn finally looks better. I stretch my arms up and my stiff back twinges.

"Oh! It's looking good, boys," Isla says as she comes through the doors with Richard. She pulls her phone out and starts taking photos of our progress.

Richard comes straight to me, handing a large tool kit and a drill over. "Apparently you know what you're doing?"

"Of course I know what I'm doing." I've been working for Jake since I was eighteen. Building decking and sheds is routine work, and it's the whole reason we've come up here so early. Richard insisted on paying for the barn to be fixed up, but Jake whacked on such a big discount that the price barely covered the cost of the materials. Jake told me and Noah that we'd be coming with him to help, but I'm starting to think that was a lie. The past few days, Jake's buggered off somewhere, leaving us to do all the work.

I show Noah how to pre-drill some holes into the hardwood, then I get to work nailing down any loose boards. I'm barely listening to the conversation going on around me, mind wandering back to yesterday again. Specifically to the way Teddy dismissed me, saying I'd made it clear I wanted nothing to do with him ... I didn't think I'd been that convincing when I broke up with him. A flare of irritation rises in me. He should've known I wouldn't have said those things unless I had no other choice.

The resentment I harboured for Teddy after he abandoned me at eighteen starts to rear its ugly head again. I feel the wood beneath my hand, coarse and cool, and count back from ten, shoving it all back down.

"You want coffee?" Richard asks, tapping me with his foot. I'm pulled away from my thoughts, which is probably for the best. I can't keep blaming Teddy for something I started.

"Please," I say.

Richard turns away and shouts across the barn. "Come on Noah, help me get the drinks."

Within two seconds of them leaving, Isla sidles up next to me. "So what's going on with you and Theo?" She hands me a nail and I line it up on the floorboard. I'd managed to avoid her for most of the week. I knew the questions would start as soon as she got me alone.

"I'm not sure what's going on." I say, gripping the hammer tighter and hitting the nail repeatedly, in rhythm with my pounding heart.

"You said you were friends in school, right? He never mentioned you ... but then I didn't keep in contact with him much when he moved. But even when he came back, he never mentioned making any friends."

It feels like there's a fist clenched around my heart, squeezing until I can barely breathe. Two whole years erased, just like that. My throat feels tight and raw as I swallow.

Placing the hammer down, I stand and face Isla. "We fell out. I told him I never wanted to see him again, and that I didn't want to be ... *friends* anymore. After that, he left."

Isla's eyebrows rise. "Must have been a pretty big falling out if he punched you twelve years later."

I frown. "I don't know why he punched me. The Teddy I knew never would have done that, even with how I left things between us, he never would have hit me. Maybe something else happened and I—"

And I *what*? I can't remember because I was out of it the night he left. Half that night is missing when I think back. I can't tell her that. So I swallow around the lump in my throat and crouch back down to finish nailing the floorboards. I struggle to see the nails as tears fill my eyes.

"What else could have happened?" Isla asks with a slight edge to her voice.

"I'm not sure, he won't talk to me about it."

Isla hands me another nail. "Did you mean it?"

"Mean what?"

"That you never wanted to see him again?"

A pain shoots through my chest, and I shake my head. "No, I didn't mean a word I said that night."

She hums then walks away. "The boats come into the harbour at two."

"What?" I look up, but she's already gone.

SEAGULLS SQUAWK ABOVE, navigating the grey clouds, as I walk down the country lane towards the harbour. I can't believe I'm doing this. It's a terrible idea. But I need to know why he's so angry with me. Whether it's something I can actually fix.

I approach the jetty, noticing Teddy's car parked on its own. I take a deep breath and head over there to wait for him.

A white refrigeration van sits by the jetty with a small boat anchored beside it. From this distance, I can only really make out the shape of people, but I pick Teddy out straight away, standing taller than everyone else, wearing a grey turtleneck jumper.

Someone locks up the back of the van and it slowly ambles out of the harbour, followed by a few cars. Teddy walks alone along the jetty, tugging on ropes that are attached to the boat. Then he picks up a duffel bag and swings it over his shoulder.

When he sees me, he freezes. For a moment, we both just stare at one another. I begin to wonder if he's trying to work out how to escape, but then he moves towards me again. His pace is quick, and the deep scowl on his face triggers my defences.

Teddy unlocks the car, throwing his bag in the boot before he slams it shut and heads for the driver's door.

"Teddy ..."

He ignores me, keeping his back turned as he opens the door.

"Please! I just want to talk," I shout in desperation, reaching out to pull the back of his jumper. He whirls around and pushes his chest against mine. I'm suddenly eighteen again. A shiver ripples through me as one of our last moments creeps forward—our bare, sweat-slick chests pressed up against one another, Teddy brushing my hair from my face, whispering that he loves me as he kisses along my jaw.

"What?" he snaps, yanking me back to the present.

I open my mouth, but no words come out. *Shit.* This hasn't happened in years. Teddy is standing so close I can't even think right. His eyes search mine, waiting.

"I ... you ... left," I stutter, trying to ignore the way my heart is racing in my chest.

He frowns and takes a step back. "I left?"

I nod.

"What are you talking about?"

"You left me ... why?" I ask, looking at the ground, cheeks aflame, embarrassed that I can't make the words come out the way I want them to.

"Yesterday? I told you—"

"No!" Tears prickle behind my eyes. "Twelve years ago. Why did you fucking leave me there?"

"I left you?" he asks. "Bailey, you told me to leave. You said you never wanted to see me again. *You* are the one who decided to punish me when I tried to talk to you. Of course I bloody left you." His fists are clenched so tight the knuckles are turning white, and the tendons in his neck strain as though he's holding himself back.

"But I didn't mean any of those things I said!" I yell, balling up my fists to stop myself from grabbing hold of him again.

Pausing, I realise what he just said. "What do you mean *punished*?"

He grabs me by the throat and shoves me against his car so fast my head spins. Getting in my face, he snarls, "I don't know what game you're playing, Bailey, but I'm not doing it again."

With that he releases me, and my legs give out. Teddy gets in the car and starts the engine. I scramble away just in time as he speeds out of the harbour.

EIGHT

BAILEY - SEVENTEEN YEARS OLD

"Where are you going?" Shane grabs my sleeve, pulling me back into the house.

"Out," I say, shaking him off.

He steps closer to me. "Out *where*?"

"The p-pub," I force out, trying to hold eye contact. I'm not sure how much longer I'll get away with lying to him. He thinks I spend every weekend working in the pub, as a pot washer. That's only on Saturdays though. On Sundays I sneak off to spend the day with Teddy.

"School's over, you don't need to keep wasting your weekends there. Why don't you hang out with me for the day?" he smiles, and my stomach drops.

"I signed a contract," I say through clenched teeth. "They're expecting me."

Shane looks me up and down. "Have you seen the Scottish boy lately?"

I swallow, scared of what he'll do to me if he finds out I'm lying. Terrified that he'll stop me seeing Teddy.

"Go," he says, jutting his chin towards the door. He

doesn't step back; forcing me to squeeze past him. Everywhere our bodies touch makes my skin crawl.

When I'm finally free, I run down the path, only to find my stepfather pulling into the drive. He rolls down the window and calls out to me. "Hey, baby boy, you off to work?"

My throat closes up completely, voice locked down tight as soon as those words leave his lips. I give a quick nod, then run far enough down the road to know they're not coming after me. Doubling over, I gasp for air, lungs burning with every breath. I rub at my chest, waiting for my heart to slow down before walking to Teddy's house.

"HEY, I thought we could go to the woods today, if that's good with you?" Teddy asks as he locks his front door. I nod, but he's not looking.

"Bay?" He turns around, and the sun reflects in his eyes, lightening them to whisky brown. I focus on them, trying to fight the knot in my throat, but the more I try, the more trapped the words get. Huffing in frustration I turn my face away from him.

He puts an arm around my shoulders and pulls me into a hug. "You not up to talking today?"

I shake my head against his chest; the movement blowing the smell of fabric softener and smoky cologne into the air.

"That's fine, take your time. You'll come back to me." He pulls back, a bright smile on his face. "Look, I got chocolate." He shoves an open carrier bag under my nose, revealing several share bags. "Come on, I wanna check out this old oak tree I saw last week. It's got low branches I think we can climb."

We? No way in hell is he getting me to climb a tree.

I follow him down the road and my hand twitches by my side, desperate to slip into his. I settle for pressing close to him instead, our arms brushing against one another as we walk. The contact, however small, is enough to settle me a little more. Teddy doesn't move away from me—if anything, I swear he leans into me as he carries on chatting away. A smile tugs at the corners of my mouth as I listen to his melodic voice.

We reach the forest and head towards the stream. Dappled light pierces through the leafy canopy, painting the water with glitter. I'm not sure why no one comes this deep into the woods, but for all the time we've been exploring here, we've never seen another person. I like that it's our secret spot, far away from everyone else.

Teddy leads the way, further than we've gone before, and just like he said, a large old oak tree stands in a clearing. Some of its roots are poking out the soil, like it's trying to break free from the earth. It's tilted to the side, hanging over the water, some of its branches low enough to reach.

I perch myself on a large rock.

Teddy chuckles. "You're not coming up with me?"

I frown at him and shake my head vehemently.

"Fine, here ... you take this." He hands me the bag of chocolate and takes his T-shirt off. I stare at him as if I've never seen him shirtless before.

I'm sure his chest looks bigger ...

"Bay?"

I shake my head and drag my eyes away from his body.

"I called you like three times, you good?"

I nod, touching the tips of my ears to see if they're as hot as they feel.

Teddy jumps to grab a low branch and pulls himself up so he's sitting with his back to me. Then he drops backwards, hanging upside down by his knees. "Throw me a chocolate!"

I grab the peanut ones and walk over to him. He shakes his head. "No, throw it, I'll catch it," he says, opening his mouth wide and sticking out his tongue.

Groaning, I turn away, subtly rearranging myself in my boxers before going back to the rock. I swear he's doing it on purpose. He never takes off his shirt like this. And now his tongue ... My cock, oblivious to the bait, twitches in anticipation.

I'm unsure how many more times I need to tell myself not to think about him that way before it sticks. My feelings for Teddy are getting too complicated. Since we first met, there's been a pull I couldn't ignore. When I hid in the woods and saw him by the stream, I was helpless to do anything but go to him.

I haven't even had the courage to tell him I'm gay. When I play the conversation through my head, I start to sweat and hyperventilate just at the thought of him not wanting to be my friend anymore. If he knew how I felt on top of that ... if he pushed me away—

Don't think about that. He's here, and he's not going anywhere.

It takes a few tries throwing the chocolates before one lands perfectly. He whoops in delight, swinging himself upright, face red from hanging upside down for so long.

"So did something happen?" he asks out of the blue. "You're quiet again. You never talk to me about—" His eyes go wide as he backtracks. "I mean when you can talk, you never say what happened ... and that's fine! I-I don't expect you to tell me anything that makes you uncomfortable. Just ... you can. You know that, right?"

I do know that, and if I could, I would tell him everything. But if he knew how scared I am of Shane ... how scared I am of myself ... I swallow down the guilt I feel for clinging to him, hating that I've grown to depend on our friendship as an escape from everything. I know it's selfish. The more time I spend with him, the more danger I'm putting him in. And yet, despite the risks, I can't stop. I draw in a shuddering breath and my chest feels tight all over again.

"Bay, it's fine, we don't have to talk about it, okay?"

I *do* want to talk about it. One day I want to tell him everything. Just ... not yet.

Teddy pulls himself up so that he's standing on the branch, wobbling as he tries to walk along it. The branch extends over the stream, but it's not overly large or sturdy-looking. He places one foot carefully in front of the other, arms spread wide.

I jump to my feet in anticipation. As if I'd be able to catch him if he fell. Then the idiot slips and my heart seizes. "No!" The word rips from my throat in a gasp as I rush towards him. He reaches up for a branch above just in time, catching it as he loses his footing, leaving him hanging by his arms.

He lets out a nervous giggle.

I stand there with my hands on my hips, watching him drop ungracefully to the ground. I'm in his face within seconds. "W-what the fuck is wrong with you?"

His mouth splits into a giant grin, and he grabs my arm, pulling me to him. "Hey, I told you you'd come back to me."

I'm stunned for a moment. "You ... you don't have to scare me half to death to bring my voice back," I grumble, rubbing my sore throat. I'm suddenly all too aware of how close he's holding me against his bare chest. I feel it rise and fall, solid yet smooth beneath my fingertips. The proximity is scalding, and I try to step away from him.

All of a sudden, my feet are swept out from under me and I crash down to the forest floor. Teddy follows, straddling my waist, digging his fingers into my sides, tickling my ribs. I struggle to breathe through silent laughter, smacking his hands and begging him to stop.

Almost certain he lets me, I manage to flip us, pinning him down. He has a shit-eating grin on his face, looking like he's exactly where he wants to be.

"You're an idiot," I say, frowning. All the tension in my body fades away, and I give myself a second to calm down. I realise staring into his eyes and counting the flecks of gold scattered amongst the obsidian doesn't help at all, so I release his wrists and put my palms against the earth, either side of his head. For just a moment, I forget Teddy doesn't know how I feel about him. My eyes dart to his lips. I've never let myself get close enough to notice the curve of them. Fascinated by the way they glisten as his tongue darts out to lick them.

When I meet his eyes again, he's frowning. I panic that he's figured out how I feel about him, that he's about to throw me off or punch me in the face. But then he cups the back of my neck, pulling me down. Our lips touch and I squeeze my eyes shut, not daring to move.

"Bay," he whispers, lips moving against mine. My rigid jaw softens and my mouth falls open in a soft gasp. The barest touch of his tongue against mine sends a bolt of electricity through me, and I stop thinking altogether. My tongue curls around his, and he lets out a deep hum that vibrates in my chest. He untangles my hairband and fists my hair, pushing me harder against him. The tug on my scalp snaps me back to reality. My best friend is kissing me ... *Teddy* is kissing me.

I know I don't deserve this—don't deserve him, but I push the thoughts away, chasing his tongue and nipping at his lips. I thread my fingers through his dark curls, holding on tight, as though he were a lifeline.

Teddy pushes a hand against my chest, forcing me to sit up. I refuse to open my eyes, not wanting to see his face. If there's regret written across it, or he says it was a mistake, I—

"Bay, look at me."

I shake my head.

"Bay." He sits upright, pushing me back so I'm sitting on his lap, wrapping his arms around me. "Please look at me."

I slowly open one eye and see his grin firmly back in place. I puff out a breath and brush my hair away from my face.

"I've wanted to do that for a while now," he says. "I didn't stop to think whether you'd want to. I mean ... you looked like you wanted to, but if you didn't then I'm sor—"

I place my hand over his mouth. "I wanted to, Teddy."

He strokes my wrist, then pulls my hand away, eyes softening. "Would you do it again?"

I don't think twice before I nod. "Would you?"

"Always," he whispers. He grabs my top, dragging me towards him, our noses nudging against one another. I'm about to kiss him again when a series of dings and vibrations come from my phone, snapping us out of whatever haze we were in.

"Sounds important," Teddy says, pulling away.

My stomach roils as I pull out my phone, knowing exactly who it'll be, seeing as the only other person who texts me is currently under me.

> SHANE
>
> Guess where I am?
>
> The pub
>
> Guess where you're not?
>
> You've been lying to me, little mouse.
> Where are you? You better not be with
> Theo. You know it's not safe for you to
> do that

I stare at the messages. He's wrong. He has to be. I've been seeing Teddy for over a year now and nothing bad has happened. I've been good ... I'm in control when I'm with him. I shut my eyes and throw my phone to the ground.

"What happened?" Teddy shifts underneath me.

I don't know what to say; there's so many secrets inside of me, any one of them could end this. Tears sting my eyes, and my lip wobbles. I open my mouth to talk, but my throat burns so badly that nothing comes out.

"Hey." He wraps his arms around me again. "Who was it?"

I bury myself into his neck, and he starts gently rocking back and forth, making me melt into him. "It was my mum. I-I don't want to go home," I croak out the lie.

He strokes my hair. "You don't have to go home, Bay. You can stay at mine, Ma and Da won't mind."

I gaze at him longingly. I've never felt more safe than when I'm with Teddy. Warning lights go off in my mind telling me this is a bad idea, but selfishly I whisper, "yes." I want him to take me away from it all.

Teddy kisses my forehead. "You'll be alright now. I'll make sure of it."

NINE

A knock on the door sends my heart leaping into my throat.

"Boys, come on, it's eleven," Ma shouts. "Get your lazy butts out of bed or I'm coming in."

I suck in a breath and look down at Bailey sprawled across my bare chest, then at the empty air mattress on the floor by my bed. "Bay, get up," I whisper, nudging his arm. His body jerks just as there's another knock on the door, and he quickly scrambles out of my bed, running to the bathroom in his briefs.

"Are you up?" Ma calls out again.

"Yes, we're up," I bark.

"Good boy."

I hear her walk away from the door, but I still shout after her, "Not a boy!"

Bailey comes out of the bathroom a few minutes later, freshly showered, skin all pink from the heat of it. I look down to the little towel wrapped around his hips.

His cheeks turn from pink to red, brows creasing. "Not now."

After we're both dressed, Bailey sits on the beanbag. He's on his phone with his knees drawn up to his chin, fingers covered by sleeves that are too long. Too long, because that's *my* jumper. My stomach flutters seeing him wearing it. I like the way he looks in my clothes ...

My words rush out of me before I can stop them. "I think I want to tell my parents."

Bailey looks up at me through his long lashes. "Tell them what?"

"About us ... that we're together," I say. He frowns, and it feels like my stomach's dropped right out of me. "We are, aren't we?"

Ever since we kissed in the woods six months ago and Bailey moved in, this thing between us has grown bigger. We're even more inseparable, especially once all the lights are out, and he ignores the air mattress to climb straight into bed, draping his body over mine like a hot blanket. It's the best part of my day.

"Boyfriends?" he asks quietly.

"If you want," I say.

He bites his lip and dips his head, muttering, "I want."

A grin takes over my face. "And you'll come to Scotland with me when I leave in the summer ... as boyfriends?"

"Yeah, I'll go wherever you go, Teddy." He smiles back at me sweetly.

Without thinking, I launch myself onto him. He screams as the beanbag explodes and thousands of tiny polystyrene balls go flying everywhere.

Shoving my chest, trying to crawl out from under me, he huffs, "Can I take it back?"

"Nope," I say, bending down, giving him a dozen kisses all over his face.

We spend way too long cleaning up the mess I made before heading downstairs for breakfast—or lunch, I guess. I grab some meat from the fridge and make us both sandwiches before heading out to the garden, where Ma is reading a book on her sun lounger and Da is weeding the garden.

We sit on the picnic table and eat but my food feels like cement to swallow. My parents have never spoken badly about people being gay or bisexual, but it's also never been a topic of conversation in the house. They've never pressured me into dating or asked why I never brought anyone home. But I don't like not knowing how they're going to react.

Bailey gives me a small smile, his hand slipping under the table to squeeze my thigh. *Fuck, okay.* "Um ... Ma, Da, I want to tell you something."

Da stands up, leaning on his spade, and Ma closes her book, both giving me their full attention.

"I'm ... I'm bisexual, and Bailey and I are kinda together." I look from one to the other trying to see any anger or disappointment in their faces, but they're both neutral.

"Kinda together?" Da asks, raising an eyebrow.

"*Are* together," I correct.

"Well we're glad you felt you could tell us, son," he says, before bending back down to the weeds.

I look at Ma, who's unnervingly silent. "Ma?"

"Are you being safe?" she says, narrowing her eyes.

I frown. "Safe?" After a second it clicks, and my cheeks burn in an instant. I stand up quickly and grab Bailey's arm. "Come on, Bay. We're leaving." That was not what I'd been expecting.

"Stop, stop, stop." Ma gets up off her lounger and rushes over before we can escape. "I'm very happy you're together, and that you told us," she says, grabbing Bailey's face so she can kiss his cheek and hug him. "Welcome to the family, love."

"COME ON, we haven't gone this way before," I say, pulling Bailey along.

"How? You've been dragging me through these woods for a year and a half, we must have seen everything by now, Teddy. Come on, I just want to hang out by the tree." He tugs my arm back.

He's lived with me long enough to know I don't like to stay in one place for too long. Besides, I'm sure I've never been this way before. I turn around to find him pouting, his plump bottom lip sticking out slightly. "That doesn't work on me, Bay." I grab his thighs, lifting him over my shoulder.

"Teddy!" he yelps.

Ignoring him, I walk through the trees until we come to a clearing, where I set him down, only to be met with a scowl.

"Happy now? You found another clearing. More trees, more grass, more moss," he says, picking some off of a nearby rock.

"Anyone would think you hate being outside," I smirk, knowing that's not the reason he's grumpy. He doesn't like when I make him walk around for hours, because he'd rather be lying under the oak tree making out.

"Come here." I fist his jumper and pull him towards me until his lips are on mine. I can taste the liquorice he devoured earlier, and something a little more familiar. We're lost in the kiss when a rancid smell floats by on the breeze, and I jerk away from him. "Christ, what is that?" I thrust my arm over my mouth and nose, resisting the urge to gag. Bailey sniffs and screws his nose up.

We follow the smell further into the clearing—it's sickly sweet and a little like rotten eggs. A shed comes into view. It looks like it could have been the groundskeeper's once, but now the wood is splintered, roof tiles are strewn across the ground, and the door is barely hanging on by the hinges. I go to take a step closer, but Bailey grabs my arm tightly.

"I don't like it," he says, pulling at me.

I point to the shed. "The smell is definitely coming from there."

He shakes his head, eyes wide and pleading. "I want to go. *Please*," he begs.

Morbid curiosity draws me away from Bailey. "You stay here if you don't want to look, I wanna see what's in there."

"No!" he shouts, digging his nails into my flesh.

"Fuck, Bay, that hurts." I try to prise his hand off me but he holds fast, pulling my arm back. "Fine," I growl, following him back through the trees. He doesn't stop walking until we get to the old oak tree by the stream. When he finally releases my arm, I look down to see little crescent-shaped indents marking my bicep.

"I-I'm sorry." He steps back from me and whispers, "I didn't like the smell."

I've never seen that kind of reaction from him before— terrified and desperate, clawing at me like a wild thing. His face has paled, and he takes a step away from me, looking over his shoulder as though he might run at any moment. I close the distance and grab his hand. "It's fine, Bay. I should have listened when you said you didn't like it."

He sniffles, looking at my arm. "I hurt you."

"It was an accident. I'm fine."

He shakes his head, voice breaking as he says, "It's bleeding."

I squeeze his hand and pull him towards me. "You were scared, it was an accident."

"I'm not safe." He pulls his hand, trying to get free of me.

What the hell is going on? I'm not sure if this is about the smell or if something else is upsetting him, but all I want is to calm him down. "You are safe, Bay. You're always safe with me. You know that."

"No. You're not safe with *me*," he cries out as he struggles against my hold, slipping his hand out of mine.

Then he runs.

TEN

BAILEY - EIGHTEEN YEARS OLD

I RUN AS FAST AS I CAN AWAY FROM TEDDY AND THE rancid smell of decay, navigating the trees without having to think. I've walked these trails so many times I could do it blindfolded. The air burns my lungs as I get far away from the clearing, but I'm convinced I can still smell rotting carcasses. The scent clings to the back of my throat, making me feel sick.

As soon as the smell hit me, I knew exactly what it was. It's something I've become accustomed to over the years. Since I was ten, I've had blackouts. Periods of time I can't remember, because, for some reason, my brain has decided I don't need to. I'd fall asleep, and when I woke, my hands would be stained with blood. I'd find dead mice hidden in drawers, in the wardrobe, under the bed. Shane would help me get rid of them, but sometimes we'd miss one, and after a while, that sickly sweet smell of rot would fill the air to the point of choking.

That's what I can smell, and the thought of what could be in that shed makes my blood run cold.

Shane said this would happen. Any chance he's had to corner me at school over the past six months, he's asked how

I've been doing. How I've been coping without him keeping me in check. Asking when I'll be coming home, telling me if I don't then there'll be no one to fix me when I break. He was right. I can feel myself breaking, and I'm all alone. There's no way I can tell Teddy what I've done.

I need Shane.

A solid weight crashes into my back and I hit the ground hard. Twigs and stones scrape along my arm. I'm rolled onto my back, and Teddy pins me in place. He says something, but I can't hear over the thumping of my heart. I struggle, trying to get out his hold, gasping for air.

"Bay, you need to calm down!" His voice floats towards me as though I'm underwater. "Why'd you run from me?"

I let out a guttural yell. Everything I've been holding in for years suddenly bursting free. Teddy releases my arms and cups my face, wiping away my tears with his thumbs. "You're safe, I'm right here. I'll always be here."

He presses his forehead against mine and we stay like that until I go numb, mind blank. My breathing slows and the tears dry up. Teddy gets off me and sits on the ground, pulling my head into his lap as he strokes my hair.

I stare up at the canopy of trees, counting the blackbirds hidden between the branches. So many things are running through my head—what I could tell him, what I *should* tell him. Taking a deep breath, I mutter, "I need to leave."

Teddy shifts under me, hand pausing in my hair. "Why do you need to leave?"

"I don't want to end up hurting you."

The view of the trees above disappears as Teddy leans over me, frowning. "How are you going to hurt me?"

"I ... I don't know. I'm just scared that I will."

"Well I don't think you will. You need to have more faith in us, Bay. More faith in yourself." He presses a finger against my chest, over my heart. "Because I do. I think you're the best thing that ever happened to me, and I want you to stay."

A single tear slips free, scalding as it runs down my cheek. Teddy leans down to kiss me gently on the lips, and it's almost too much. I want to believe him, but just one blackout could end everything. Us ... me. I wouldn't be able to live with myself if I hurt him.

Stop it, I growl to myself. I've known Teddy for a year and a half and I haven't hurt him. I've lived away from home for six months and nothing bad has happened. Everything bad that's ever happened has been in that house. Away from it— away from my family—I feel safe. In control.

"Okay?" he whispers against my lips.

I nod. "Take me home, Teddy."

ELEVEN

HE'S AVOIDING ME, AND EVERY DAY THAT PASSES, I feel like I'm losing a grip on myself. Something really bad must have happened the night Teddy left me, and I hate not knowing what. My mood's plummeted, I'm struggling to eat, headaches are a daily occurrence, and I had my first nightmare in nine months last night.

I roll over in bed and come face to face with Noah. His eyes are closed, and his mouth hangs open with quiet little snores filling the silence. He's been sharing my bed since he was fifteen; just crawled into it one night, and refused to leave. Even if he does like to sleep diagonally and take up eighty per cent of the bed, in times like this, when I'm so in my head like this, I'm glad I'm not alone.

I poke his face. "Get up, Noah. It's eight." He groans as I slide out of bed, bending down to retrieve my anxiety pills from my suitcase. I pop one in my mouth and wash it down with water.

"Why?" Noah complains.

"You asked me to wake you up to go jogging before breakfast." I don't think I can actually stomach any food, but if we get to the farmhouse early enough, I might bump into Teddy.

"Fine," he grumbles, throwing the duvet off and getting dressed.

I follow him out of the house and he jogs off ahead of me. When he looks back, I plaster on a fake smile and overtake him.

Running usually helps to clear my mind, but the silence surrounding me lets the monsters in.

"You're never good, Bailey. Never," my brother's voice carries on the wind. My light jog turns into a run, Dean's voice chasing me also: *"Hey, baby boy."* I pick up my speed until I'm sprinting, pumping my arms and legs as fast as I can until my lungs burn and my knees feel like they might buckle. My stomach cramps, and I come to an abrupt stop, grabbing my stomach as I double over, retching.

Noah eventually catches up with me. "No more," he gasps. "Come on, you're done." He marches me all the way to the farmhouse, telling me I'm stupid for doing that on an empty stomach. Once inside, he forces me to sit on the stool and tells Teddy's gran I need a double portion of bacon. I roll my eyes, about to protest, but Mary shoves a plate under my nose before I can say a word.

"Gran!" someone yells from another room.

Mary rolls her eyes. "I best go see what Isla wants." She unties her apron and hangs it up before leaving the room.

"Have you got therapy later?" Noah asks.

I freeze with my fork almost to my mouth, suddenly nauseous. "No. Carol said we could pick it up again when the wedding's over. Unless I—unless I feel like I need her."

Noah raises an eyebrow, and I know he thinks I need her.

Everything is starting to unravel in the worst possible way. What's worse is that I'm the one doing the unravelling, and I know I'm not going to stop until Teddy tells me what happened—even if I destroy myself in the process.

Even if I do need my therapist, I can't tell her about *this*. I haven't told her everything about my past. I'm not ready for it. I may never be. I'm fucking terrified that if the whole truth comes out, they'll lock me up and throw away the key.

I put the fork down and rub my temples to try and ease the god-awful throbbing. Noah bumps his shoulder against mine in comfort, but remains silent, knowing not to push me.

"There's the unhappy couple," Richard says as he walks into the kitchen. "We're all going to the pub later, you're coming right?"

"Who's *all?*" Noah asks.

Richard steals a sausage from Noah's plate. "Me, Isla, Theo, and Robbie," he mumbles, chewing.

"You think that's a good idea, with ... you know." Noah nods his head to me. "Theo isn't going to want Bailey there."

"Isla spoke to Theo; he said he's fine with it."

That seems hardly likely after what happened the other day at the harbour.

"I was there," Richard says. "He's fine."

The brothers look at me, two sets of grey eyes, waiting for me to make a decision. I'm not sure what would be worse: not going and acting like I have a problem with Teddy, or *going* and risking him shouting at me again.

This might be my only chance to get him to talk. I nod to Richard. "Sure, we'll go."

THE SMELL of wood smoke fills the air as we walk down the lane towards the pub. The closer we get, the more my palms sweat, and I can feel Noah's questioning gaze on me without even having to look at him.

When we reach the entrance, I push the door open, gesturing for him to go first, then follow him, ducking under the frame. Inside, the ceiling isn't much better. I bend my neck to avoid hitting my head on the low exposed beams adorned with hops.

We approach a large table at the back of the pub. Richard and Isla are sitting on chairs on one side, with Robbie and Teddy on a bench opposite.

"Hey strangers," Robbie calls out, face lighting up with a big grin. He climbs out from behind the table and gestures for us to sit in the middle. I look at Noah, expecting him to sit between Teddy and I as a little bulwark, but he just stares right back at me.

"What?" I ask.

"What?" he replies.

I frown, then cast a quick look at Teddy. He's eyeing me warily, but doesn't protest when I slide onto the bench next to him. I leave a big gap, but Noah sits so close to me that I'm forced to move over. He moves with me, so I shift again until I'm pressed right up against Teddy—thigh to thigh, shoulder to shoulder. The moment we touch, I feel his body stiffen, as mine prickles all over.

I push Noah back, but he seems just as squashed, with Robbie practically sitting on his lap. Noah looks up and opens his mouth to say something, but Robbie flashes him a grin, highlighting the barbell in the middle of his bottom lip. Noah quickly averts his gaze, a slight blush blooming on his cheeks.

"Comfy there?" Robbie asks, prodding Noah gently with his elbow, making him fall against me again. I'm pushed further into Teddy and quickly turn to apologise, but he's already staring at me. The words turn to ash on my tongue and I look away.

"There's clearly not enough bloody room; get a chair and sit on the end," Noah snaps.

"I'm good here, thanks." Robbie stretches an arm along the back of the seat, behind Noah's shoulders.

"Anyway," Isla interrupts, glaring at Robbie. "As I was saying, a dog walker found a body in some woods down in Surrey. They think the amount of rain they've had recently unearthed him." She gags dramatically. "The police searched the area and found *two more* bodies."

"Shit," Robbie says, screwing his nose up. "Do they know who did it?"

"Not a clue so far. But they've shut down the entire forest to see if there are any more bodies. They said the victims were likely killed years apart, due to the different stages of decay."

"Lovely," Richard mutters next to her.

"It could be Peter Sutcliffe all over again." Isla nudges him with her elbow. "The Surrey Ripper is at large," she says in a deep, serious voice, mimicking a news presenter.

"Have your parents said anything?" Robbie asks Teddy.

He looks around me to answer. "No, but I haven't spoken to them for a few weeks."

I should probably be concerned for my own family, but I haven't spoken to them since I ran away. I changed my last name specifically so that they couldn't find me. When I let my mind wander to picture something happening to them, I feel nothing.

"So, you two were friends back in England?" Robbie asks, changing the subject. "How'd you manage to win him over? Theo hated making friends when he was a kid. Still does as an adult, actually," he chuckles.

I look at Teddy, unsure of what I'm allowed to say. My throat closes up from the fear of saying the wrong thing.

He holds my gaze, warm whisky eyes sweeping over my face. "We dated for a year," he mutters.

"What!" Robbie bellows. Noah jumps at the volume, covering his ears.

"What?" Teddy asks cooly.

"A boyfriend? You never told me about a boyfriend, Theo." Robbie complains.

"It was nothing." Teddy frowns, eyes turning cold again as he picks up his beer.

I stare daggers into the side of his head, but he avoids meeting my eye.

It was not *nothing*.

Is this my punishment? Him announcing to everyone that I had been such an insignificant part of his life? Maybe I deserve it. I threw him away first—told him I'd never loved him.

Except I was lying when I said all those things. I'm not sure I can say the same for him.

"Excuse me." The table falls silent as Teddy stands up before making his way to the bathroom.

TWELVE

THEO

ALL WEEK IT'S BEEN EATING AWAY AT ME THAT there's something not right about Bailey. How he acted at the harbour reminded me of when I first met him. The way tears glistened in his eyes as he struggled to talk; *that's* the Bailey I'd forgotten. The Bailey I'd cleaned up in the woods when no one else gave a shit. The Bailey I wanted to protect from his shitty mum. The Bailey I swore would never hurt me.

I want to know why he's acting like he doesn't remember the night I left. That's why I came here. But being that close to him was like sitting next to an open fire. Warm and familiar at first, then gradually getting hotter until it felt like the flames would consume me. I don't know why I thought I'd be able to get through tonight.

I turn the cold tap on and splash my face to cool down just as the bathroom door flies open, banging against the wall.

"What the hell was that?" Bailey demands.

Nope. I was definitely wrong to think I could talk to him. I freeze at the sound of his raised voice, staring at my reflection in the mirror. I see my eighteen-year-old self, wide-eyed and scared looking back.

"Teddy, we need to talk about this, because I don't know what's wrong. This is more than just the break up."

Of course it's more than the fucking break up.

"I didn't mean to end things between us, I swear. It was Shane—"

I turn to face him. "What was Shane?" I snap, feeling like I'm vibrating out of my skin.

"Everything! He said I didn't deserve—" He cuts himself off, then grabs my arm, stepping into me, backing me into the corner. "Just tell me what I did, *please.*"

I put my hand on his chest to stop him getting closer, unable to think or look at him. He's messing with my head, like he did all those years ago.

"Come on Teddy, you *know* me. I wouldn't have said those things to you if I had no other choice. I loved you—"

"No. You don't do that to someone you love, Bailey. We were kids. Neither of us knew what love was, but that wasn't fucking it." I push his chest again but he doesn't move. "I wish I'd never met you," I rasp. A sharp pain shoots through my chest as the lie leaves my lips. However much I hate him now, I *know* I loved him once. I must have, or else it wouldn't hurt so bad. I've never felt anything close to it since.

Bailey's mouth goes slack, and he puts his hands on the wall either side of my head. "You're a liar ... you don't get to say the time we had together meant nothing to you, Teddy. I was there too. It was everything."

I'm shaking my head before he's even finished. My breath hitches as I meet his gaze. Tears threaten to spill from his eyes, light bouncing off rings of gold. Memories of that night try to push through, but I close my mind to them and try to focus on breathing.

His chest rises and falls quickly as he draws short breaths. He looks terrified, and so much like the sixteen-year-old Bailey I remember that I find it hard to piece the two versions of him together. Fractured moments slip through: the first time he spoke to me, the first time I kissed him ... the first time I told him I loved him.

Bailey rests his forehead against mine, and I freeze at the contact, trying to swallow around the lump in my throat.

Tears stream down his face as he holds the knife to my throat. "You made me do this!"

"Move," I say hoarsely.

Ignoring me, he leans closer, breath puffing against my lips. "No."

"Move!" I shout over the high-pitched wailing in my ears.

Bailey growls in frustration. Tearing himself away from me, he punches the mirror, glass shatters everywhere, and I collapse to the floor with my arms over my head, a whimper falling from my lips.

Flames burst through the glass windows climbing up to the roof. A blistering heat bites at my ankles as the ropes catch on fire.

"Jesus ... I-I'm sorry, Teddy," Bailey chokes out. He touches my arm hesitantly, and I flinch away from him, trying to back myself further into the corner.

"Fuck," he breathes.

Head still buried in my arms, breathing through the nausea, I listen to him pacing the bathroom.

"Shit ... okay. I don't know why I did that ... I don't know what the hell is going on." The desperation in his voice is palpable. "Should I get Robbie?"

I look up and shake my head. If Robbie finds out, he won't stop to think before going for Bailey. My ears have stopped ringing, and I don't feel as though I'm going to throw up anymore. With a clearer mind, I focus on Bailey. Trying to reassure myself that if he wanted to hurt me again, he would have done it by now.

"I really think I should get him," Bailey repeats.

"No," I manage to say through a tense jaw. Rubbing a hand over my face, I take one last deep breath before gripping the sink to pull myself up. I'm hit with a headrush and sway, trying to catch my balance. Bailey stays as far away from me as he can in the small room. I look around and see there's blood splattered across the floor and amongst the shards of glass—dripping from Bailey's fist clenched tightly at his side.

"Clean yourself up," I say calmly, as though I didn't just break in front of him.

I open the door and hear a choked sob. When I look over my shoulder, Bailey's wiping away tears roughly with his undamaged hand. My chest tightens at the sight of it.

He said he doesn't know what happened to me the night I left England, and I think I'm starting to believe him. I'm not ready to unpack what that would mean, so I slip out and let the door swing shut between us.

AN HOUR PASSES as I roll from side to side, moving the cover off, then on, then off again until I've had enough. I jump out of bed, heart thumping and body vibrating with energy. I check my phone and see Isla's posted a few pictures from the pub last night: Rob and I deep in conversation, Rob winking at the camera, me frowning. Then a bunch of photos from the barn restoration. I pause on a photo of Bailey kneeling, hammer held mid-air as though he's about to bring it down. An Alice band pushes his hair away from his face, his brow creased in concentration. He seems so normal ...

I storm into the bathroom and turn on the shower, hoping to clear my mind, but once I'm under the water it goes straight back to Bailey. How terrified he looked when he begged me to tell him what he'd done.

A growl of frustration escapes me as I press my fists into my eyes. I don't want to think about what it means that he can't remember. Was it such an insignificant time in his life that he just forgot? Whilst I have to relive it every time I close my eyes. My head spins, and I lean against the cold bathroom tiles. I just need to fucking sleep then I'll be able to think more clearly.

My cock throbs uncomfortably, and I look down to find that I'm hard. It's been weeks since I've had any kind of relief. I want to ignore it, but the release might actually help me get to sleep, so I pump a little conditioner into my palm and reach down to massage my aching balls. My cock kicks at the sensation, and I slide my hand up the length of it, taking a firm grip.

I try to think of nothing; just feeling my hand work over my shaft in a steady rhythm. My thighs tense as my foreskin rubs over the sensitive head, each pass of my fist dragging me closer to the edge—then the memories flood in again. They flash through my mind so quickly it makes me dizzy.

Bailey lies under me, and I grip his sweat-slick thigh. He clings to my shoulders as we grind against one another desperately. Then he's suddenly leaning over me, eyes filled with tears. My wrists and ankles are bound tight by rope, the sickly sweet scent of death thick in the air.

I gag and release my softened cock, slapping my hands against the cold tiles. The echo ripples around the bathroom, and I collapse to my arse, letting the shower wash away my tears.

THERE ARE no clean cups in this bloody house. I slam another cupboard door shut and groan when I see the mountain of washing up. It's eight in the morning and I've had little to no sleep; I just want a coffee. I do the only sensible thing I can think of—ignore the mountain and pluck out a cup and a teaspoon.

"Morning." Robbie's voice, gruff from sleep, fills the silence. I watch as he walks into the kitchen ... wearing just a jockstrap. I freeze with the kettle in my hand.

"Close your mouth, you'll catch flies," he says, pushing two fingers under my chin.

I smack his hand away.

"So, you and Bailey, huh?" he asks, leaning against the counter, crossing his arms.

"I'm not talking about Bailey." I keep my head down and finish making my drink.

"Why? Was it that bad? Isla seems to think—"

"Yes! It was that bad," I bristle, turning to point at him. "You and Isla need to mind your own business. I mean it."

"Why didn't you tell us? Or me, at least. You know, out of everyone, I would understand. Twelve years Theo, and you said nothing about making friends, or having a *boyfriend* while you were in England. Now I'm thinking you've been hiding other shit from me, because when you came back to Skye, you were a different person. If that had something to do with him, then I want to know," he says with a bite to his words.

And that's exactly why I couldn't tell him. I doubt much would have stopped him from going straight to Surrey to find Bailey back then. He would have got in trouble and I'd have been dragged into the spotlight. I didn't want to relive the experience over and over with every person I told. Because it wouldn't just stop at Robbie, or Isla. I'd have to tell my parents, my grandparents, the police. It's my fucking story and I should be able to decide if I share it or not.

For twelve years I let it fester beneath my skin and haunt my dreams. But now ... this is the most I've consciously thought about that night since I came back to Skye, and I'm not sure my memories can be trusted anymore.

"I can't take you seriously when you have your arse hanging out," I say.

"Stop changing the subject," he counters. "Tell me why you hate him so much?"

My grip on the cup tightens. I'm done. I need to get out of here, to go for a fucking walk or ... something. "I'm leaving now."

"No, you're not. Talk to me," he says more softly, taking a step towards me.

Not again—my body feels fit to burst. I'm trapped, and he's not going to let me leave.

"Let me help y—"

"I said no!" I yell.

Shit. Coffee drips down the white wall and the shattered remains of my cup lay scattered across the stone floor.

"Okay ..." Robbie says, staring at the mess I made. "You're not doing this shit with me, Theo. Not again. Go get your gym clothes, we're going out."

"I don't want—"

"Theo," he says, raising his voice. "Go get dressed."

I leave the kitchen like a scolded child and go upstairs to get ready. I hadn't even realised I'd thrown the cup until I saw it broken on the floor. It's been years since I've been this out of control. My memories are bursting at the seams, threatening to consume me. I stare at my reflection in the wardrobe mirror, determination flickering in my eyes—I think I'm finally ready to pull on the thread.

When we get to the gym, Robbie heads to the punching

bag, handing me his spare boxing gloves. "You need to work some of that anger out. You need to talk to me ... or someone. *Anyone*, Theo. You can't keep it inside like this." He stands behind the bag, holding it steady. "Start punching."

I'm silent as I hit the bag, each punch jarring as it sends a dull ache through my arms and shoulders. I keep going until the adrenaline I felt earlier releases in short bursts of energy.

"I met him when I was sixteen," I say, "about a month after we moved to England. We played a game of football together and his brother made a bad tackle. Fucked his nose up." My breathing speeds up as I pick at the old wound. "I helped clean him up, and should have left it at that, but I wanted more. I wanted to be his friend." *Punch.* "I wanted to look after him." *Punch, punch.* "I fucking fell in love with him, Rob, and it made me weak." *Punch, punch, punch.* "His brother warned me not to get close, and I ignored him."

The memory of that day comes to me so fast, I have to stop punching, feeling as though my heart might explode. It was the last time I'd spoken to Shane ...

"Bailey likes to play games. Just be careful, yeah?"

I search his face, not believing a word coming out of his mouth. His ice-blue eyes hold my gaze, cold and unblinking, lips curling up into a grin.

The memory shifts to the night that destroyed me.

Ice-blue eyes stare back at me, wet from tears, yet cold and distant.

Blue.

Always blue.

My breath hitches as I meet his gaze. Tears threaten to spill from his eyes, light bouncing off rings of gold.

They have different eyes ...

I gasp for air, leaning heavily against the punching bag. Either my memories are so distorted they're playing tricks on me. Or Bailey wasn't ...

"Hey, are you okay?" Rob asks, putting a hand on my shoulder. I shake my head, stepping away from the bag.

"I'm done." I bite the velcro on the gloves to rip them off, feeling sick. If Bailey wasn't there, then that would mean Shane—why the hell would he have done that?

I only just make it up Robbie's stairs to the en suite in time for the contents of my stomach to come up. As I wipe my mouth with the back of my hand, there's only one thing on my mind.

I need to speak to Bailey.

THIRTEEN

BAILEY - EIGHTEEN YEARS OLD

Teddy's breathing is slow and steady as he lies facing me, dark curls cascading over his forehead. Not wanting to wake him, I gently twirl the curls around my finger then release them, watching as they spring back up. Even though we're officially boyfriends now, I sometimes forget that it's okay to touch him like this. I gently stroke the arch of his brow while running my thumb over his cheekbone, studying his face. The more I stare, the harder it is to push away the guilt. I still haven't told him the truth about everything. I'm too scared that he'll kick me out and send me back to my family. It's been almost a year since I've had contact with them. I've managed to avoid Shane, for the most part, by sticking to Teddy like glue whenever we leave the house. And I haven't spoken to my mum at all since leaving. She hasn't even tried to call Teddy's parents to ask if I'm okay. I guess she's glad to be rid of me.

Teddy's eyes flutter open, and I'm caught with my fingertip tracing his bottom lip. "Are you being a creeper, baby?" he asks, voice like gravel. His mouth curves up into a bright smile, eyes latching onto mine.

As soon as that word comes out of his mouth, memories of my stepdad bleed into my thoughts. I pull my hand away as if I'd been burnt. "Don't call me that."

"What? You don't like me calling you baby?"

God, why won't he stop saying it? I shake my head furiously, trying to stop myself from remembering the way Dean's hand would rest on my lower back, and his hot breath would tickle my ear as he whispered, "*Hey, baby boy.*"

Teddy grips my chin between his fingers, forcing me to look at him. "I'll call you whatever you want." He rolls on top of me, caging me in, his larger body pressing down into mine, warm and solid. He kisses my forehead and says, "Darling," with a deep Scottish burr.

Then a kiss to my cheek. "Honey."

On my neck, sending a shiver down my spine. "Love."

Pulling back, his eyes jump to my lips, and he leans down to kiss me, tongue flicking along my bottom lip. My cock twitches, pushing eagerly against Teddy's thigh as he shifts over slightly, erection hard against mine as he rolls his hips.

"I think ... *mo leannan*," he whispers.

I can't focus. The torturously slow movement of his body isn't enough for me to find release, so I grind myself against him quicker, in desperate motions.

"What does that mean?" I pant, looking into his eyes. When I see how dark they've got and the smirk dancing on his lips, a whimper escapes me as warmth floods my body.

Teddy chuckles, pushing off me, making his way down my body. His hands stroke across my chest, down to my hips. "It means 'my sweetheart.'" Pausing his movements, his face is serious as he asks, "Is that okay?"

I nod, my brain flatlining when he hooks his thumbs into my briefs, drawing them slowly down. My cock pulses as the fabric drags along the length, catching on the head roughly. It springs free, slapping back against my stomach, pre-cum smearing in the hair there. I lift my hips, desperate for his mouth. Teddy dips his head down and runs the flat of his tongue from my balls to my tip. I let out a choked cry, running my fingers through his hair, grabbing a fistful of curls. His tongue rolls around the head of my cock as he pushes back the foreskin with his lips. Then he takes me fully into the tight heat of his mouth.

I know I'm not going to last long, and thankfully Teddy doesn't seem to have much patience either. He moves up and down quickly, quietly gagging when he takes me too deep.

"Teddy!" I gasp as he pushes all the way to my base, his throat squeezing so tight as he swallows around me that I lose what little control I had. "I'm gonna—" His hand moves from my hip to my thigh, lifting my leg onto his shoulder. Then, he drags a finger over my hole. My breath hitches as he starts sucking me harder, his finger pushing against my opening, and as soon as I feel it slip through my tight ring, I lose it. White spots blind me for a moment. "Teddy, I'm gonna ... fuck, I'm coming," I pant. My cock kicks in his mouth with every spurt of cum.

Teddy pulls his finger out slowly and crawls up my body. He leans over me, fisting his cock, tapping it against my lips. "Open up, mo leannan."

My eyes flash to his, seeing them glint with mischief. I hold his gaze and open my mouth, letting my tongue loll out.

Teddy grips the headboard above me with one hand, while the other starts running over his length. He keeps the head of his cock resting on my tongue, and I hold still, watching his face as the smirk fades, replaced by a deep frown. He pulls his bottom lip between his teeth, biting down as his hand movements jerk out of rhythm. He grunts and pitches forward, arms shaking, and I feel the hot splash of his cum hit my tongue, and swallow it all down.

I feel his tongue drag across my stomach, then he collapses

onto the bed, pulling me against him. He pushes his tongue into my mouth, feeding me my cum, and I groan at the taste of us mixed together, salty and a little sweet.

I never want to leave here.

WITH TEDDY WORKING at the coffee shop, I wander around town aimlessly, wasting the hours until he finishes his shift. I'm about to go into the bookstore when my phone rings. I freeze. No one ever calls me—Teddy would usually text. I look at the number and see Unknown flashing across the screen. Letting it go to voicemail, I slip my phone into my pocket and walk back towards the coffee shop instead, with what feels like the weight of a heavy stone in my stomach.

My phone rings again, and this time I hesitantly answer, holding it to my ear. "H-hello?"

"Hello, am I speaking to Bailey Townsend?"

"Um, yes?"

"Your mother was admitted to hospital this morning. She had a little accident and was brought in by the ambulance. She's okay now and ready to be released. Would you be able to come pick her up?"

I overheat in an instant, and slip down a side road to lean against the cold brick wall. "W-what about my stepdad or brother, she won't want me to—"

"We tried to get hold of your brother but there was no answer, and your stepfather is currently here on duty and can't leave. He said we should try to contact you."

Shit. Shit shit *shit*. I shouldn't. I should make her wait there until Shane answers his damn phone. I hate that I'm instantly worried about her. I can't help it. My body feels like it's going into shock. "What happened?"

"She was found by a neighbour unconscious in her garden, and had sustained an injury to her ankle. Just a bad sprain, she'll be okay after some rest ... so are you able to pick her up?"

"Okay," I say, hanging up.

When I get to the hospital, I see my mum sitting in the reception area. Swallowing down my fear, I tell a member of staff I'm here to take her home. She looks up at me with watery blue eyes, barely focusing, and I can tell she's been drinking again.

"Shane?" she asks.

I help her up and hand over the crutches the hospital provided before leading her out to the bus stop. She comes willingly, and I stay silent the whole way back to Banstead. Luckily, she sleeps for most of it, and I tell myself I'll see her to the front door then go straight back to Teddy's.

Once the front door's unlocked, I turn to leave. "Bye Mum," I say, voice cracking. Everything I've been holding together snaps, knowing that I mean forever. I never had the chance to say goodbye when I moved in with Teddy. Not that she deserved it. She'd checked out of being a parent straight after Dad died.

"Bailey?" she says quietly.

I turn to look at her, tears blurring my vision. "Yeah."

Her face turns to stone, and she shoves the door open, stumbling over cans and bottles that litter the floor as she makes her way to the living room. I can't help but step inside, taking in the mess before me. Nothing's changed. She's still drinking, and no one's bothering to keep the place clean. The place stinks of stale beer and cigarette smoke.

"This is all your fault." She points to her leg.

I freeze in the doorway.

"I found what you hid in the treehouse," she slurs, "caught

my ankle as I was trying to get down from the ladder. You're sick, Bailey. I don't understand where we went so wrong with you. Shane had told me you'd stopped doing it."

A spike of fear lances through my chest as she picks up her phone, pointing it at me.

"Why did you come back? You should have stayed away."

A breeze hits the back of my neck as the front door swings open and Shane comes in. "Hey, look who came home. Do we need to make a welfare check on Theo?" he says seriously.

I flinch at the accusation. I wouldn't—I would never hurt Teddy.

"Shut up Shane," Mum barks, glaring at me. "I want him gone. He's fucked in the head—doing it all over again."

Shane squints at me. "What's happened?"

I open my mouth to speak, but invisible fingers wrap around my throat, making it impossible.

"Your brother is a fucking psychopath. Animals in the treehouse, mutilated. Just like what I used to find in his room." Her face turns thunderous as she looks me dead in the eye. "I should have told the police years ago what happened to your father. I protected you because I wanted to believe it was an accident. But it wasn't, was it? This shit has been going on for *years*." She pushes the keypad on the phone three times, looking past me to Shane. "He's never going to stop."

I can't breathe.

"What are you doing, Mum?" Shane asks, shoving past me.

She puts the phone to her ear. "He's not going to stop, Shane!" she chokes out, tears welling up in her eyes. "It's not my fault, whatever's wrong with him. He's eighteen; the police need to deal with him."

Shane moves quickly, wrestling the phone off her and ending the call before it can connect. "We don't need to call the police. Come on, Mum, I won't let him do anything. Let me talk to him, find out what's going on."

She looks up at him, face red with frustration, then back to me. Her blue eyes turn dark, and I see no love in them at all. The last threads of her maternal instincts fraying until they snap completely. "I want him out of my house," she spits.

"Here," Shane says, pulling a clear zip bag from his pocket. He hands her a pill, and she takes it quickly, lying back on the sofa. She throws an arm over her eyes and mutters, "Get out."

Shane grabs my arm in a vice-like grip. "It's been too long, little mouse. I think you're due a reminder of why you should behave."

After dragging me up the stairs, Shane nudges me toward the bed. "On your stomach."

I hear the bedroom door lock, and ice-cold tendrils wrap around my body. Tears well up in my eyes as I wonder how I let myself get here. My tongue sticks to the roof of my mouth, and I force my heavy legs to move. I don't know how long those animals have been in the treehouse; I'm sure I haven't had a blackout since living with Teddy. He hasn't mentioned me disappearing or doing anything out of the ordinary. I've been stuck to his side twenty-four-seven.

I swallow down the bile as it creeps up. I thought I'd been good since moving out. That being away from here made me better.

"Shirt off," Shane says calmly.

My hands shake as I pull my T-shirt over my head and let it drop to the floor. Over the years, I've learnt that if I behave then this will all be over quicker. I lie on the bed and bury my face in my duvet so Shane can't see the tears streaming down my face.

"Do you understand why you need this?" he asks. A hand brushes over my lower back and I flinch. Even though my scars have long since healed, the phantom pain cuts through me all the same.

I nod my head twice.

"I think you need an extra punishment this time." The bed shifts and Shane straddles my thighs, pinning me in place as he leans across my back. His breath is hot against my ear as he says, "You shouldn't have left me, little mouse." Then he grabs my wrist and fastens a rope around it, attaching the other end to the headboard.

I let out a startled cry. He hasn't had to tie me down in years; I don't need it—I'll stay still and be good! I open my mouth to tell him no, but my throat tightens, making it impossible. He grabs my other hand, and the only thing that comes out of my mouth is a whimper.

"You need this, Bailey. It's going to be so much worse this time, but it's for your own good. You need to feel the pain you caused those defenceless animals, don't you? It's the only way to get you to stop—at least for a little while."

I pull on the restraints, but they don't budge. Between them and the weight of him pinning me down, the fight starts to bleed out of me. I'm breathing so hard and fast that I feel light-headed.

"Do you think Theo cares about you the way I do? That he would stay if he knew what you were capable of? He wouldn't know how to manage your episodes." Shane pushes, sowing that seed of doubt I'd tried so hard not to let take root.

I hear the flick of a lighter and flinch, pressing deeper into the mattress.

"What do you think will happen if you leave me? If there's no one to keep you under control? What happens when animals aren't enough and you want to hurt someone?" He leans closer, whispering. "What if you hurt Theo?"

The moment the cigarette touches the bare skin of my lower back, I slam my eyes shut and suck in a breath. It never used to be like this. When we were much younger, he would try pinching, or stabbing with drawing pins. Holding teaspoons over candles and pressing them to my skin. Anything he could think of to show how those animals had suffered because of me. When we were fourteen, he tried using cigarettes for the first time. It would work for a while. For a few months I'd be good. No blackouts. No dead animals. No punishments.

I lose track of time. My face is stuck to the sheets from a mix of tears, snot and drool, body devoid of any feeling except for the blistering heat on my back. Shane climbs off of me, and I hear him throw the empty cigarette packet in the bin. My body shakes from the pain and adrenaline. I try to draw in a deep breath but it's hard with the thick smoke lingering in the room, bitter and acrid. Thankfully, Shane opens the window to let in fresh air.

"That was punishment number one," he says.

I can barely turn my head to look at him as the movement pulls at the burnt skin.

"Now for punishment two," he says, flicking open a small knife.

"No," I rasp out as I pull on the restraints again, ignoring the pain rippling across my back.

Shane places a hand on my ribs. "Just a little something to remind you of who will always be there for you, even when everyone else turns their backs," he mutters.

White-hot pain sears against my side as he pushes the knife into me. It doesn't go too deep, but after the first slice, my body gives out, except for the occasional involuntary flinch. I can't stop the whimper that escapes me when I realise I won't be going home to Teddy tonight.

TEDDY

Hey, just got home, I thought you were
meeting me at the coffee shop?

I SHOULD BE grateful Shane left me with my phone and
untied my wrists, but that's no use to me when I have no idea
what I should tell Teddy. This was all my fault. I chose to get
my mum from the hospital. I chose to come into this house
again, after swearing I wouldn't. And I chose to hurt those
animals. I deserved the punishment. And now I have to wait
until my injuries heal before I can see Teddy again.

If I see Teddy again.

I know I shouldn't. Shane is right; if Teddy ever found out
about this, he'd never talk to me again. He'd probably call the
police, just like Mum wanted to do, and if I go back and keep
silent about it, then one day it might be him I end up hurting.

I sniffle at the thought, eyes and nose burning from
holding back tears. I don't want to deal with that yet. Ignoring
the text, I slowly peel myself off the bed and limp over to the
mirror. A sob breaks free, and my vision blurs through tears as
I look at the amount of cigarette burns on my back, red-raw
where the skin's peeled off, blisters oozing. I gag at the sight
of it.

He's ruined me.

Something else catches my eye. Just under my arm, across
my ribs, is the evidence of my second punishment.

Jesus Christ ...

My breathing speeds up as I watch a trickle of blood run
down from the jagged 'S' he's carved into me. I turn away
sharply, unable to look at myself anymore.

I lay back on the bed, and grab my phone.

ME

My mum was in the hospital and I had to take her home. I need to stay here for a while

TEDDY

Shit, is she okay? Do you know how long you'll be there?

ME

I'm not sure. A few weeks maybe

TEDDY

What? Send me the address and I'll come stay with you there

Prickles burst along my head and fingertips as fear spikes through me. I don't want him anywhere near this house, or my family—but fuck, I need him so bad. I swipe the tears from my cheeks and smack my hand against my head several times, getting frustrated with myself because I know—I fucking *know* I'm not going to be able to let him go. After all this, I still see Teddy as my safety. I just need time for my back to heal, and then I'm going straight back to him, because I'm too weak to stay away.

ME

No, it's just a few weeks, I need to try and fix things between me and my mum before we leave for Scotland.

I don't like lying to Teddy. There's no making amends with my mother.

TEDDY

Fine. I'm not happy about it though. They haven't given a single fuck about how you've been doing since you moved out. But it's your choice. Video call me tomorrow?

ME

Okay. Night, Teddy

TEDDY

Night, mo leannan

I jump awake at the sound of my bedroom door opening, gasping in pain as the skin pulls taut on my back. My hand closes tight around my phone, and I slide it under the pillow, so that whoever comes in doesn't take it away. I must have fallen asleep straight after texting Teddy.

"Hey baby boy, what happened?"

The sound of my stepdad's soft voice brings my anxiety back tenfold. At least with Shane, I know what to expect. There's a mutual understanding that it's something that needs to be done. But with Dean, I'm instantly on edge, my muscles tensing in anticipation.

My skin feels so tight around the burns. Every movement pulls on them, threatening to burst the blisters. I can't risk infection if I want to get back to Teddy. So I lay still.

"Shane really did a number on you." Dean's finger brushes against my hip, and I flinch at the contact. He avoids the burns, but pain shoots through me all the same. He hushes me and strokes my hair. "It's alright, I'll clean you up now."

Shortly after Shane switched to cigarettes, Dean found out what was going on. He came home early one day and found me on my bedroom floor, passed out, hot and sticky from a fever. He injected me with something, and when I woke up feeling better, he was hovering over my bed, stroking my cheek. I couldn't speak. Just laid there in silence. Since then, Dean lingers whenever Shane hurts me. He tells me that he'll help keep my burns clean from infection, and that we can leave Mum and Shane out of it. That it will be just our little secret.

There's a familiar sound as the first aid kit clicks open, and I jump when the cold antiseptic cream touches my raw skin. It hurts like hell, yet soothes at the same time. A sigh of relief escapes my lips before I can stop it.

"That's it, you'll feel better soon," he coos as he massages the cream into my hips. I feel him pause before saying, "This is new," as he rubs the cream over the cut on my ribs.

The first aid kit is closed back up, and I squeeze my eyes shut, hoping that's it. He'll leave the room and let me rest. But he grabs my waistband, pulling my joggers down slowly, exposing too much of my body. "Everything feels better once I fix you up, doesn't it?" He strokes a hand over my arse cheek. "You're going to stay quiet for me, aren't you, baby boy? You wouldn't want anyone to find out why you let your brother hurt you, would you?"

I thread my fingers through my hair, tugging so hard it stings my scalp. I'm exhausted and in so much pain, I don't have the energy to push him away. Don't have the voice to tell him no. I try to tell myself that it'll be over quickly—he usually just caresses me a bit and then covers me back up. It will only be a couple of minutes, and then he'll be gone.

Except this time, as he starts to touch me, his fingers slip between my crease, and I feel them brush against my hole. My body freezes up again, and I'm panting for air, squeezing my eyes shut, begging for my mind to black this out.

FOURTEEN

THEO

"Where's Bailey?" I ask, moving to stand in front of television. Isla and Robbie both lean to the side, trying to look around me.

"Well, good morning to you too, Theo," she deadpans. "Why do you need to know where Bailey is?"

"I need to talk to him about something."

"Sure, because that's just what we need, even more injuries before the wedding," she scoffs, rolling her eyes.

My stomach turns over at the reminder. If I find out I was wrong all these years, blaming him for something he never did, then I don't know how I'll forgive myself.

"Shush a minute, this shit in Surrey is getting wild," Isla says, pointing to the TV.

"*... East Surrey Hospital said that they have a zero-tolerance policy and have suspended a member of staff based on the allegation that medical supplies had been taken without authorisation over a period of time. They will be conducting their own internal investigation. However, after toxicology reports showed traces of propofol in one of the bodies found in Banstead Woods,* *police are not ruling out that the two investigations may be linked."*

"I don't give a shit about what's going on in Surrey, Isla. Where is he?" I ask again through gritted teeth.

"Gone. You missed him," she says, casually sipping her coffee like that one word didn't just slice through my chest.

"Gone *where*?"

"There's been issues at the office. Jake needed to go back to Cumbria to speak to his staff about the temporary manager. Bailey offered to go instead."

"He's gone home? How long ago did he leave?"

"I'm not sure, to be honest. Richard was told like an hour ago. Apparently Jake offered Bailey the car, but he insisted on taking the train. Said he needed the time to himself to think about some things. What's going on?"

"Text me his number and address," I shout, already jogging up the stairs. I'm working on autopilot, practically vibrating out of my skin as I throw clothes into a bag. There's no plan. I just need to find him.

"Do you want me to come with you?" Robbie makes me jump, standing in the doorway, arms crossed, looking far too serious.

I shake my head. This is between me and Bailey. "No, Rob. I'm good."

"You sure?"

Zipping up my bag and throwing it over my shoulder, I turn to him. "I need to figure something out. I'll make sure we're both back in time for the wedding, it'll be fine." My phone dings, and I see Isla sent me Bailey's details. "I gotta go —can you let Luke know I'm going to be off work tomorrow and that I'll call him when I get to Bailey's?"

"Of course I can." He pulls me to a stop. "Theo, I don't like it. If he's the reason you were so messed up when you came back to Skye, I—"

I put a hand on his shoulder. "Stop. My head's so fucking messed up right now, Rob. I thought Bailey did something bad, but I think I was wrong. We need to work that out together, *alone*."

He frowns at me. Then, slowly, his face relaxes. "Fine, but I want a hug before you go."

"You don't need a hug."

"I want a hug, Theo."

"No."

"Yes. Or I'll tell Isla that you lied when you said you liked her wedding dress."

"I did not lie! I just—" My eyes narrow. "Fine, hurry up." I stand still and let him wrap his arms around me, squeezing me tighter than a boa constrictor. I pretend it doesn't affect me, and that I'm not ten seconds away from hugging the clingy bastard back.

We pull apart and head out to my car, followed by Isla. As I throw my bag in the back and get into the driver's seat, I'm met with twin looks of concern. I sigh and turn the engine over. "It'll be *fine*. I'll tell you everything when I get back."

Isla leans in through the open window, smiling sweetly. "If either of you come back with a black eye or split lip, Theo, I'll slap you both myself."

I frown, then put my hand on her face, shoving her away from the car. "Goodbye, Isla."

After setting the satnav for Bailey's home address, I pull out of Robbie's drive and head down the A87. Only a few minutes pass before I'm debating calling Bailey to ask how far he's got. I wonder whether I should warn him I'm coming, or just turn up on his doorstep. I'm not sure if he'd turn me away after how I acted yesterday.

As I pass a bus stop, a flash of blonde hair snaps me out of my thoughts. I slam on my brakes, then reverse back. Bailey stares, wide eyed, hands gripping onto the bus stop seat.

"Get in," I tell him.

"W-what?" He stands up hesitantly. "I need to get the bus to—"

"I know, you need to go home. I'm driving you, get in."

He pulls his bottom lip between his teeth. I wait patiently, trying not to snap at him to just get in the fucking car. My heart is already racing at the thought of being in such close proximity to him.

Bailey finally moves; he puts his bag in the back and slides into the passenger seat. I thought I'd have several hours to myself so I could think of what I want to say to him, but now I'm drowning in the silence, unsure how to approach any of this.

"Why are you driving me?" Bailey asks, just as I finish crossing the Skye Bridge.

"We need to talk."

I can feel his gaze burning into the side of my head, but I keep facing the road. It's hard enough to concentrate with him sitting so close, let alone being tempted to check if his eyes are the ones from my nightmares.

"I tried to talk to you yesterday, but you wouldn't let me," he says, voice tight.

"I *couldn't* talk to you yesterday."

He's silent for so long that my eyes drift over to him. He's facing away from me, staring out the window, left hand balled into a fist under his chin, and his right, bandaged up, resting on his thigh.

"I've done some thinking since, and I think we need to—"

"My therapist told me that I should remove myself from a situation when I feel overwhelmed." Bailey interrupts. "I should have left when you said you wished you'd never met me. I knew I wasn't in control, but I kept pushing. I'm sorry, Teddy—I didn't mean to scare you, but that fucking hurt." His voice breaks, and when I look at him, he's staring right back at me with tears in his eyes. "I haven't felt like that since the night you left. Like you shoved your hand into my chest and ripped out my heart—throwing everything back in my face like that."

I bristle at the accusation and turn back to face the road. "Why can't you remember anything?" I ask through a tight jaw.

"I didn't want to do it," Bailey says, so quietly I almost miss it.

"Do what?"

He lifts a hand to swipe at his cheeks, and I shift in my seat, instantly uncomfortable. My mind decides to assault me with images of a younger Bailey breaking down, crying in my arms. I had always been the one he could rely on to hold him together, and now I'm the one breaking him apart. I try to tell myself that he broke me first, but it feels like a lie. The truth is staring me right in the face. I just need to piece it all together before I let myself fully pull down the walls I've been struggling to hold up for so long.

"I didn't want to break up with you. Shane made me do it."

What? "How did Shane make you break up with me?" That's the second time he's mentioned his brother in two days. When Bailey moved in with me, he cut contact with not just his mother, but Shane also, as far as I was aware.

"I thought that he'd hurt you." His breathing gets louder, coming in quick bursts, until he's gasping for air. "Pull over!" he says suddenly.

I drive another few hundred yards, then pull into a lay-by, stopping just in time as Bailey swings the door open and jumps out. He doubles over with his hands on his knees, sucking in air. A few seconds pass by as I war with myself over whether I should help him or not.

My body moves before my mind's made up, rushing over

to him, hovering by his side. Being this close to him settles me slightly, but I can't bring myself to touch him.

"Why would he hurt me?" I ask.

Bailey rocks back, collapsing onto his arse, resting his head in his shaking hands. "He didn't want me getting in trouble, so he said that if I didn't break up with you and come home, he would make sure you'd never want to go near me again."

"He *what*?" My jaw clenches tight. I feel my reality dissolving around me, the edges of my vision darkening. "Why would you get into trouble?" I stare down at him, waiting for an answer, heart pounding in my chest. When he finally looks up at me and we lock eyes, I see it again—rings of gold, flaring out into a sea of blue. Something I'd never thought too hard about when I was a kid. I'd known he was beautiful, but I'd never paid enough attention to his face. I saw him every day for a year, yet somehow I missed *this*. He was just Bailey. *My* Bailey.

I should have paid more attention. I should have counted his freckles every day, should have noticed the patterns in them, the curve of his lips. I should have realised that those weren't the eyes staring back at me while I begged for my life.

I grab Bailey by his good hand and haul him up. We stand inches apart, and for the first time in a long time, I'm not scared. "Get in the car."

I need to tell him what happened to me that night, and if what I'm thinking is correct, then it's something he deserves to know.

Bailey gets back in the car, and I slam my door. I'm not dealing with this in a lay-by on the A595.

FIFTEEN

BAILEY - EIGHTEEN YEARS OLD

"Finally," Teddy says as he flings his front door open, grabbing my shirt and pulling me into him. He wraps his arms around me and picks me up. The skin on my back pulls tight and I suck in a breath. I've waited an extra couple of weeks to come home so that my burns would heal enough, but everything's still sensitive. I do my best to ignore the pain, wrapping my legs around his waist, clinging to him, burying my face into his curls, and breathing him in.

"Are you able to talk?" he asks as he carries me towards our bedroom. I shake my head. I haven't said a single word in a month.

"That's okay. You always come back to me eventually, right?"

I nod, hoping he's right. Whenever I get like this, I'm scared my voice has left me forever. It feels impossible to fight the knot in my throat. My mouth finds its way to Teddy's neck, kissing him there, tongue slipping out to taste him, making sure this is real.

When we get to the bedroom, Teddy lets go of me like he

expects me to drop onto the bed, but I can't make my arms and legs release him. He laughs, but I don't find it funny. I've missed him, and I can't even tell him. Tears roll down my cheeks onto his neck. I know the moment Teddy feels them because his arms envelope me, squeezing tight. He turns us around and sits on the edge of the bed, pulling me closer, rubbing circles on my back. "I know you can't get your words out right now, but I'm ready to listen whenever you can." He gently pulls me away from his neck, cupping my face so he can kiss my forehead. "Something bad happened at your mum's?"

I nod, avoiding his eyes, not wanting to see pity there. I know it was all my fault. I should have controlled myself and not hurt those animals, should have left Shane to deal with Mum, should have fought against Dean instead of letting him touch me like that.

We sit in silence for a while, and I use my sleeve to dry my eyes. Teddy wouldn't be comforting me if he knew everything. He wouldn't want to touch me. I'm terrified that I'm putting him in danger by coming back here. Though I want to believe I would never hurt him, I *have* to believe that, because he's the only thing that keeps me grounded. I feel so fucking fractured, and nothing feels as right as when I'm with him.

"You're alright now, just—just don't leave again, Bay, it's not worth it," he says cautiously. He kisses my neck, up to my jaw, and along to my lips. I close my eyes and let him consume me. The feel of his hands on my thighs, the scrape of his stubble against my chin, the way his hard length presses against me. I want more. I want him to take everything away.

He pulls away and we lock eyes. A silent understanding passes between us, and in a rush of movement, Teddy flips me onto my back. He kicks his trousers off, then his hands go straight to my jeans, peeling them off me. I grab the hem of his T-shirt, desperate to touch him, and he lifts his arms. I break the kiss so I can pull it off over his head, but when he reaches to do the same to me, I slap his hand away.

"What?" he asks, startled.

I've never had an issue taking my top off before, but he'll notice the new scars and realise I lied to him. All I can do is shake my head as I reach for his boxers. His hands fall to the bed on either side of my head and his breathing picks up as I rub his hard cock, hot and heavy, through the fabric. Hooking my thumbs into his waistband, I pull his boxers down as far as I can. Teddy kicks them off the rest of the way, then rids me of mine. All the while I'm reaching for the bedside cabinet, rummaging around for the lube he keeps in there, somewhere. My fingers finally brush against the cool plastic bottle and a foil packet. I pull them out and hold them out to him.

He takes them from me and frowns. "What do you want?"

In the month I spent away from him, he was all I thought about. Not a day went by that I wasn't glued to my phone texting him. He was in my head when I was awake, and in my dreams when I slept. He's everywhere, and everything. I've been ready for this for a while now, and If I hadn't gone back home, I'm sure it would've happened sooner. I swallow around my sore throat and manage to croak out, "You." It comes out too quietly and makes me cough. "I want … you."

Teddy's brows knit together as he looks down at me, "You already have me, mo leannan."

I shake my head at him, the tips of my ears burning from embarrassment. "Inside … of me."

His eyes go wide and he doesn't move, just hangs over me, so I grab the back of his neck and pull him down so that his body blankets mine, our lips almost touching. "Please," I whisper.

He seals our lips in a kiss that takes my breath away, but it's over too quickly, my mouth chasing him as he pulls away.

His large, warm hands run up my thighs, over my stomach, stroking me everywhere, making the hairs on my arms stand up and my body vibrate in anticipation. He wraps a hand around my hard cock and strokes me slowly while dipping his head to deliver open-mouthed kisses to my hips. I squeeze my eyes shut, trying not to think about my back rubbing against the mattress, but I find myself counting each scar as we move.

I'm ripped from my thoughts by the shock of being pinched on my thigh. My eyes fly open, and I frown at Teddy.

"Eyes on me, Bay."

A small whimper escapes me at the command and I nod.

"I need to know you're okay with what I'm doing. If you're struggling to talk, then I need to see your face."

I nod, watching as he reaches for the lube and pours some onto his fingers. He grabs the back of my thighs, pushing them up towards my sides.

"Grab hold," he says, nodding to them.

I grip under my knees and pull them up. Feeling cool air brush over my hole, I suck in a breath, feeling exposed all of a sudden. Teddy exhales a shuddering breath and brushes a finger over my hole while wrapping his free hand around my cock. He puts pressure against my rim and I slam my eyes shut, body going taut.

"Bay," he says sternly. My eyes snap to his deep brown irises. I can see heat in them, mixed with concern. "I need you to watch me." His finger slides into me, and my breath hitches. I can do that. I can keep my eyes open if I focus on Teddy and how he feels inside of me.

He slides his finger out completely, then presses back in with a second. The sting is more brief than the initial intrusion, and I quickly feel pleasure overtake the discomfort. I only realise I've lost my erection when he starts stroking me slowly, and I feel the pressure of the blood rushing through me again.

He twists his other hand around inside of me and curls his fingers up. My stomach tenses, and I gasp.

"That good?" Teddy chuckles.

I nod eagerly, never taking my eyes off his face. He carries on stretching me open, taking his time while driving me insane. My hands grip onto my legs so hard I'm sure they'll leave bruises, and by the time he removes his fingers from me and lets go of my aching cock, I collapse back onto the bed, panting as though I've run a marathon.

Teddy shuffles forwards on his knees, stroking my legs as he stares into my eyes, nervous energy bouncing between us. I wriggle on the mattress in anticipation. He opens the condom and rolls it down the length of his cock. "Ready?" he asks softly.

I nod and reach for his arm, tugging on him until we're chest to chest, my lips finding his. He shifts his hips and moves his hand down between us, rubbing the head of his cock against my hole in firm circles. All my attention focuses on where our bodies meet. My mouth hangs open, lips pressed against his, both of us panting out short, shallow breaths.

He pushes forward. The prep he's done helps a little, but the further the head goes in, the more it stings. Sharp pain slices through me, and I cry out as the head finally pops through my tight ring.

"Hey," Teddy says, freezing. "Do you want me to stop?" He pushes himself up off my chest, sounding panicked. I shake my head, tensing experimentally. Teddy lets out a shaky breath, squeezing his eyes shut.

"More," I breathe.

He pushes a little harder, and my body gives way to let him slide in fully, making us both groan. When I look up at him, there's a bead of sweat at his temple, and his jaw's clenched tight.

"Okay?" he asks.

"Y-yes."

He pulls out carefully then pushes back in, the lube making his movements glide as he does it over and over again. Gripping under my knees, I open myself up to him more. The pain eases off, and I can finally focus on the feeling of him inside me. The way it sets my whole body on fire.

Teddy leans forward, hooking his elbows under my knees, forcing me to release them as his mouth comes down on mine again. I grab hold of his bicep, feeling the muscles flex with every pump, and thread my fingers through his curls, gripping on for dear life when he starts to speed up. Desperate sounds fall from my mouth, and he swallows them while sweeping his tongue over and under mine. Every stroke of his tongue matches the thrust of his hips, making my cock pulse desperately.

As though he can read my mind, Teddy rips his mouth from mine and sits back on his knees. He pulls my hips so my arse is in his lap, then thrusts into me. My vision goes white for a second, and my whole body tenses as he hits my prostate. I yell out, and Teddy's eyes snap to mine. My teeth clamp down on my bottom lip, hoping to trap any other noises that try to escape. When he realises the yell was from pleasure and not pain, his mouth curls into a wicked smile. My stomach clenches, cock leaking. He thrusts again, hitting the same spot over and over.

"You're doing so good, Bay," he pants.

I shake my head. *I'm not good.*

"You are, mo leannan. I've never felt anything like this. You're so tight and hot around my cock; I don't know how much longer I can last."

I wish he'd stop saying that I'm good. Guilt tries to push its way through the ecstasy, and I shut my eyes again, hot tears slipping down my cheeks.

"Shit. Have I hurt you?" Teddy stops immediately, his voice wavering. I feel him slip out of me slowly, and if I could, I would scream at him for stopping right now. I scramble upright and take his cock in one hand, tugging him towards me.

"Please," I whine. I know I don't deserve any of this. But I want him. I *need* him. I'll deal with the consequences when they come, but no way in hell am I stopping now. I was so close.

"You want to carry on?" he asks.

I nod with determination.

"Did I hurt you?"

"N-no," I rasp.

He looks sceptical at first, but the frown lines smooth as I hold his gaze. Lining up his cock, he pushes back into me. My whole body jolts and I collapse back onto the mattress, reaching up to hold on to the headboard. My cock slaps against my stomach with every thrust. I'm so close, the feel of him inside me is like nothing I've felt before.

"Okay—okay, fuck. Bay, I'm close. Are you?"

"Yes," I pant, the word clawing its way out of my throat.

Teddy wraps his fist around me and pumps in time with his thrusts—and I'm done. My body tenses, and then the dam breaks. A wave of ecstasy crashes over me. It almost feels like it's washing away the touch of my brother and stepfather. My cock pulses, and cum shoots all over my stomach and chest.

As I start to come down from my orgasm, everything starts to feel oversensitive. Every thrust leans towards discomfort over pleasure. Then Teddy's movements stutter. He hunches over me as I feel his cock pulse inside me. He collapses onto me, chest covered in sweat, sliding against the mess of cum on mine. His mouth goes straight to the side of my neck, kissing me, making my whole body shudder.

After a moment he gently pulls out and goes into the

bathroom, coming back with a warm, wet flannel to clean us up. He tosses it to the floor when he's done and settles next to me, pulling the duvet over us. We lay there in a tangle of limbs, facing one another as he strokes his thumb across my nose and cheeks, tracing my freckles. "Bay," he whispers. "I love you so much. You know that, right?"

It feels as though there's a vice closing around my heart—I didn't know that. I want to say it back, but it won't come out. My breathing speeds up the more I try, and I stare at him desperately, hoping he'll understand. He meets my gaze, smiling nervously. The words still won't come. I make an undignified sound of frustration and roll onto my back, pushing the heels of my palms into my eyes.

"I know," Teddy says, pulling my hands from my face. "Hey, I know, okay? You'll say it back when you can. Don't force it." He kisses me softly, pulling me against his chest.

Eventually, the noise of his rhythmic breathing fills the room. I lie there on his chest, counting his heartbeats, and whisper weakly. "I-I love you too."

THERE'S HALF an hour to go until Teddy finishes his shift at the coffee shop. He only has a couple more weekends to work his notice, and then we'll be packing up and moving to Skye. The closer we get to it, the more nervous I feel. I'm not sure how I'll cope being somewhere new. If I lose control while I'm up there ...

Shaking my head, I try to push the thoughts away. It's just the anxiety messing with me. I carry on walking down the high street towards Teddy's work. At the last minute, I notice a puddle and sidestep it, slamming into something hard. When I look up, Shane's staring back at me. Silent, with his arms folded across his chest. "We need to talk," he insists.

"N-no, Shane, I haven't done anything this time." I haven't seen him in three months. There's been no more blackouts—I'm sure there hasn't been.

Desperate to get away, I push him and run. If I can just get to Teddy, then everything will be alright.

Shane grabs my arm, pulling me to a stop, then drags me down an alleyway.

"Get off!" I yell, tugging against his hold. "I haven't done anything, I swear! I've been good, Shane. Get off me, please."

He steps into me, baring his teeth. "You're never good, Bailey. Never."

I flinch at the accusation.

"You can't stay with him. You know that. What the hell do you think you're playing at?" His grip on my arm tightens, and I cry out in pain.

"I'm leaving," I gasp out. "You're wrong, I-It's not me … it's that house. I'm fine when I'm not there. I'm good with Teddy! When he goes back to Scotland, I'm … I'm going with him."

Shane releases my arm, a flash of something on his face morphing from concern to rage, then back again. "You can't. If something happens when you're up there, what do you think will happen?"

I shake my head. I don't want to think about what ifs. "I love him, Shane," I cry.

His nostrils flare and his jaw tenses. He grabs me by the throat so fast, I can barely take a breath. I claw at his arm, but he slams me against the wall, my head bouncing off the bricks. White spots dot my vision and dizziness overwhelms me.

"You're going to break up with him—"

"I will not!" I shout, struggling against his hold.

"You *will* break up with him, Bailey," he repeats. "I swear to God, if you leave me ... if you go up there and fuck up, they will arrest you. You'll be thrown in prison, and you'll never see the light of day again. Is that what you want? Is he worth that?"

My heartbeat pounds so hard, I swear I can hear it. I hate that he's echoing all my doubts and fears.

"If you don't do it, then I'll make sure he never wants to go near you again. I'll tell him all about your sick secrets. About what you did to Dad."

I freeze, hands going limp where they were trying to pull him off me.

"How much will it hurt him to know he's been fucking a psychopath. That you've been lying to him for two years. That you put his life at risk because you have no self-control." He puts more pressure on my throat until I can't draw breath. Blood rushes to my ears, and my head swims. "If you leave with him, and he ends up hurt—or worse—then you'll have to live the rest of your life knowing you could have stopped it. You don't deserve him. You've done nothing good in your life to deserve that happy ending," he growls.

I don't deserve Teddy ...

"Come home with me," Shane says, releasing my neck.

I collapse to the floor, dragging in sharp, ragged breaths. "I-I can't go back there, Shane," I rasp. I won't go back to a mother who hates me and a stepfather who touches me when I'm too weak to stop him.

"Then we'll leave together," he says, crouching so we're eye to eye. "Just you and me; we'll go somewhere. I'll make sure you're safe, and you'll never have to worry again. You belong with me, Bailey."

I look up at him through eyelashes heavy with tears. Going with him isn't an option, either. He thinks that hurting me keeps me under control, but it doesn't. I can't deal with it anymore. Every punishment strips something from me, and I know if I go with him that eventually there'll be nothing left. I'd rather be on my own.

MY STOMACH ROILS like the sea in the midst of a storm as I stand in Teddy's bedroom with my bags packed at my feet. The front door bangs closed, and I hear the thumping of Teddy's feet as he runs up the stairs.

"Hey ... what's up?" he asks slowly, eyes darting to the bags.

Oh God. I don't want to do this ... if I open my mouth right now, all that's going to come out is the contents of my stomach. My throat tightens painfully as I swallow.

"I-I need to talk to you," I start, begging my voice to hold out. Teddy stays silent, staring at me. I'm sure he already knows what's about to happen. "I want ... I want to end this." I motion between the two of us. "Us ... I want to end us."

His eyes go wide at that, and I realise I'm wrong. He has no idea where this is going. Of course he doesn't—he's being completely blindsided. We're happy together. Why would he ever think it would end so abruptly?

"I don't understand ... Did I do something wrong?"

No, Teddy. You did nothing wrong. It's all me.

I clamp down on my bottom lip to stop those thoughts coming out of my mouth. "I just can't be with you right now. I-I don't want to go to Scotland with you, and living—" I swallow back a sob, choking on my lies. Blinking rapidly, trying to hold back the tears for just a little longer. "Living with you has been too much."

"What?"

"I'm not ready! We're only eighteen for fuck's sake, Teddy."

He just stands there, letting me spit vitriol, looking so calm, while I'm static in the air before a lightning strike. I hate not knowing what's going on in his head. Why isn't he fighting for me to stay? It's a selfish thing to think—I know I'm doing this for *him*, but does he not care if I walk out of his life?

I take a deep breath before carrying on. "I'm not ready for all of this. I don't ... I don't want to be with the first boy I fucked forever." I don't even know what's coming out of my mouth. It's all lies. I'm always lying to him. Ever since I first met him.

Teddy's face crumples, finally. "You said you loved me—"

"I lied!" I yell, feeling my cheeks heat.

He flinches. "I ... I don't believe you," he says, looking me up and down as though he can see the lies written on my skin.

I love him. More than I thought possible, and I'd choose his safety over mine, every damn time. He's not safe with me. I'll never be able to tell him the truth about me without breaking us both. At least doing it this way, he'll be free to move on with his life. I'll just be that arsehole ex that broke his heart.

Broken hearts can be fixed—I can't.

"Believe me, Teddy, I'm leaving." I pick up my bags and try to step around him, but he puts his arm out to stop me.

"Please, Bay," he whispers. We're so close, I'd just have to lift my chin to kiss him one last time. His eyes wander over my face, then go wide. "What happened to your neck?" He hooks a finger into the turtle-neck jumper I'd stolen from him. I grab his hand to stop him. My neck's still tender from when Shane grabbed me. In my panic, I shove Teddy back and he loses his balance, collapsing to the floor with a grunt.

I'm out of the house within seconds, already at the end of his driveway when I hear him.

"BAY!"

I start to run.

"BAILEY!" His voice breaks, and so does my heart right alongside it. I run as fast as I can, knowing if I stop for even a second, I'll crawl back to him and beg for forgiveness.

And that will destroy us both.

SIXTEEN

THEO

AFTER AN HOUR OF DRIVING IN SILENCE, I PULL OVER and park outside a lilac-coloured two-up two-down. We get out of the car and I follow Bailey to his front door. My body's vibrating with anticipation. I know as soon as I cross the threshold, there's no turning back.

Steadying myself on the door frame, I watch as Bailey walks through the open plan space to the kitchen, dumping his keys onto the counter. He keeps his back to me, oblivious to my mental tug of war. I slowly step inside and shut the front door behind me.

"You can't remember that night," I say, voice too loud, cracking through the silence.

He turns to me and shakes his head. "I remember some of the night, but part of it's just … gone. Like a-a blackout."

"What *do* you remember?"

"That we broke up … I regretted everything I said and wanted to talk to you. But by the time I got back to your house, your dad said you'd already left."

My dad? He never told me. I rub a hand down my face. "Do you know where Shane was?"

"He ... he was with me for some of it." His brow creases, and he pulls his jumper sleeves over his hands. "Why?"

"After the blackout?"

"What do you mean?" he asks, voice wavering slightly, putting the cuff of his sleeve into his mouth.

I close the distance between us, and pull his hand away. "Did you see Shane after you blacked out?"

"N-no, I ran away."

Okay ... okay, fuck. I believe him. He was always a terrible liar, avoiding eye contact like the plague. But I'm staring right into those blue irises, laced with gold, and he's holding my gaze. He looks scared, like he wants me to reassure him that it's not as bad as he's thinking. I'm going to have to tell him that it's so much worse. I have so many questions for him, but first I need to swallow down my fear and tear that wound right open again. I need to tell him what happened to me, exactly the way I remember it.

SEVENTEEN

THEO - EIGHTEEN YEARS OLD

"BAY!" I YELL AFTER HIM AS HE RUNS FROM ME. "BAILEY!" My voice cracks, and I choke on my tears. He doesn't look back once as he disappears down the street. I want to chase after him, but my feet are rooted to the ground, legs barely holding my weight.

What the fuck was that? Everything was good. *We* were good. I head back inside, slamming the front door shut, rushing up to my bedroom. The last five minutes play on repeat in my head.

He told me he loved me before I went to work this morning, to turn around and say he'd been lying—he couldn't even look at me. I'd like to see him try that again. I'd make him look me in the eye and tell me I meant nothing to him.

I don't believe him. The boy I've lived with for the past year would never have done that. And yet, it's not the first time he's run from me ...

Jesus, my stomach hurts. I sit on my bed and pull out my phone, debating whether I should call him. I need more from him than the 'not wanting to be with my first boyfriend forever' bullshit.

I call him and it rings through to voicemail, so I try again. And again. Growling in frustration, I text him instead.

ME

We need to talk, you can't just leave like that, Bay

Minutes go by, and the message sits unread.

ME

Where are you? I'm not angry, I just want to understand

I'm not sure how much time passes, but I'm lying on my bed, feeling numb, when my parents get home. My throat burns from holding back tears. I'm going to have to tell them that Bailey's gone. I desperately try phoning him another three times, but all of them go through to voicemail.

ME

Let me see you one more time, please?

A knock on my bedroom door makes me jump.

"Boys, have you had dinner?" Ma shouts through.

"Yes," I say weakly.

"Theo? Is everything okay?"

Sniffing and wiping away my tears, I choke out, "Yeah, everything's fine, Ma. I'll talk to you later."

"You sure?"

"I said it's fine, Ma!" I shout, frustrated that she won't leave.

"Okay, honey. Come find me when you've calmed down."

Great. Even without telling her anything, she probably knows what's happened. Exhausted and emotionally drained, I close my eyes for just a minute.

Vibrations shock me out of my sleep. I sit bolt upright,

hands seeking my phone. When I unlock it, there's a text from Bay.

BAY

Meet me by the shed in the woods.

I FOLLOW THE RIVER, retracing my steps from a few months ago, until the shed comes into view. I try not to question why he wants to meet here when he had such a bad reaction to it last time. The sickly sweet smell is still thick in the air, getting stronger the closer I get. I can't see him anywhere in the clearing, so I approach the shed slowly.

"Bay?" I whisper, pushing the door open slowly. It's pitch black inside, other than the fading light of the setting sun slipping through the doorway. The smell is so much worse in here —cloying, hot, and thick, coating the back of my throat, making me retch. I scan the room, letting my eyes adjust, but the door snicks shut and I'm plunged into darkness. Something hits the back of my head, and I drop to the floor.

I try to stand up but my head swims. Hands grab my wrists, binding them, pulling tight. I kick out, desperate to break free of whoever the fuck is touching me. They squeeze my arm tight, and I feel something sharp pinch inside the crook of my elbow. "Bay!" I call out, hoping he's somewhere in the clearing, close enough to hear me. Everything feels warm and heavy. All the fight bleeds out of me until I can't keep my eyes open.

This is wrong ...

Everything feels so wrong.

Fighting to stay conscious, I try to yell, but nothing comes out. The silence is suffocating.

THE WORLD TILTS wildly as my eyes flutter open. Everything's still dark and hazy. I feel like I'm buried under a hot blanket. Gasping for air, I try to move, gagging at the rancid smell. I can't move my arms or legs—I pull and tug, but my wrists and ankles are restricted by tight ropes that scratch and dig with every movement. My skin crawls, and I break into a sweat.

I manage to roll over, and whatever was on top of me shifts, thudding onto the wooden floor. As my eyes adjust to the darkness, I see the door is still cracked open, a slither of moonlight illuminating what I'd been buried under. My breath catches in my throat. Bright copper fur, stained red, numerous vacant eyes staring back at me. I squint, fighting double vision as I start to identify different animals: foxes, rabbits, a couple of cats, and at least a dozen mice mixed into the mound.

There's a buzzing sound, increasing in volume, that draws my attention to a cloud of black hovering over the carcasses. Flies zip and dive through the air before landing on the decomposing flesh. Something shifts in the pile, and I hold my breath, searching the bodies for the source of movement, terrified that there's something alive in here with me.

A fox moves, and I scramble further back. It's missing a whole eye. The socket and cheek ripple and undulate. Squinting, I can just about make out a sea of white, hundreds of maggots wriggling in the gaping hole.

I roll away from the horror and retch again, bringing up

the contents of my stomach, acidic bile burning my tongue as I spit it out. I begin to shake, my breathing too fast ... there's not enough oxygen. The hum of the flies disappears. I'm deaf for a moment before a high-pitched wail pierces my ears, getting louder and louder until everything goes black once more.

"WAKE UP."

A hand strokes through my hair, and I lean into it as my head pounds. Moaning, "Bay."

"Yeah, I'm here."

My stomach clenches as though it's on a hair trigger, ready to expel its contents again. I peel my eyes open. Seeing Bailey so close to me, I jump, biting my tongue, then rush out, "Bay, help me, I don't know—"

"Why didn't you let me go?" he interrupts. "I told you it was over, and you wouldn't stop calling."

"I-I needed to talk to you. Please, you need to get these ropes off me, there's someone—"

"No."

"No?"

Ice-blue eyes stare back at me, wet from tears, yet cold and distant. "I told you that I'd end up hurting you. I said I was scared that I would, and you ignored me. I wanted to leave and you made me go home with you. Forced me to stay."

"I didn't force you—"

He pulls a knife from his pocket and yanks my head, exposing my neck. I suck in a breath and hold it there, too scared to move an inch.

"This is all your fault. You should have just let me go when

I ran from you in the forest," he says, voice cracking, eyes welling up with tears.

"Please," I breathe.

The knife digs into my skin. "I can't do this anymore, Theo. I can't pretend that I'm normal, that there isn't this fucking monster hiding inside of me, just waiting to escape."

"You don't have to do this, Bay," I gasp.

I stare as tears stream down his face. "You made me do this!"

I swallow, and the knife scrapes my skin. I've never felt so helpless. I don't know what he's on about, there being a monster inside him. He's not violent. He's not—whatever the fuck this is.

"Go home, pack your things, and move to Scotland. I'm not coming with you." He drops the knife on the floor. Panting, he stands up and walks out. As soon as he's gone, I shuffle along the floor towards the knife, turning and trying to grab it between my fingers. Just as I have it secure in my hand, the door bangs open fully and more moonlight streams in. Bailey comes back in holding a petrol can.

"W-what are you doing?" I shake my head as he walks over to the pile of animals. "Bailey." The smell hits me immediately as he starts to douse them. I try to use the knife to free myself.

"Can't leave evidence behind," he mutters, walking back to the door. He wipes the tears from his eyes and pulls a lighter from his pocket. "I tried to be good for you, Theo. I know you'll get out of this, just ... just leave, okay? And never come back."

He flicks the flint with his thumb and a flame jumps to life, dancing in the slight breeze coming from the open doorway. "I'm sorry," he whispers as he throws it onto the petrol-soaked carcasses, then turns, walking out the door.

I watch the flames surge upward and suck in a breath,

fingers halting their progress on cutting through the rope. My heart stops as the pile of furs are engulfed. The cloying smell of the animals melds with petrol and charred flesh, forcing bile up my throat.

I shake my head so I can focus, frantically sawing through the rope again. My hands suddenly snap apart, and I immediately start on the ropes around my ankles.

The flames lick up the walls and along the floor. Too close. Too hot. Black smoke starts to settle, making it hard to draw in air. There's no time to free my legs. I hold the knife in one hand and start dragging myself out of the shed.

When I get outside, I gulp in fresh air. There's no time to stop—I hear the timber crack, and part of the roof collapses. Rolling onto my back, I scramble away just in time to see the flames burst through the windows. Shattered glass sprays outwards. I cover my eyes with my arm as tiny shards hit me. A blistering heat bites at my ankles, drawing my attention away from the shed. The ropes around my ankles have caught on fire. Fumbling the knife, I cut myself free as quickly as I can, tossing the rope away, burning my fingers in the process.

Dizziness hits me like a freight train as I push to my feet. I wobble, grabbing hold of a nearby tree to steady myself. I drop the knife and push myself forward, trying to run, stumbling over rocks and roots as brain fog consumes me.

When I finally get home, I head straight for the bathroom, and turn on the bath tap, forcing my throbbing ankles under the water for a few minutes. I dry them off then wrap them in cling film. Giving myself no time to think about what's happening, I shove everything I can think of into bags, grab my phone charger and wallet, and head back out.

My brain hasn't caught up yet. I don't know what the hell Bailey injected me with, but I feel sick, and my vision still won't focus properly. My arm itches, and when I look down, there's a little bruise on the inside of my elbow. I pull my phone out and block Bailey's number, letting out a choked sob as I make my way to the train station. I just need to get to Skye and everything will be okay. I'll be safe.

I'll never have to see that psychopath again.

EIGHTTEEN

BAILEY

No. I try to process what Teddy is telling me, feeling like I might throw up. I said I would never hurt him. I was *sure* I would never hurt him. But as he goes into detail about the animals and the fire, I back away from him. Further and further, watching his face shift from pain to anger to frustration as he recounts the horror. By the time he's finished, his chest is heaving.

That's what I blacked out?

I grip the kitchen counter to steady myself. I thought that had all stopped. *Nothing bad has happened for twelve years! I'm sure ... I—I've been good.*

My world shatters. Everything I thought I knew about the night Teddy left me collapses in on itself until there's nothing left.

You're a monster.

Fuck, Shane was right—I need him. My back throbs in anticipation. I don't think there's a punishment great enough to make up for what I've done to Teddy. "It was my fault," I whisper. Realising that all these years I've blamed him for abandoning me, wondering why he would leave me behind without a second thought ... it was all *my* fault.

"What?" Teddy asks.

"I was supposed to be better!" I yell, chest feeling like it's about to collapse in on itself. He flinches and I break a little more. I close my eyes for a moment, trying to stop my head from spinning. He shouldn't be here with me. I don't want to hurt him again. "Get out," I gasp.

"I'm not going anywhere. We need to talk Bay, I don't think—"

"Get out!" I yell. My eyes dart to the knife block on the counter. If he won't leave, then I'll make him. I'll be the monster one more time so he'll never want to come near me again. The disease inside of me is never going to go away. I pull a knife from the block and turn to face Teddy. He shifts away from me slightly.

"What are you doing?" he asks with a slight waver in his voice. "Put the knife down."

I'm tired. Tired of trying to stay good only to find out I fuck it up every single time. It's completely out of my control —like sharing one body with a stranger—but it never should have got to the point where Teddy got hurt. I made the choice to find him in the woods the first day we met. I made the choice to become friends with him, to kiss him back ... to fall in love with him and refuse to let him go.

All. My. Fault.

"Leave, Teddy." I stalk towards him, knife in hand. He backs up until he hits the front door, reaching behind him to grab the handle, never taking his eyes off me. Once he opens it, I step back, ready to let him go once and for all. "I'm sorry ... for everything." My hand tightens on the knife, and I run my fingertip along the sharp edge of the blade until I feel that familiar sting of pain as it pierces my skin.

Teddy freezes in the doorway, staring at me intensely, eyes

flicking down to the knife. My hand shakes, and I feel blood drip from the cut. I look him in the eye and take a shuddering deep breath, knowing this will be the last time I see him. As I reach for the door to shut him out, his eyes widen, then he lunges at me, catching me by surprise. He wrestles the knife out of my hand and throws it clear across the room, then grabs my arms, pinning them to my sides. Fear lances through me when I realise I can't move.

"No! No, Teddy, please!" I choke out. "I can't ..." I struggle against his hold, but he doesn't give an inch. "I need to be punished," I sob.

"What the hell, Bay!" he shouts over me.

Suddenly it's Shane who is holding me down, telling me I'll never be good. Telling me he knew I'd hurt Teddy. Telling me I need to be punished. "I'm sorry I was bad!" I yell. Throat so dry, every syllable burns. Tears blur my vision as I continue to pull against his hold. We collapse to the floor and my body gives up.

"Fuck, Bay." The familiar Scottish brogue washes over me, and thoughts of my brother dissipate. I realise it's not Shane holding me down. I'm sitting on Teddy's lap with his arms wrapped around my chest, unbendable, like iron.

"Stop," he orders.

Sobs rack my body so violently it makes my head pound. I try to breathe, but I can only manage quick, sharp breaths that scratch at my throat, until I finally give in to exhaustion, going limp in his arms, letting my head fall back against his shoulder.

Teddy's hold on me loosens ever so slightly, and I feel his panting breath in my hair as he rests his cheek against the top of my head. "Just stop," he whispers.

NINETEEN

THEO

My ex-boyfriend is cradled in my lap, and I have no idea what the fuck is going on. The moment I'd started to recall what happened to me that night, I realised it wasn't Bailey who had hurt me. Small things I'd never let myself think about before crept to the surface, things I hadn't noticed even as they were happening. I'd been so out of it between the drugs and fear that I hadn't paid enough attention to what was happening—which I guess is exactly what Shane had wanted.

I recognised that look in Bailey's eyes a moment ago. I've seen it once before, when we first found the shed in the woods. He'd run from me, fear and desperation pulsing off him in waves. Then when I caught him, he shook like a leaf in my arms until he went deathly still. Just like he is now.

A section of the wall I'd built around my heart cracked seeing him break like that again, and now it feels like something's trying to crawl back inside. I know I'm not strong enough to push it out. Not sure if I even want to, not now I have my hands on him again. He's bigger than I remember, but it still feels the same as it did. *He's* still the same, lying in my arms, solid and warm.

I rest my chin on top of his head and squeeze him a little tighter. My heartbeat hasn't slowed down since he stopped fighting me. If anything, it's getting worse because my gut feeling was right—Bailey had nothing to do with what happened to me, and I've despised him for it for years. Bile rises to my throat, and I swallow it back down. My thoughts flit between wondering why Shane would have done that to me, and why Bailey can't remember part of the night.

"Bay?" I call out to him gently, the nickname rolling off my tongue naturally. I realise I called him that earlier too, the familiarity of it comforting. I lean around him to see his face. His eyes are closed, eyelashes sweeping down towards the freckles that sprinkle his nose and cheeks. I gently maneuver one arm around his back and one under his knees, then push myself up off the floor. My legs shake as though they could give out at any moment. "Holy shit, you're heavy, Bay," I mutter to myself. "This was a lot easier when we were kids."

I make my way over to one of the sofas and lower him down, blowing out a breath as I look around the flat. My eyes go straight to the knife, then back to Bailey. I lift his hand, seeing a small cut on the tip of his finger, then let it go again, not sure what to think about that. I pick up the knife, then go to the kitchen and grab the whole knife block. There's a cupboard full of random shit, from winter coats to board games. I shove the knives as far back as I can, burying them amongst the mess. Whether Bailey just wanted to scare me into leaving, or if he was planning on using the knife to hurt himself, I'm not taking any chances, not with how he was screaming and yelling that he needs to be punished.

I head upstairs to the bathroom, grab the two shavers on the sink, and hide them in another cupboard. It's enough to settle me slightly. If I fall asleep, there's nothing he can easily get his hands on. When I leave the bathroom, I come face to face with two doors. One of them is Bailey's bedroom.

I bite down on my bottom lip, knowing I shouldn't. He *could* technically have something dangerous in there, but that's not the driving factor behind me opening the doors. I need to know more about the man who feels both like a stranger and someone painfully familiar.

Inside the room on the left, everything's tidy: there's just a double bed with navy bedsheets that look untouched. There are no personal items to show if this is Bailey's or Noah's room. I close the door and open the one on my right instead. I'm immediately hit with a mix of colognes, rumpled charcoal bedsheets on a larger bed, and clothes strewn across the room. My chest feels tight as I cautiously step inside. There are pillows with creases and dents on either side of the bed. Any intention I had of looking for things Bailey could use to harm himself is quickly abandoned. I pick up two T-shirts that were left on the end of the bed and look at the collars. One is a medium, the other a small. I scrunch them up, and throw them back. I'm sure Isla said Bailey and Noah are just friends. The tightness in my chest won't go away, and my stomach twists itself into a knot. I don't like that I know nothing about the man he's become, and after everything that's happened, I realise I didn't really know the boy he was before.

I leave the bedroom and head back downstairs. Bailey's in the same position on the sofa, knees tucked up to his stomach, arm covering his head. I take his shoes and socks off then grab a blanket, draping it over him as little whimpers fall from his lips. I collapse on the sofa opposite him, trying to force myself to sleep, but my heart starts thumping against my rib cage again so hard that it hurts. There's too much I need to know —to understand what he hid from me the two years we were together, because right now I'm terrified that I missed something big.

TWENTY

BAILEY

I WAKE UP, BODY STIFF AND MIND HAZY. THE memory of me screaming as Teddy held me on the floor comes back, and my cheeks heat instantly. I didn't want to break in front of him, that's exactly why I wanted him to leave.

Rubbing my eyes, I force myself off the sofa, head spinning as I make my way to the kitchen, each step sending a shockwave of pain through my head. I take two ibuprofen and swallow them down with some water, trying to chase the headache away before it turns into a migraine. My hands are shaking as I put the cup down. More fractured moments from last night push their way forward—Teddy's face as he told me I'd tried to kill him. Me yelling at him, threatening him with a knife. Being held down. Wanting to be punished.

My eyes dart to the kitchen counter where the knife block should be but it's not there. I frown, searching the kitchen. It's gone—so is the knife I'd picked up yesterday.

Teddy...

There's a weight sitting in the pit of my stomach. I've never hurt myself before; not when Shane was always there to do it for me. I shake my head, making myself a cup of tea on autopilot, trying not to think about how letting him do it was just as bad as doing it myself.

I don't know how to fix it this time. I know nothing I can do will be enough for him to forgive me—let alone forgive myself. I stir my tea and go to throw the spoon into the sink, pause for a moment, then put it back in hot liquid. When I pull it out again, I press it against the inside of my forearm. The burn is sharp and fast, but the spoon cools down too quickly to do much else. It's not nearly enough.

"What are you doing?"

I jump and throw the spoon in the sink. "N-nothing." I keep my back turned, afraid to look at him. *Why is he still here?*

"We need to talk," he says, voice firm but gentle. I shake my head. I don't want to. I can't. He touches my shoulder, and I flinch so hard I drop my cup. Hot tea splashes up my legs, rooting me to the spot.

"Jesus," Teddy mutters, yanking me back from the spill. As he uses a tea towel to dry my feet, the world tilts off its axis, and I sway, grabbing hold of his shoulder to keep myself upright. I look down at him for a moment, then push away, running for the door.

I've been here before, running from Teddy as if my life depended on it. Except that's not it at all. I run from him because *his* life depends on it. Every second I spend with him puts him in more danger. I'll never be able to escape the monster that dwells inside me.

I reach the bus stop at the end of the road and stop to catch my breath, leaning against the shelter.

"You okay, mate?" A middle-aged man steps into my line of sight, cigarette in hand. He takes a drag while looking down at my bare feet, raising an eyebrow. My chest rises and falls quickly as I stare at the red cherry glowing. He blows the smoke out the side of his mouth away from me, but the smell hits me instantly. My stomach churns, vision darkening.

"What do you think will happen if you leave me? If there's no one to keep you under control? What happens when animals aren't enough and you want to hurt someone?" He leans closer, whispering. *"What if you hurt Theo?"*

"No!" I yell. "I didn't ... I wouldn't." I stumble over my words, throat closing up for the first time in years.

"Get away from him." Teddy is suddenly next to me, putting himself between me and the stranger.

"Hey, man, I was just asking if he was alright."

"He's fine."

"He doesn't look fine. He looks out of it."

My ears ring, and I slide my back down the bus shelter until I'm sitting on the cold, hard ground. My hands go to the asphalt, and I focus on the loose pieces, rolling my fingers over them, trying not to breathe through my nose with the man smoking still too close.

"I'm taking him home. Everything's good." Teddy squats next to me and places a hand on my knee. I stare at him, struggling to focus. "Come on, Bay, get up. Let's go home," he whispers. I shake my head. "Yes, you can do it." He stands and holds a hand out.

I stare at it for a long time, focusing on the dark hair that dusts the back, the veins that run up towards his wrist. Maybe my punishment was never meant to be physical. I take his hand, letting him pull me to my feet. Maybe my punishment will be having him shout at me as he tells me I'm sick and wrong. Words will cut me so much deeper than any knife could, anyway. Slowly, I put one foot in front of the other, following Teddy back to my house, his hand never leaving mine.

When we're back inside, I'm made to sit on the sofa with a blanket wrapped around me. I don't argue. I'm shaking so hard my teeth start to knock together. He leaves me, and I hear the noise of the kettle boiling, a teaspoon clinking against china. A cup is pushed into my hand and Teddy sits next to me.

"You okay?" he asks.

Of course I'm not. I just found out that I did the one thing I swore I'd never do, and now my body is on alert, waiting for a punishment. Waiting for Shane to show up and knock on my door after I hid from him for twelve years. I don't even bother trying to answer Teddy—my voice is locked up tight.

"Look. What happened—it wasn't your fault."

I frown at him. I may not have realised what I was doing that night, but choosing to stay with him for so long, knowing hurting him was a possibility—*that* was my fault. Shane warned me, but I didn't listen to him, ignoring my own fears, wanting something I knew I couldn't keep.

"I was wrong," Teddy says quietly, looking away from me. "At the time I thought it was you, Bay. When I woke up, whatever drug that was used on me was still in my system. Everything was hazy, and I was terrified. I didn't realise ..." He takes a deep breath. "It was Shane."

I shake my head.

"Yes. I fucked up, Bay." He swipes away a tear on his cheek.

I count to ten in my head, slowly and steadily, trying to control my breathing, focusing on letting my voice out. "N-no." It couldn't have been Shane. Everything Teddy told me is exactly something I would have done. The animals. The fire.

Me.

Always me.

I stand up quickly, dropping the blanket. "That's—that's not true. Y-you shouldn't be here alone with me. You need to go."

Teddy gets up, following me. "You're not listening to me." He raises his voice slightly. "It was Shane."

I back away, and he grabs my arm.

"There's things you don't know, Teddy," I say desperately, trying to pull free from his grip. I don't want to tell him. Don't want to admit everything I've done.

"So tell me!"

"Because it's so fucking easy!" I snap. "J-just open my mouth and tell you everything?"

"We had two years together, Bay, and you never told me a thing, except that your mum was an alcoholic. This is more than that, and you hid it from me."

My face crumples. "Because I couldn't!" I choke out. "I had to hide it. I was s-scared."

"I know ... fuck, I'm sorry, okay. Just—just tell me what I'm missing here, *please*."

I look into his eyes, two pools of warm whisky staring right back at me, imploring. "It's not the first time," I say, looking sharply away from him.

"What's not the first time?"

"The blackouts. I had them on and off throughout my childhood." Teddy's grip loosens, and I finally break free, putting distance between us. "The first was when I was t-ten. There was a house fire, and the only thing I remember is Shane telling me that I—that I started it on purpose. M-my dad never got out." I turn away from him and look up at the ceiling, my eyes burning as tears escape. Teddy's gone deathly still behind me. If this is what it takes to make him leave for good, then I'll tell him everything. And if he calls the police on me, then maybe that will be punishment enough. At least there'll be no more secrets between us.

"After that, I would start waking up to find dead mice in my room. In my bed, in the wardrobe, everywhere." I dare to turn around and look at him, expecting to see disgust, but all I see is confusion.

"That never happened when you lived with me."

"Yes, it did! When I went home after mum was in hospital, she'd found animals in the treehouse! I don't know when I would have ... I was with you the whole time, but they were fresh, and I-I—"

Teddy's eyes narrow for a moment, then his face twists into rage. "Bailey," he growls. "Why the hell did you stay there for a whole month after that?" He takes a step towards me.

"I couldn't trust myself around you. Shane said I'd hurt you," I whimper. "I tried to stay away, Teddy, I promise. I was scared I'd hurt you, but I couldn't stay there in that house with them. I just wanted to come home to you," I cry out. "I ended up hurting you, just like he said I would. My stupid fucking brain made me forget about it." I gasp for air, pulling my hair until my scalp stings. I step towards him and shove his chest, making him stumble back. "Just *leave*, Teddy!" I yell. "I want you to go. Get out!" I push him again, but he catches my wrists, shoving me against the wall with his thigh wedged between mine, holding me in place.

"Get off me!"

"Not until you listen," he snaps, leaning so close that our foreheads are almost touching. "Has any of this shit happened since you moved to Cumbria?"

My body stills. It doesn't prove anything. I could have done something at any point in the past twelve years and have no clue. And yet ... "N-no."

"Has Noah or Jake ever said you've blacked out? Sleep-walked? Have they ever found any animals? Have you?"

"No." I realise he's right. His hands around my wrist feel like shackles. I try to move out of his grip, but I can't. "Teddy, please—"

"So why would you think you did anything wrong?" he asks softly.

"I-I don't know, I don't ..." None of it is making any sense.

I can't think straight.

Can't breathe.

"Teddy, let go, please," I gasp.

He ignores me, pushing his forehead against mine. I'm reminded of the night in the pub when I did the same thing to him. Ignored the fact he was struggling. Pushed and pushed until we both broke.

"It was Shane." He doesn't completely let go of my wrists, but he lowers them so they're between us. Rubbing circles where his fingers had dug in. I stare into his eyes, unable to look away.

"You can't know that," I whisper.

"I can. I've never let myself think about that night fully because it makes me feel sick. Anytime the memories try pushing their way forward, I shove them back down, only for them to return in fragments in my sleep." He pauses, then asks, "Shane has different coloured eyes to you, doesn't he?"

I nod slightly. It's the only way Mum could tell us apart sometimes. I have a ring of gold around my pupils, like my dad. Shane has pure light blue, like Mum.

Teddy lets go of my wrists and cups my face, wiping away tears with his thumbs. "Shane held the knife in his left hand. You're right handed."

My breathing picks up.

"When I last saw you, you had bruises on your neck." His fingers run along my jaw and brush against my neck. "Did Shane do that to you?"

My bottom lip wobbles, and my throat burns as I force words out. "Yes."

"He wore a crew neck. No bruises."

I swallow.

"What's my name?" he whispers.

"What?" I breathe.

"Tell me what my name is."

"T-Teddy ..."

"He called me Theo," Teddy chokes out, "I'm so fucking sorry, Bay. I should have realised."

I wonder if this is how it feels to have a heart attack. My chest feels like it's been struck by lightning.

"What haven't you told me? Why can't you remember that night?" Teddy asks.

I take a shuddering breath and sink to the floor.

BAILEY - EIGHTEEN YEARS OLD

I FIND MYSELF BACK HOME, UNSURE WHERE ELSE I can go. I know I can't stay here, but I need money. I'd hidden my wages from the pub under my mattress before I moved out with Teddy. Hopefully they're still there. I gently push the front door open and step inside. It's quiet ... I let out the breath I'd been holding, thankful no one's home.

I keep an ear out as I head up to my bedroom and straight to my bed, shifting the mattress to find the money's still there. The movement blows up the stench of death, and I freeze. Prickles scatter over my body, and I forget how to breathe. I look around my room, wondering where it's coming from. The smell gets stronger when I get near my bedside table, and as I pull the drawer open, I retch. Four dead mice lie there in various stages of decay. I slam the drawer shut, but it does little to dull the stench.

They weren't there the last time I was here, three months ago. I haven't been back since. I'm sure of it. None of it makes sense—the treehouse, this. Teddy would have noticed something, I'm sure of it. Why would I keep coming back *here* just to kill these animals?

A floorboard creaks behind me, and my head snaps up to find Dean leaning against the door frame with his arms crossed over his chest. I quickly shift the mattress back over the money out of habit. Hiding it was necessary before, with Mum's drinking habit. If she'd found it, she would have taken it all. If Dean found it, he would have given it to her, because if she passed out drunk, she wouldn't be paying attention to what he was doing.

"Bailey, what are you doing here?" he asks, voice soft and low. Walking over to me where I'm kneeling by my bed, he places a hand on my shoulder.

I freeze immediately, my body starting to shut down. "I-I just came to get something. I'll go." I shake my shoulder, trying to dislodge his hand, but his fingers dig in deeper, making me wince in pain.

He's never hurt me before.

"What did you need?" he asks casually.

"Just—just some more clothes," I lie.

His hand slips under my armpit, and he yanks me up, spinning me towards him. There's a smile on his lips, but it doesn't match the glint in his eye or the tone of his voice as he says, "I think you're lying to me." He drags his calloused thumb across my cheek, making me flinch. "You've been gone for so long; I missed you, baby boy."

I try to pull away, but he grips me tighter. I'm taller than he is, but he's stronger, making it impossible to fight him off. My mouth opens, but nothing comes out.

No. Not again.

Dean pushes me onto the bed, and it feels like I'm still falling, even with my back against the mattress. He pulls his tie loose and whips it from under his collar. In an instant, he's holding my wrists, tying them together.

No!

He's never done anything like this before, never been

aggressive. My stomach drops, feeling that this is going to be so much worse than last time. His movements are jerky and desperate. I kick my legs and lift my knee, trying to get him off me, but he jumps out of the way.

"That wasn't very nice." He grabs my legs and flips me over, pulling the long end of the tie up to the headboard, securing it in place.

This isn't happening. I'm not really here.

I fight until my muscles burn, but Dean's too strong. He puts a hand on my back, pushing me down into the mattress, while his knees knock mine apart. I try to scream, but it just reverberates inside my head, never finding a way out.

No one's coming to save me.

I'm alone.

I hear a zipper opening, and think, not for the first time, that I want to die.

I'M LYING on my back, my hands are untied, but I can't move. My mind is just ... gone. I feel like a ghost hovering over my limp body, praying I never reunite with it.

I want Teddy. I want to get up off this bed and run to him.

The smell in the room is putrid, but I'm too exhausted to move. My whole body aches. I just need to close my eyes for a minute ...

"Bailey."

I jolt out of my sleep, jarring my muscles at the sound of Shane's voice.

"Do you have something to tell me?" he asks, sitting on the edge of the bed.

My chest hurts from holding my breath. I swallow and

concentrate on getting the words out. "I-I broke up with him." The words tumble out, clumsy and stilted.

"I know that, little mouse. It's a good thing you did, because I don't think he'd like to know what you just did." Shane starts stroking my hair, twirling the ends around his finger.

My heart thumps hard and fast, and the walls close in on me. "W-what do you mean?" I whisper.

"I saw you. You dump your boyfriend and in less than twenty-four hours, you're bending over for fucking *Dean*? Are you that desperate for attention? What would Mum say?" His hand tightens in my hair, and I choke out a sob. *I didn't want to do it, I didn't let him ... I—I tried to get him off of me.*

I shake my head and try to say no, but everything's locked down again.

"Roll over."

I know what's coming, but I don't understand why. I've done nothing wrong this time. It wasn't my fault. I shake my head. I can't deal with this, not on top of what Dean just did. Shane leaves me no choice, wrestling me onto my front, and I find myself in the same position as earlier. He grabs my wrists and pulls them above my head.

"No!" I croak out. He's never done this without me agreeing to it first. He isn't listening to me.

I feel a needle pinch into the crook of my elbow as he whispers, "Keep quiet, little mouse."

WHEN I WAKE UP AGAIN, my stomach lurches, and I throw up where I lie. I'm so nauseous I feel like I'm on a boat rather than on my bed. My back is on fire, burns throbbing with any slight movement, and the smell of stale cigarette smoke lingers in the air. I glance around the room, relieved to see that Shane isn't here.

I push myself up on unsteady arms and turn over, wincing as I sit on the edge of the bed. I feel my pockets, but my phone isn't there. Turning to look for it, I hiss at the pain before snatching it from the bedside table. I check the messages, but there's nothing from Teddy. It's three in the morning, so he won't see if I text him. I stand up, the skin on my back pulling taut. Shane left my shirt on this time, and I can feel where it's stuck to some of the blisters, every movement tearing them open again. I push the mattress over and grab my money, then limp to my door, opening it quietly. The house is silent again. I make my way downstairs, gripping the banister to steady myself, legs barely holding me upright. As I get to the living room, movement makes me jump so hard that pain shoots through my chest. When I look at the sofa, I see Mum asleep, facing away from me. I shuffle to the front door, wondering if she was in the house when everything happened. Whether she would care, or if she'd think it was what I deserved.

I close the front door quietly and slowly make my way to Teddy's house. A walk that usually takes about ten minutes takes me half an hour or more. The lights are off, so I make my way into the back garden. Faced with a trellis that leads to the top of a flat-roofed extension, I cry out in pain as I put one foot on the wood and pull myself up. Finally, I'm facing Teddy's bedroom window. I press my cheek onto the cold glass to try and cool down before I collapse.

I knock on the window, but there's no answer.

I knock again. Still nothing.

"Teddy, please!" I shout in desperation.

A light comes on from the room to my left, and I jump when the window opens.

"Who's there?" Teddy's dad, John, shouts sternly, popping

his head out. He groans when he sees me, rubbing a hand over his face. "Bailey, what are you doing here?"

"I need Teddy," I say quietly.

John stares at me, the furrow in his brow softening. "I'm sorry, but he's gone."

Gone?

"Decided to go to his grandparents early, he left in a rush a few hours ago."

He wouldn't ... he wouldn't just give up on us that quickly and leave.

"He texted me once he was already on the train, so there was nothing we could do about it. You two had a falling out?"

"Y-yes."

"Right, well maybe he just needed some headspace. If you can't go home, you can come in. Ellen would rather you stay here, I'm sure."

Teddy's parents know I have issues with my mum, but not much else. I can't stay here though, not on my own. It doesn't feel right. I shake my head and climb down the extension, biting my lip so hard from the pain in my back that I draw blood.

I make my way down the road, looking over my shoulder to make sure John isn't following me, then pull my phone out, weighing heavily in my hands. I feel numb, not wanting to believe he's actually left. I pull up Teddy's number and ring him. Before it can even ring once, an automated voice says, "This number is unavailable." I pull the phone away from my ear and stare at it in disbelief, then open my texts and type out a message.

ME

Teddy, I'm sorry. Please, I need to talk to you

UNDELIVERED

Fuck, fuck, fuck. I pull my hair, barely registering the sting. I try another messenger service, typing out the same message, but the same thing happens. He's blocked me on everything. I have no way to get hold of him. The ground collapses out from under me, ready to swallow me whole. I don't know what to do—where to go. My fist tightens around my phone, useless to me now. "You left me behind!" I yell, as I throw it across the street, watching it shatter. Then I scream at the top of my lungs until there's no air left. Collapsing to the ground, scratching the tarmac.

THEO

I watch Bailey carefully, waiting patiently for him to open up to me. The feeling of dread that sits heavy in my stomach hasn't left me since yesterday. I want to know what happened to him and why he hid it from me. After what Shane did to me I can't help but jump to conclusions about what he could have done to Bailey. It was too easy for him. The animals had been building up in that shed for months. He had petrol ready to go, some type of drug and a syringe; he was organised, he'd planned it. He's fucking psychotic. And Bailey had been living with him for *years*.

"Shane caught me trying to get rid of the mice, not long after it started. He said he'd help me. H-he got rid of them for me, but said that I needed to understand the pain I'd caused them." He pulls his fists up into his sleeves, rubbing the cuffs together. "It started with him pinching me until I bruised. Then drawing pins, pushing them into my thigh—"

"He what?" I snap, unable to stop myself from reacting.

Bailey stares right through me. "It wasn't constant. A year would pass, but then it would be nine months, six months.

When we turned fourteen, he said he needed to try something new because it wasn't w-working anymore."

I'm suddenly too hot. I let go of his knee and stand up, needing to move.

"I'd lie down on the bed and he'd—he'd burn me with cigarettes on my back and hips, over and over, to try to get me to stop being bad."

I stop and look at him, remembering something from years ago. "Stand up."

He looks up at me, eyes wide, as if he's scared of *me*. I'm too far gone. Too desperate to see what I already know. "Get up, Bay."

On shaky legs, he pushes himself off the ground. I turn him around, and he goes limp, as if there's no fight left in him, leaning against the wall as I lift his shirt and suck in a breath at the sight. His back is littered with little circular pink and silver scars. Puckered, with raised edges, they're a stark contrast to his usual smooth, lightly tanned skin. I brush my fingers along them, and he flinches. The last time I saw him, there were a few concentrated on his lower back. But now—there are dozens.

"Why?" I choke out. "Why did you tell me they were from chicken pox?"

"If I had told you about them, then I'd have to tell you why. I was scared you'd leave me. You *would* have left me if you knew what I'd done," he says, voice muffled from where he's got his sleeve in his mouth.

"But you didn't do anything." I pull his shirt back down and turn him around so I can see his face.

"I did!" he shouts, face going red. "I let him do it—he'd ask me if I wanted it and I said y-yes! He was trying to fix me." He gasps for breath.

I cup his face. "You never needed fixing, Bay. Shane fucked with your head so that you'd think it was you, but those animals had been in that shed for *months*. I would have noticed if you'd been sneaking off to do that. It would have taken time. He'd planned it all. Have you ever used a syringe? Have you ever found one in your room?"

He frowns, then shakes his head, rubbing the inside of his elbow.

"Th-the last time I saw Shane he used one on me, but he'd never—he'd never done that before."

"The same night he injected me?"

"Y-yes."

I want to shake him. Shout at him and say, 'Don't you get it now?' But I can see he's still trying to process everything. I can't even begin to imagine how he feels right now. It's bad enough that for years, I blamed him for something he never did. But he's been carrying all this pointless guilt for far longer. How the fuck did Shane manage to get that much control over him?

I feel sick. The evidence of it all was right there in front of me the whole time. I hadn't paid enough attention to my boyfriend—missed all the warning signs. The mutism, the scars, the way he ran from me in the woods and screamed until he couldn't fight anymore. I thought that just being there for him to lean on was enough, but it wasn't. I didn't show up when it mattered most. I left him.

What the fuck does that say about me?

I can't stay still, can't offer words of reassurance right now. I prise myself away from him and run my hand through my hair, trying to remember the two years we were together. Wondering how I got it so wrong. Why hadn't I pushed him for answers when he said he'd had a bad day at home and couldn't speak? Pacing back and forth, I drag in deep breaths. "Your mum did nothing?"

"She didn't know."

"What about your stepdad? Didn't he notice anything? You said he was a nurse."

I watch as Bailey's face pales, and his lip trembles.

"What?" I step closer to him. Wanting to touch him. Hold him. Anything to close this chasm between us.

"He found out when Shane started with the cigarettes."

"And?"

"He gave me antibiotics and cleaned me up."

"He didn't call the police? Or tell your mum?" I shake my head in disbelief.

"No. He used the excuse of cleaning up my burns to—" Bailey rubs his face, looking exhausted.

"To what?"

"He'd touch," Bailey says so quietly I almost miss it. The reality of everything sinks in. How helpless he was. How no one showed up for him. The people he should have been able to trust took advantage of him or abandoned him. It's all fucked.

I feel sick. I want to grab hold of him and never let him go again, but I don't have the right to. "Jesus, Bay."

BAILEY

Everything Teddy's saying makes sense, and I think I hate him for it. He's shattering my perception of reality with every word. Telling me all the guilt I've harboured since I was a child was never mine to carry. And it hurts. It hurts so fucking bad, because until that night I told Shane no, I thought he'd been trying to help me. That he really was the only one I could trust with it all, because he was my brother, and he said he'd keep me safe.

I don't know how long I've been sitting on the floor. Teddy's leaning against the wall next to me, and all I want is for him to touch me. I want him to tell me it's okay. That I'm not too broken to be held. I'm too scared to look at him, let alone ask for anything like that. We've both calmed down at least. The tears have dried, and the silence is comfortable, like we're both processing everything that's happened in the past forty-eight hours. So even if he isn't holding me, at least he's still here.

I push to my feet, and my whole body feels like I've gone too hard at the gym. Every muscle is fatigued, and my eyesight feels blurry. I start walking to the stairs when I hear movement behind me.

"Where are you going?"

I look over my shoulder, finding Teddy's face pinched with concern. "I need to go in to work. That was the whole point of me coming here."

He grabs my hand before I can start walking again, pulling me to a stop. "No you're not. Not after all that."

"I need to do something, Teddy. I'm not going to sit on the floor and marinate in it all. I can't."

"Go tomorrow." His eyes are pleading. I know I can't say no to him.

"We've already wasted one day, the wedding—"

"Fuck the wedding," he growls.

I frown at him and shake my hand free. "You don't mean that."

"Yes, I do. The wedding isn't as important as this. We're both exhausted, and I'm not driving when I feel this way. I just want—"

"Want what?" I ask, nervous all of a sudden.

"I want us to be okay."

I suck in a breath. If I thought Teddy being angry at me was confusing, it has nothing on this. He can't just turn all that off and start being nice again. I can't trust it's real. Even if it was Shane who hurt him, I started it. If I'd ignored Shane and told Teddy I wanted to leave to go to Scotland, instead of dumping him, it never would have happened. I run up the stairs and into the bathroom, locking the door.

Teddy follows, knocking on the door. "Bay, come on."

I switch the water on and strip out of my clothes. "I-I'm showering, go away." He doesn't answer me, so I assume he's done as I've asked. I climb into the bathtub and lean back, letting the hot water hit my face until there's not a thought left in my head.

THE DAY PASSES SLOWLY; Teddy forces me to eat toast and drink coffee. We sit on the sofa together, and he puts some cartoons on. In a silent agreement, we don't talk about the past. We don't talk at all, really. I'm pressed against the armrest, trying not to draw attention to myself, scared that he'll bring it all up again.

After a while, Teddy grabs my arm, pulling me until I'm laying against his chest. It's warm and solid, his heartbeat so familiar. He wraps his arms around me, and I cry quietly while he holds me.

"I'm sorry, Bay," he whispers for what seems like the hundredth time. Old thoughts of blaming him for abandoning me resurface for an ugly moment. I used to hate him for leaving me behind, but now I start to think about how he mistook me for Shane. He couldn't tell us apart when it mattered, even though we'd lived together for a year. He was so willing to believe I'd hurt him that he ran away and never looked back. Never once questioned it all.

I hold the burst of anger inside, focusing on the now. Teddy is *here*—in my house. He's holding me, just like I wanted. It wasn't his fault.

"How did you end up in Cumbria?" Teddy asks, pushing my hair back from my face.

"Jake," I smile at the memory. He walked into my life, grabbed hold of me, and unlike everyone else in my life, never let go. "I made it to London but didn't know where to go. I wanted to go to Scotland to try and find you." I sniffle, wiping my eyes with my sleeve. "I didn't have enough money for the ticket, so I stupidly tried to jump the barrier. A guard stopped me before I could, and he was telling me to leave the station when Jake turned up. He said I was his nephew and then offered to buy me a ticket to Carlisle so that I could travel up North with him."

Teddy shifts under me. "And you *let* him?"

I frown, not liking his tone. "Yes, I let him, he was very nice. I sat with him on the train, and after talking for a few hours, he offered me a job and a place to stay."

"Seriously? After everything you went through, you just went off with a stranger."

I push myself up and glare at him. "You've met Jake. He's fine."

"I know I've met him. But you didn't know him; anything could have happened, for fuck's sake."

"But it didn't. I moved in with him, where he was living with his brother and nephews. Other than Noah, Jake's all I've got, so don't judge things you don't understand. You gave up the right to worry about me when you left," I snap.

He opens his mouth to argue, but quickly shuts it again, jaw ticking. We fall into silence, a little more awkward than before. I don't lean against him again, and he doesn't reach for me. My eyes are on the cartoon, but I'm not taking anything in.

"I should go to bed," I mutter, getting up from the sofa. As I walk past Teddy, he grabs my trouser leg.

"Can you sleep down here again? I don't want you out of my sight, not after last night."

I look at my fingertip, remembering what I'd done—what I'd considered doing if I'd managed to make him leave. I slap his hand away. "I'm not sleeping on the sofa when I have a perfectly comfortable bed upstairs. I'll get you some blankets, or you can sleep in Noah's bed. He barely uses it anyway, so the sheets are clean."

He stands up, following me up the stairs, into my bedroom. "I don't want to leave you."

"What do you mean? You—you can't sleep in my bed." I say, staring at him, bewildered.

He nods. "We've shared before."

"I know that, but we were *together*."

He just stares back at me, breathing louder, chest rising and falling quickly. Looking like he's a second away from a panic attack if he's forced to sleep in a different room.

"Fine," I mutter.

We strip off our clothes quickly. Teddy gets under the covers before me, and I flick the light off, joining him. We lay still like bookends on the edges of the bed.

"This is weird," Teddy says in the dark.

"Yep."

He shuffles closer to me and reaches out until he finds my hand, then threads his fingers through mine, holding them between us.

"Night, Bay."

I let out a soft breath. "Night, Teddy."

BAILEY

"I told you that you'd hurt him. You're sick, Bailey. Look what you've done; he's lying there tied up and the fire's coming. Why would you do that to him when you said you loved him? Maybe you're incapable of love ... he's going to die, and it's all your fault." Hands curl around my wrists, holding me down. *"Are you ready for your punishment, little mouse?"*

There's a yell in the distance, drawing my attention away from Shane. Two warm hands wrap around my body, pulling me against a solid chest. I almost break the surface of consciousness. Heart racing, I try to shake whoever it is off, dragging myself to the edge of the bed.

Shane lied to you.

No, he didn't. He tried to make me better.

He tried to control you by fucking with your head.

He—he was trying to fix me.

You never needed fixing.

"Bailey, wake up!"

Everything starts to come back to me. The arms surrounding me are thick and strong, and the body that's curved around my back and thighs is larger than mine. I breathe in deeply, and I'm hit with a burst of amber and sandalwood. Something familiar lingers beneath it, something fresh and a little salty. I wonder if this is what it's like to be held by the sea.

Slowly opening my eyes, I look down to see two hands pressed against my chest. Dark hairs on tanned forearms, and veins that fork up from the wrist. I focus on them and blow out a shaky breath.

"Shh, it's fine. I think you had a nightmare."

I cling to Teddy's arms. "It wasn't me? I didn't hurt you?" I whisper, voice cracking.

He shifts closer, squeezing me tighter. "It wasn't you. You didn't hurt me, Bay."

I'm struggling to process everything that Shane did to me. He lied to me for years and made me believe I was going crazy, just so he could ...

"My head is fucked," I mutter.

"I know, maybe you shouldn't go to work today. Just take one more day—"

"No. I need to go to work so I can sort everything out for Jake," I say, pushing his arms away so I can get out of bed. I'm feeling restless all of a sudden, like I need to be moving ... need to be doing *something*. "I can't sit in this house for another day, thinking about everything. We should head back to Skye once I'm done." I look over at Teddy. He's lying on his back with one knee up, rubbing his face.

"Fine," he huffs, throwing the duvet off. He gets up to gather his clothes, and I suck in a breath, choking on air as he bends down, presenting his arse to me. Two perfectly firm globes stretch the cotton of his briefs. My gaze trails over his body, from his broad back down to his thick thighs, then back up again. He looks over his shoulder, and I quickly turn my back to him, my cheeks burning. I quickly get dressed, then lead the way downstairs.

"I'll be gone for a couple of hours," I say as I pour hot water into my travel mug.

"I'm coming with you."

"Why?"

"Because, Bailey." He shoves his feet into his boots, then stands by the door, waiting.

I hate that my brain tries to trick me into thinking this is the same as when we were kids. We were inseparable for the whole two years we had together; it was easy, and we were happy that way. But this isn't the same. This isn't him wanting to be near me because he likes me. I can see it in how he stands —rigid, tapping his fingers against his thumb. He's anxious about me ... or for me. Maybe both. Either way, I don't like it. I've survived years without him. I have methods to regulate myself; I have Noah, and I have a therapist. I don't want him fussing over me like I'm breakable.

But then I think about how he held on to me while we were in bed, and that didn't feel so bad. It felt more familiar than anything else in the past two days, his body curled around mine, warm and strong. I shake my head; there's no point in thinking about him that way. We'll soon be heading back to Skye for the wedding, then I'll come back to Cumbria and he'll stay there.

"Come on then," I say, giving in all too easily.

THE HEADLIGHTS COMING toward us become more and more infrequent the further into the Highlands we get. With the sun setting behind the Munros, shadows jump across the landscape, making my head spin. I try to close my eyes, but the motion of the car makes my stomach churn.

Shane comes to my side and places a hand on my ribs. "Just a little something to remind you of who will always be there for you, even when everyone else turns their back."

"Pull over, please," I beg, already opening the passenger door.

Teddy slams on the brakes, and the seatbelt pulling tight across my stomach is the final straw. One hand over my mouth, I unbuckle myself and jump out of the car, spilling the contents of my stomach over the tarmac. A hand touches me as I hunch over, and my spine jars as I flinch away from it.

"You okay?" Teddy asks, rubbing circles on my back.

I focus on the heat of his palm and count his fingers as they push into my skin. I nod, trying to stand upright again, but the blood rushes to my head, and I collapse to the side, right into Teddy. He catches me and lowers me back to the ground, then goes back to the car.

I close my eyes, unable to stop thinking about Shane. The relief of knowing I hadn't hurt Teddy was stripped away with the realisation that Shane had manipulated me. The monster I thought lingered inside me turned out to be a monster I'd lived alongside for years, instead. It didn't matter that I'd been in therapy for the past five years, discussing how my mum hated me and my step father had raped me, when I'd never realised Shane was the catalyst for my trauma.

Teddy nudges my shoulder, handing me a bottle of mouthwash. I take a swig, then spit it onto the ground. He's messed with my head too, Teddy. All that aggression and hostility he held because he thought I'd hurt him—replaced with this need to look after me—is giving me whiplash. Two days alone with him is all it took to throw my world out of balance. It's like my mind is a ball of wool that's been rolling around for years, tying itself into more and more knots. I can't even find the end to know where to begin untangling it. It's hard to believe Shane had tricked me into thinking I'd done all those bad things when I *felt* like I had. It's making me doubt everything I thought I knew about myself.

"I know it's been a lot, the last two days. But when we get back to Skye, you'll—you'll at least have Noah there to help you," Teddy says through clenched teeth.

I look up at him, noticing he's scowling. "Do you not like Noah?"

"Why would I not like Noah?"

"I don't know—that's why I'm asking. It sounded like you didn't like the idea of Noah helping me. Maybe I misunderstood—"

"Are you in a relationship with him?"

What?

"Noah's my best friend."

"I was also your best friend."

"Excuse me," I say, voice low and measured. "That's completely different."

"His things were in your bedroom—" He turns away sharply, growling to himself. "Never mind, it doesn't matter."

I watch, open mouthed, as he storms back to the car, slamming the door shut behind him.

Yes, it does matter. There's never been anything but friendship with Noah—he's like a brother to me. I push to my feet and get in the car.

"Sorry," Teddy mutters as he starts the engine.

"It's different because I fell in love with you," I say bluntly. Teddy keeps his eyes on the road, pulling his bottom lip between his teeth.

"Noah and I both struggled with nightmares for years. When I moved in with him and Jake, I'd cry out in my sleep, and I'd wake up to find him in my bed. He isn't big on affection, but he didn't like being alone when he slept, and I think he wanted to be close to me when I was going through that.

We still share a bed most nights; it's not sexual at all. A little co-dependent, maybe ..."

Teddy releases his lip, glancing at me, looking abashed. "I didn't mean to be ..." He sighs and rubs his face. "I have nightmares too, ever since that night—they come and go. Sometimes I can go a few months with none, and then I'll have a whole week of no sleep where I'm scared to close my eyes."

Guilt eats away at me. "Sorry," I whisper, looking out the window.

"You have nothing to be sorry for. It was Shane."

"If I hadn't been determined to get to know you, then Shane never would have hurt you. It's my fault that I stayed with you for so long."

"It doesn't matter whether you chose to stay with me or not. I would have kept chasing you because it's what *I* wanted too, Bay. No one forced me to fall in love with you."

Tears sting my eyes, and I wipe them on my sleeve.

"Are you still in contact with him?" Teddy asks.

"No. The night I ran away, he—he hurt me even though I hadn't done anything wrong. I went home to get some money I'd hidden in my room, and Dean found me." I keep staring out the window, finding it easier to say all of this without having to look at him. "He tied me to my bed and raped me."

The car swerves violently, and I grip the door handle. My head whips around to look at Teddy, his mouth hangs open as he watches the road, knuckles white from gripping the steering wheel tightly. "Fuck," he says, catching his breath.

"Don't do that again." I demand as I rub my chest.

I watch him swallow and glance over at me. "Go on."

"Shane came into my room not long after. He said that I dumped you, then willingly fucked Dean for a-attention."

I barely notice the car stopping as Teddy pulls over. The tears are flowing freely down my cheeks, and my vision is too blurry to focus on anything. "He said it's a good thing I dumped you, because you wouldn't want to know what I'd just done. Then he tied me to the bed and injected me with something that put me to sleep." My chest heaves at the memory of it all. How scared I was. How desperately I needed Teddy. "I woke up and my back was messed up again. I managed to get out, and tried to find you, but you'd already gone."

The sound of his door opening makes me jump. Then he throws my door wide and leans over, unclipping my seatbelt, pulling me out of the car. He holds me tight as I break against him, hands fisting his jumper as he kisses my head.

"None of that was your fault, Bay. Your brother is sick, and your stepfather ... you didn't deserve any of that, and I'm so fucking sorry I didn't realise what was going on."

"I told them no, but they didn't listen," I sob with my face buried against Teddy's neck.

"I know. Fuck, I know, Bay, but you're safe here. They can't get you, and I'm not going anywhere. I won't let you go again, I swear."

Time slips by as we lean against the car wrapped in each other's arms. I pull away from him, sniffing. "It's getting late. I just want to get back to yours."

Once back on the road, I keep drifting in and out of sleep. I'm not sure how Teddy is staying awake, but the next time I look out the window, I can see we're approaching the Skye Bridge. My phone vibrates, and I see a message from Noah.

NOAH

> Are you staying home another night or coming back here?

ME

> We're coming back to Skye. About an hour away.

NOAH

In one piece?

ME

Yes, both in one piece. We've made up ... I think

NOAH

Okay, I'll see you tomorrow then

ME

Why tomorrow?

NOAH

I've been staying at Robbie's

"What?" I say out loud.
"What?" Teddy asks immediately.
"Noah's apparently been staying at Robbie's."
Teddy groans, and I go back to texting.

ME

Why are you at Robbie's?

NOAH

You and Jake abandoned me and I didn't want to sleep in that cottage all on my own. Robbie invited me to his for some drinks, and let me stay over the last couple of nights.

"Apparently Jake has disappeared, and Noah didn't want to be in the house on his own," I tell Teddy. I don't have the energy to message Jake and find out what he's been up to for the past two days.

"So my house is currently unoccupied?" Teddy asks.
"I guess so ..."
"Good."

THEO

My phone alarm pulls me from a deep sleep, and I throw my arm out to stop the damn thing. The room goes silent, but there's no chance of me falling back asleep; all I can think about is Bailey.

I roll over to find him staring back at me, wide eyed. "Morning," I say, voice rough from sleep.

"Morning," he mutters.

It didn't take any persuading for him to share a bed again last night. We got in at around eleven and were both so exhausted that we headed straight to my bed, passing out pretty much straight away.

The morning light drapes over Bailey, making his hair lighter and his freckles stand out. I realise I've missed this far too much. Even though he's right here with me, it's not the same as it used to be. There's an ocean between us, and I have no idea how to navigate it.

"We have a wedding to get ready for," I say, hating to end this moment, but time is against us. He nods, not saying a word or making any effort to move.

"Five minutes?" I say, and he nods again. I reach out for

him and he shuffles forwards until we're chest to chest. Since the truth has come out, I'm struggling to keep my hands off him. Feeling fiercely protective, just like I did when we were kids, I want to wrap him up in my arms and never let him go. But I don't deserve to be that for him. I left him when he needed me most.

"Teddy?" he says, nuzzling under my chin.

"Yeah?"

"Stop worrying, please."

I huff and push my cheek against his soft hair. "I can't help it."

"I know."

I let go of him reluctantly, getting up and pulling my suit bag from the wardrobe. Bailey does the same, then we take turns showering and getting dressed in jeans, so that we can change into our suits at the farmhouse later. Before I know it, we're out the door and on our way.

Breakfast is in full swing by the time we get to the farmhouse. Gran greets us with a smile, pushing bowls of porridge into our hands, corralling us into the dining room.

"There's my boy," Ma stands up and rushes over, giving me only a second to put my bowl down before she wraps her arms around me. "We got here yesterday and then found out you were in Cumbria of all places."

"Hey, Ma. There was something I needed to deal with," I say, nodding to Bailey.

When she pulls away, she looks behind me and squints. "Bailey?" she gasps, pushing me to the side.

"Hey, Ellen," he breathes.

Ma looks back at me, and I can see the hesitation in her eyes.

"It's alright, we've made up."

She barely waits a second before pulling Bailey into a tight hug, cooing over him, saying how long it's been and how big he's gotten.

I take a seat next to Da and leave them to it.

"This is a surprise," he says.

Frowning, I drag my eyes away from Bailey. "You never told me he showed up the day I left."

He coughs awkwardly, taking off his glasses and cleaning them on his jumper. "I didn't say anything at the time because you left in such a hurry; I was worried something bad had happened between the two of you."

Something bad *did* happen. Not that I'd ever tell him that.

"I heard that he ran away shortly after you left. No one knew where he'd gone, and his phone kept going through to voicemail when we tried to get hold of him. Your mother tried to talk to his mum, but she said, 'Good riddance,' or something to that effect," he mutters under his breath so Bailey can't hear. "When you never mentioned him again, I just—I didn't think you'd want to know that he'd moved away."

Well, he's right. If I had known Bailey moved north, my paranoia would have been much worse. But then, if I'd *stayed*. If I'd confronted him about that night as soon as I'd got myself free, then maybe I would have—no. Staying was never an option. Shane made sure the message got through. If I didn't leave, he wouldn't have left me the option to free myself next time. And I'm certain there *would* have been a next time. It hurts, though, knowing I left Bailey with him.

"I never told you before, but when you left, your mother was heartbroken, Theo. Understandable, considering her eighteen-year-old son buggered off without even a goodbye. But it wasn't just you she lost." He nods to Bailey, and I turn to look at him, chest tightening. Ma is cupping Bailey's face so firmly that his freckled cheeks are smooshed.

"She loved him too, you know. We both did. So it was hard when he ran away. I told him he could stay with us, but he left anyway. Your Ma filed a missing person report. It took a while, but they did tell us he was safe and well. They just couldn't tell us where he was."

"Really?" I ask, feeling warm all of a sudden. I never thought about the effect all this had on my parents. I'd been scolded for leaving so suddenly by Ma, but I didn't think about Bailey being taken from them as well—all because of Shane. I grip my spoon so tight it hurts my fingers. Bailey lifts his head, and our eyes meet. I hold his stare and bury the anger enough that I'm able to give him a soft smile. His lips turn up at the corners before he turns his attention back to Ma.

The way my chest aches for him, I realise all the feelings I'd buried are surfacing again. For the first time in years, I'm feeling something. I don't just want things to be alright between us. I want to get on my knees and beg for his forgiveness. I want him to tell me everything will be alright. And even though I don't deserve it, I want him back.

THEO

"Hey, Grumpy," Isla calls out as I walk into my grandparents bedroom. I can't see her face through the veil of bright copper waves. It takes a moment to realise she's tilting her head, trying to plait her own hair, blindly shoving bobby pins in as she weaves it in and out. I sit on bed, watching her struggle.

Just a week ago I was desperate for the wedding to hurry up and be over so that Bailey would leave, but now I'm wishing for everything to slow down. After today, there's nothing keeping him here, and I'm running out of time to make things right.

"Seriously, breathe louder, Theo. I almost forgot you were there."

I frown at the sarcastic bitch. "Come here, let me do it for you," I say, grabbing her hand to take the pins. "It's painful watching you try to do it yourself."

Isla huffs and pulls the rest of the bobby pins out, then shakes her hair out. I wiggle my finger in a circle at her. She turns her back to me, and I set about combing out the knots she made.

"You okay?" she asks.

I hum in response.

"Did you manage to sort things out with Bailey? You seem to be getting close again."

"What? What makes you say that?" I mutter.

She sighs. "Really, Theo? There are no secrets on this farm. I know that Noah's been shacking up with Robbie, and Jake has been staying with Luke."

"He—what? Why's Jake been staying with Luke?"

"I don't know *why*. I just know that you and Bailey were all alone in your house last night." She looks at me in the mirror, waiting for an answer. "So ... did something happen?"

"You're a nosey bitch, you know that."

"Excuse me!" she splutters. "I was rooting for the two of you! I think I have the right to know how it's going."

"That's really not helping your case," I say, pushing a bobby pin into her hair, jabbing her in the head accidentally on purpose.

"Bloody hell, Theo!" she yells, rubbing the sore spot.

There's a moment's silence, and I gather my thoughts, wondering how much I can tell her. Nothing's changed. I don't want anyone knowing what happened to me, especially since telling Bailey felt like it hit a raw nerve.

"We became best friends shortly after I moved to Surrey," I say. "Feelings developed between us ... naturally, I guess. I realised I liked him more than a friend, and that he felt the same way. He had a shitty home life; his mum hated him and drank a lot—" I swallow, realising now that his mother was the *least* of his problems. I struggle to get the next bit out. "Something happened, and I blamed Bailey. I left him without warning. Ran away and never looked back. Then spent the last twelve years despising him."

"That's ... a lot."

"So when I saw him again the other week—"

"You thought you'd punch first, talk later, like the logical man you are."

"Actually, my first thought was to kill him, so I'd say I *was* thinking somewhat logically when I clocked him in the jaw instead. Are you listening or judging?" I ask her.

"Always both," she replies instantly.

I roll my eyes and continue. "We talked about everything when we were at his, and I realised that I'd been blaming him for something he didn't do all these years."

"Who did it then? Whatever this 'it' is."

"He has a twin brother."

She gasps and turns her head so quickly, I lose grip on the plait. "Isla, for fuck's sake."

"Sorry. But you said he has a *twin*. I didn't know that—I don't think Richard even knows that. What the hell?" She turns back again and stays still as I finish the plait. "And you're not going to tell me what happened?"

"Nope." Not yet, anyway. Maybe one day …

She lets it rest and looks at herself in the mirror. "Hey, you did a great job!"

"Yeah, well it's hard to forget when you used to make me do it any time we sat down to watch cartoons."

She huffs. "You say that like you hated it, when we both know it's the only way you'd sit still long enough to watch the whole thing."

She's got me there.

"So where are you now?" she asks, turning to face me.

"What do you mean?"

"Do you still like him?"

The question drops between us, growing bigger and bigger until it sucks all the oxygen from the room. I can't explain how or why I still do. I haven't felt this way in so long, but it feels easy with him. Like I don't have to get to know him, or learn to trust him again from scratch. The ghost of all those feelings is still inside me. As soon as I realised I was safe to be close to him again, the wall that I'd built to protect myself crumbled completely.

"Yeah," I murmur, avoiding eye contact. "I still like him."

I SIT to the left of the aisle, next to my parents, watching Isla with her hand in Richard's at the front of the church. He's sliding the ring onto her finger, and I try to pay attention but my eyes keep wandering to my right. Bailey's sitting just across the aisle from me, dressed in a fitted black suit, with his hair tied up into a neat bun, showing off his long, slender neck.

He turns and catches my eye, cheeks turning pink when he notices me staring. He quickly looks back to Isla and Richard. Reluctantly I do the same, tuning in just as they finish making their vows, then join everyone standing up, clapping and cheering as they leave the church. Guests start spilling out into the aisle to follow them, and I let Bailey go first, my gaze sweeping down the length of his back to his arse, watching as it jiggles slightly in his tight trousers with every step he takes.

"What are you doing?" Rob appears out of nowhere, pressing himself right up against me, drawing my attention away from Bailey.

"I'm just walking."

"Looked to me like you were checking out your ex-boyfriend's arse," he says quietly so only I can hear him.

"You shut up and mind your own business. What have you been doing with Noah?"

He grins at me and shrugs. "Wouldn't you like to know?"

No, actually I would not like to know. Robbie has fucked

his way through this island and now he's apparently determined to conquer England too.

When we get back to the farm, I'm dragged and pulled about as the photographer gets every pairing possible of the guests. My jaw is sore from smiling by the time we finish, and my stomach grumbles, demanding attention.

I head into the barn, finding my name card and sitting down at the table, waiting for the rest of the guests. Bailey comes and sits next to me, and Ma takes her seat next to him, much to her delight. She spends the entire meal chatting his ear off, asking him what he's been up to since moving away from Surrey.

I sit quietly and listen to them talk easily with one another. Bailey explains how Jake helped him by giving him a job and supporting him while he did a part-time degree in horticulture, and that when he finished, he and Noah spent a year travelling in South America. Ma gasps when he tells her they did the Inca Trail in Peru.

He's had a whole life without me. Memories we could have shared, ripped away, all because his brother wanted me as far away as possible. The room fades away, and I only have eyes for Bailey. Staring at his profile, I watch his lips curve up into a genuine smile when Ma tells him how adventurous he is compared to me.

At some point, my hand slips under the table and grabs his knee. He jumps at the contact and looks down at his lap, then up at me. I look away as I move my hand to his thigh and squeeze.

"You okay?" Ma asks him.

"Y-yes, sorry I missed the question." He relaxes his thigh, and doesn't push me away.

"I asked when you're going back to Cumbria? I don't think I'm quite ready to say goodbye."

You and me both, Ma.

"We have one more week here, then unfortunately, it's back to the grind."

Isla's Da stands up at the head table and taps a knife gently against his champagne glass, drawing our attention. He starts off the speeches, but I quickly tune him out when I feel Bailey lay his hand over mine. I spread my fingers wide, my breath catching in my throat when he doesn't hesitate to slide his between them. I can't hear a thing. Can't see anyone but him. There's just his hand in mine, and something too big for words pulsing between us.

Bailey stiffens, squeezing my hand a little tighter, snapping me out of my daze. When I focus on the head table again, I notice Richard's in the middle of his speech.

"... I wish Mum could have met Isla." He reaches down, and Isla grabs his hand, kissing the back of it. Richard's voice wavers slightly, and he smiles at his dad before continuing. "And I wish that Jamie could have stood behind me with Noah as a groomsman. This has been the hardest yet happiest day of my life, and I believe that somehow they were here with us—"

I don't hear the rest, because my attention is drawn to Noah. He stands up suddenly and storms out of the barn. Bailey untangles his hand from mine and slips out of his chair to rush after him. I stare at the door, waiting for them to come back, but eventually the speeches are finished and the food is cleared away. The band sets up on the stage, and the first dance is about to begin—there's still no sign of Bailey.

"THEO?" Emmy tugs on my shirt as I dance with her little feet on my shoes. I haven't seen my cousin Joy's kid since she was a shy little three-year-old. Now she's an eight-year-old with attitude, demanding dances from me—we're already on our third.

"What's up, Ems?" Looking down at her, I notice a frown wrinkling her forehead. She looks to the right, and when I follow her line of sight, I realise she's staring at Bailey. I hadn't noticed him coming back into the barn, but he's there, dancing with Noah. My chest tightens when Bailey grins at him, one hand on his hip. I have to restrain myself from holding Emmy tighter as my whole body tenses.

"Why does ... um, what's his name?" she asks, pointing to Bailey. "That blonde man, he called you Teddy earlier, but your name is Theo." She scowls as though Bailey has personally offended her by giving me a nickname she wasn't privy to.

I chuckle at her indignation. "I've known him a very long time. He's just always called me Teddy." My head snaps back to him. Something clicking into place. He'd insisted on calling me Teddy because everyone else called me Theo. He didn't want to be just anyone to me.

And he isn't.

Fuck, he'd been everything to me. The last few days, I've barely stopped thinking about him, and I feel like I'm right back where I started, when I realised there was something more between us.

"I need to go, Ems. Gotta cut the dance short, sorry." I give her one last dramatic twirl in the air and place her feet back on the ground, then I'm pushing through the other guests, making my way towards Bailey and Noah.

"Mind if I cut in?" I ask, placing a hand on Noah's shoulder. He startles, looking up at me, then rolls his eyes and nods, stepping away.

Before he can get too far, Robbie sweeps in from nowhere, scooping him into his arms. Noah doesn't protest, and I notice the moment his body relaxes as they slowly dance together, putting space between us.

I breathe out, trying to steel myself. Bailey's rigid by the time I'm standing chest to chest with him. I put one hand on his hip, pulling him into me, the other clasps his hand, and he responds by placing his free hand on my bicep, squeezing slightly.

"Hey," he says awkwardly.

"Hey."

"What's going on?" he asks, breath hitching.

"Am I not allowed to want to dance with you?"

"That depends."

"On what?" I ask, swaying to the music.

"On whether you actually want to, or whether you're just trying to keep an eye on me."

I frown at that. Is that what he thinks I've been doing? "If I wanted to keep an eye on you, I could have done that from over there," I say, nodding to the tables.

"Then why?" He looks off to the side. Just like he used to when he was anxious about my intentions.

"Look at me."

Slowly, he meets my eyes again, brows creased with concern. I stop moving and cup his face, eyes flicking down to his lips, then back up again. His eyes blow wide and I think he realises what I'm about to do, but I wait a moment, giving him the chance to pull away. Then I lean forward so our lips are barely touching and whisper, "I've missed you, mo leannan."

BAILEY

I'M SUDDENLY EIGHTEEN AGAIN. TEDDY'S LIPS ARE on mine, and they're hauntingly familiar—soft as they move slowly against mine. It feels like no time has passed. The only thing different is the scratch of his beard against my cheek. I let out a sound of protest when he pulls away, and dig my fingers into his arms to make sure he doesn't get too far.

"Want to go home?" he asks, grinning.

"Yeah," I breathe. He drags me off the dance floor and out the barn doors, all the way back to his cottage without pausing or saying a word.

Once the front door opens, Teddy slams my back against the wall, making me suck in a breath. Then, finally, his lips are back on mine, and this time it isn't slow or hesitant—he forces my mouth open, hands stroking down my back, cupping my arse as he pushes his tongue deeper into my mouth. A moan rips from my throat. His arms are the only thing holding me up as I melt into the wall. I grab at his jacket, trying to undo the buttons, but he pulls away.

"Upstairs?" he asks.

I nod, still trying to catch my breath, and follow him.

Once we're in his bedroom, he pulls me against him again, and my fingers weave into his hair so tightly that I'd have to be cut free before I willingly let go. The back of my thighs bump the end of the bed, and he pulls away, wiping the corner of his mouth with his thumb. "Not quite the same as I remember," Teddy says, as his eyes rove over my body, burning as his mouth curves up into a smirk. He places one hand on my chest and shoves me onto the bed, then steps away, undoing his jacket. His dark hair frames his face in soft waves, curling around his ears, with his fringe hanging just above his eyes, brushing the bridge of his nose.

Teddy removes his shirt and waistcoat and throws them to join his jacket on the floor. His muscles tense, and my cock twitches in response.

"You're bigger," I mutter under my breath. But in the silence of the room, he hears every word, cocking an eyebrow at me.

"So are you. Now take your shirt off," he demands as he stalks towards me.

I undo a couple of buttons on my shirt and pull it over my head in one sweeping motion. Teddy rakes his gaze over me slowly, and I barely have time to draw a breath before he's on the bed, prowling towards me. He straddles my waist, his kilt pooling around my lower body. I reach out to touch the rough, warm wool, stroking the bright yellow stitching that runs through deep blues and greens.

"I can take it off," Teddy says, fiddling with the buckle. I quickly put my hand on his to stop him.

"No."

"No?" He frowns.

"Leave it on." I've never seen him in a kilt before. It's definitely doing something for me. I'd spent most of the wedding staring at his bare knees and the shape of his calves in his knee-high socks.

Teddy looks down at himself, and I chuckle, hesitantly reaching out to touch his chest. His pecs are large and warm as I palm them, stroking the dark hair and travelling down to brush his soft stomach. My body relaxes, being able to touch him like this again.

"I've missed you so much," Teddy says softly as he leans down, dragging his nose up the side of my neck, making my body tighten as he breathes in deeply. My cock kicks eagerly against him, and we start kissing again, slowly, taking the time to explore one another. My hands work their way back into his soft curls, while his frame my face, thumbs stroking my jaw.

It takes me a moment to realise he's grabbing my wrists, moving my arms above my head. I freeze up, but he doesn't realise. He's too busy leaving a trail of little kisses along my jaw and neck. My eyes sting, tears trail down my cheeks, and he finally looks at me.

"That wasn't very nice." He grabs my legs and flips me over, pulling the long end of the tie up to the headboard, securing it in place.

"No," I whimper.

"No? No, what?" Teddy asks. But I've lost my words, and I can't find them in the darkness.

Shane leaves me no choice, wrestling me onto my front, and I find myself in the same position as earlier. He grabs my wrists and pulls them above my head.

"No!" I scream. My chest is collapsing in on itself, and I can't breathe.

TWENTY-EIGHT

THEO

"Bailey?" I jump off the bed, watching as he lies still, chest rising and falling rapidly. He stares up at the ceiling, jaw clenched tight, with tears streaming down his face.

Fuck, what have I done? He said no twice, and I took too long to stop. "Bailey, I didn't mean to ..." I say, fighting my instincts to go to him and hold him, not sure if that would make things worse. Guilt eats away at me as I watch him for a few minutes. His hands eventually come up to cover his face, and he rolls onto his side away from me, letting out a choked sob. I can't hold back any longer, climbing onto the bed and curling myself around his back. He doesn't flinch as I wrap my arms around his waist—he leans back into me as his body shudders.

"You're safe with me, you know that, right? You've always been safe with me," I say, kissing his head. He holds onto my arms so tight that his nails dig into my skin. I lose track of time, listening to his breathing slow down until I follow him into sleep.

I'm startled awake as Bailey pushes me off him and climbs out of the bed.

"What are you doing?" I ask, getting up.

"We should get back to the wedding," he says, picking up his shirt.

I put my hand on his to stop him. "We're not going back to the wedding. Why the hell would we do that?"

"Noah will wonder where I went," he says stiffly, jerking out of my hold.

"Fuck Noah. What happened earlier? Was it something I did?"

"I'm fine, I just want to ... I want to go back to the wedding." His voice cracks, and I know he's lying to me.

"Bailey, please, I just want to help."

He whirls around, face furious. "You want to help?" he scoffs. "There's nothing you can do now. I needed you twelve years ago. Where were you then? When my brother held me down and tortured me, over and over, telling me no one will ever care about me as much as he did—that I'm safe with him."

I open my mouth to speak, but he cuts me off immediately.

"Where were you when my stepdad waited for an empty house to tie me to the bed and rape me?"

I wince as his words hit me like daggers. He jabs a finger into my chest as he continues to feed the guilt that consumes me. "Where were you when I went to your house in the middle of the night, begging you to take me with you? You fucking left me behind, Teddy."

My tears are so hot they leave a blazing trail down my cheeks.

"I don't need your help now. I did it all myself. I worked through my shit alone, and I shouldn't have had to. I needed my best friend," he chokes out. "I needed my boyfriend."

It's as though he's shoved his hand into my chest and ripped my heart out. I know I fucked up not realising how bad things were for him, but he also hid it from me. I get that he was too scared to tell me what was happening, but I was just a kid; I didn't know ... I swallow, reminding myself that he wasn't Shane's only victim, and a flare of anger rises in me, unbidden. "You know where I was for at least part of that, Bay."

He flinches away, and it douses the fire within me in an instant. I grab his wrist, pulling him against me before tucking a loose curl behind his ear and cupping his face so I can see he's paying attention. "I had to live twelve years thinking you tried to kill me. That my boyfriend—that the boy I *loved*—wanted to hurt me. Shane messed with my head after just one night, and it hasn't gone away in all this time. So for him to have been fucking with your head for years, Bay ... I can't even imagine how you're feeling right now." I hold his chin, tilting his head up a little. "But I'm not going anywhere." I kiss his hot forehead. "You have to believe me, mo leannan—I'm not leaving you again."

BAILEY

My body calms in Teddy's embrace. I know what happened earlier wasn't real; he wasn't trying to hurt me. I focus on his fingers pressing into my back, and the familiar smell of his smoky cologne. Shane and Dean can't hurt me anymore. Not here. Here, I'm safe. I take deep breaths until I feel more whole again.

"Come on," Teddy says, pulling free of me. He heads to his wardrobe and pulls out a pair of grey tracksuit bottoms and a hoodie, passing them to me. "It's getting cold outside. Put these on."

"Why are we going outside? I changed my mind, I don't want to go back to the wedding, I can't—"

"We're not going back to the wedding. You slept for a few hours so it's likely finishing up anyway. Get dressed."

I frown at him, confused, but do it anyway, pulling the front of the hoodie up over my nose and inhaling deeply. When I look up, Teddy's staring at me with an intensity that makes my stomach tighten and my heart beat harder. He pulls the drawstring of the joggers, forcing me to take a step closer to him, lips brushing mine in the gentlest of butterfly kisses as he deftly ties a knot. I lean in, but he moves away before I can kiss him properly, taking his suit jacket off and putting a hoodie on too. Then he leads me down the stairs to the back door, where he grabs some wellington boots and bangs them upside down against the wall. "Just in case of spiders," he grins, handing them to me before sliding on his own.

We head outside into the cool evening breeze. The sound of pipes and fiddles in full swing fills the air as we walk along the shingle path that runs behind the barn, towards the fields.

"Where the hell are you taking me?" I murmur.

We approach a stile, and he places one foot on the stone step, then swings the other over, hopping off into the field. "Over you come," he says, holding his hands out as though to catch me. I maneuver over the stile and jump, purposefully avoiding his arms, making him chuckle.

We traverse the muddy field, getting closer to the trees that run all along the border on the far side. Amongst the trunks, I can just about make out two giant boulders in the twilight. "What is that?" I ask, squinting.

"*They* are Heather and Rosie." He makes a clicking noise, and two giant Highland cows come out of the shadows, trotting over to us. Imposing horns stretch outwards, and gorgeous caramel-coloured hair covers their eyes in a sweeping fringe. I hold my breath, worried they'll charge, but Teddy steps in front of me. He holds his palms out, and they instantly push their noses into them, snuffling, letting out large snorts, shaking their heads. "They're harmless, just a bit old and grumpy."

"Like you, then," I reply before I can stop myself. My jaw drops, and I take a step back from him. "I didn't mean that ..." I start, but Teddy's already turned around and closed the distance.

"Did you just call me old?" he asks, voice deep and gravelly.

"No, I'm the same age as you!" I put my hands on his chest to stop him getting closer, but now my mind is wholly fixed on his firm pecs as they flex with his movements. "I was calling you grumpy," I say, biting my lip to stop myself from grinning.

"I brought you here to see the lassies and the first thing you do is insult me?"

I look back at the cows, and they raise their giant heads from the grass, watching us closely. Just the sheer size of them puts me on edge.

Teddy takes a step back. "When I came back to Skye, I'd get into these phases where I was angry all the time, often at the smallest of things. The rage would consume me so quickly I'd have no way to stop it. I only realised I'd broken or hit something *after* I'd done it." He frowns, looking away from me.

"What?"

"I thought I had it under control for a while, but maybe it never went away. The day I saw you in the barn ... I've never felt so angry. I need to apologise properly. I shouldn't have hit you like that." He runs his thumb along my jaw where the bruise has since faded.

"I don't blame you for that, not after everything you went through. Besides, I think I got a little carried away too." I say, fiddling with the hem of Teddy's jumper.

His lips curl up into a grin. "You've got a mean right hook, though."

"Shut up." I shove him away from me, but one of the cows moos loudly, startling me back into his arms.

"They're gentle." Teddy goes over to one of them, stroking its side. "Whenever I feel overwhelmed, I come and sit with them. It soothes me. Come here." He pulls me until I'm standing in front of him, then guides my hand to the thick hide. I wiggle my fingers and find it's coarser than I was expecting for how soft they look. Teddy pushes my hand deeper until I find downy fur beneath, soft and warm.

My concentration flags as I became all too aware of the length of Teddy's body pressed against my back. I feel his hard cock settle against my arse as he pushes closer to me, one arm wrapping around my waist, tight. I'm suddenly wanting to be anywhere but here.

"Take me home."

THIRTY

THEO

I FUMBLE THE KEY, TAKING FAR TOO LONG TO OPEN the front door. Bailey's hanging off me, grabbing my face and pressing his lips against mine, determined to make it impossible for me to find the damn lock. His teeth latch onto my bottom lip, holding me in place. "Shit, Bay. Let me get us in the bloody house," I groan, ripping my mouth free. A second later the door swings open, and after we kick our boots off, I bend down and lift him over my shoulder, carrying him into the house.

I just about manage to get up the stairs before dropping him onto the bed. His hands go to the waistband of his joggers, and he starts undoing the knot.

"What are you doing?" I ask, suddenly uncertain.

"I'm going to bed," he says. "Are you?"

I kneel between his legs and place my hands on his hips, tucking my thumbs into his waistband, pausing just in case I'm misreading the situation, and he doesn't want me to touch him again.

"Yes," he nods.

I ease his trousers down over his thighs, pulling until

they're completely off and he's lying there in tight red briefs. The curve of his hard cock is prominent, with a wet patch at the tip from where he's leaking. I get up and take off my hoodie and shirt as he does the same. Then my hands move to the fastenings on my kilt. His mouth hangs open slightly, and he stares at me with hooded eyes as I let it fall to the floor with a heavy thud. When I look up, Bay is staring, a blush creeping along his cheeks.

"Not what you were expecting?" I chuckle.

"No," he pouts.

I leave my boxers on and climb onto the bed, suddenly in uncharted waters, nervous to touch him.

"Why are you all the way over there?" he asks.

"I don't—I don't want what happened earlier to happen again." I look at him, and he's frowning at me.

"I'm not delicate, Teddy," he snaps.

"I didn't say you were."

"I'm fine, just—"

"You're not fine." My voice rises slightly despite trying to remain calm. "A few days ago, I had to wrestle a knife from you. You've had numerous panic attacks since, and you freaked out when we made out earlier. So tell me when, amongst all of that, you've been *fine*."

His face scrunches up, hurt by my words. That wasn't my intention at all. I'm just fucking scared of ruining this. I rub my face. "I'm sorry, Bay."

Silence blankets us for a moment.

"What do you want, Teddy?" he asks.

Him. I don't want to watch him go back to Cumbria at the end of the week. But I can't ask him to stay. He has a whole life down there. I reach out and brush his cheek with my thumb. "I want the last twelve years back. I wish I'd figured everything out sooner so that I didn't have to bury my heart and leave you behind."

Bailey swallows, and I grab the back of his neck, pulling him towards me. "What do *you* want?"

I see the moment fire ignites in his eyes. "You. Always you. Just—just don't hold my arms down, please."

I lie back, dragging him on top of me. Bailey's quick to straddle my hips, hands falling either side of my head. Then we're nose to nose. I wait for him to make the first move, body thrumming with energy as he breathes against my lips, his cock long and heavy, pushing against mine.

But he's still not moving ...

"We don't have to go any further. We can stay like this the rest of the night." I reach for his hand and bring it to my lips, kissing the rough, healed cuts on his knuckles. "You set the pace, and I'll meet you halfway." I barely get the words out before his lips crash down on mine.

I'm quickly overwhelmed by the weight of him pushing me down into the mattress, his hips grinding into mine, making my cock pulse with want.

I slip my hands down the back of his briefs, feeling the globes of his arse bunch and flex with his movements. I knead them, remembering the curves and dips, the crease between his cheeks and thighs. Bailey's tongue flicks over mine—every movement makes my balls tighten, and my cock throb. I feel a wetness between us, but I'm not sure if it's me, him, or the both of us combined.

"Teddy," he breathes, pulling away.

"You okay?" I ask.

He nods a little frantically. "Please, I want you," he whimpers, pushing his face against my neck, mouthing at it, making my toes curl and my eyes roll back. His little noises get louder, and his hips grind more frantically as he murmurs another 'please' into the crook of my neck.

I tug at his underwear. "Take these off."

Bailey sits up, quickly dragging his briefs down. His cock

springs free, pink and smooth, long with a thick vein running underneath. I shuffle out of my boxers, then grab his thighs and pull him so that he has to knee-walk over me until his cock is resting against my face. I stick my tongue out and lick from his base to the tip. Using my hand to guide him into my mouth, I close my eyes, feeling the weight of his cock as it brushes my tongue and grazes the back of my throat. My eyes sting for a moment; I'm not sure if it's from my gag reflex being tested for the first time in a while, or if this is exactly how I remember him. The shape, the taste—it's all the same.

Bailey jerks, pushing his cock deeper, making me gag. "Sorry!" He rushes to pull out, cock bobbing in front of my face, a string of saliva trailing from his tip to my lips. I pant, catching my breath.

I want more.

"Turn around," I growl, giving him a push to speed things up. He catches on quickly and does as I ask, straddling me backwards so that his cock is dangling above my face. I feel him rub his cheek against my thigh; the scratch of his stubble makes my stomach tense and pre-cum leak from my tip. I try to focus on guiding his cock into my mouth, when I feel him push his nose into my groin and inhale deeply.

Oh fuck.

A loud groan escapes me as he gives an open-mouthed kiss to the side of my cock. "Bay." I slap his arse to get his attention before I lose all my senses.

"Mmm?" is all the response I get, sending vibrations straight to my balls.

"Can you control the pace?" I ask, hoping he understands.

"Mhm," he confirms. Swallowing me down to the root, then thrusting as he comes up, his cock brushing against my chin.

"Fuck," I grunt, squeezing his arse cheeks.

Bailey whimpers, and I feel pre-cum drip from his tip onto

my neck. I fist his cock and lick the head, a burst of salt hitting my tongue, before I relax my throat and swallow him down. His hot mouth pulsates as it moves up and down my length, while he simultaneously cuts off my air supply, thrusting deep into my throat, making my brain glitch.

Bailey's thrusts start to speed up. I draw my knees up for purchase on the mattress as I push up into his mouth. We both lose any sense of control, moans and whimpers mixing as we near the edge. Bailey shouts around my cock as hot cum pulses out of him, straight down my throat. I finally let go and release into his mouth. We both drink one another down, and then Bailey pitches forward, collapsing onto me, arms wrapping around my legs.

His fingertip traces the scar on my ankle as we lie there catching our breath.

"How?" he whispers.

"When the ropes caught fire, I couldn't get them off quick enough. They were made from plastic, so it melted to my skin," I say, sobering up way too fast. He makes a soft noise, then I feel him press his lips to one, then the other, making my heart ache. I can't believe I ever thought someone so gentle could have hurt me.

This is exactly where we belong—together.

THIRTY-ONE

BAILEY

A LOW HUM VIBRATES AGAINST THE SIDE OF MY neck, and I'm pulled from my sleep, floating close to the surface. Teddy's squeezing me so tight I can barely take a full breath. He pushes his nose into my neck, breathing in, sending a shiver down my spine. I wriggle against him, trying to get away from the tickle of his beard, but end up brushing against his hard cock. His hand stroking along my hip pauses, and he grips me hard when I grind my bare arse against him.

"What time is it?" I mumble.

"Ten. You slept like a rock." He kisses the underside of my jaw, continuing to rub his beard all over me. My morning wood aches, feeling tight and oversensitive. I clasp my hand around it, pumping a few times to take the edge off.

"What are you doing?" Teddy asks, lifting the duvet. "Are you needy, Bay?" His large, rough hand replaces mine, as he grinds his erection between my arse cheeks.

"Fuck, Teddy," I groan.

"Roll over," he whispers in my ear. I feel him move away, and when I turn around, he's on his back, the duvet pushed off. His stiff cock lying against his stomach, twitching as he reaches for me. He pulls me onto his lap and cups my arse, digging his fingers into my flesh, dragging me along his body until our cocks grind against one another. A deep rumble comes from the back of his throat as he thrusts up against me at the same time.

"Use me," he says on a breath.

"What?" I lean against his pecs to brace myself.

"Make yourself cum." He squeezes my arse again, forcing my hips to work, and I rub myself against him, stomach tensing as the friction pulls me deeper. One of his hands wraps around our lengths and tightens, while the other runs up my hip and side until it's on my pec. He pinches my nipple between his thumb and forefinger and I gasp, squeezing my eyes shut.

"Do you want to cum?" he says softly. When I open my eyes, he's looking up at me through hooded eyelids, cock throbbing against mine. Every time I thrust, my foreskin rolls down and my head catches on his.

"I'm—I'm close," I pant.

He starts to pump us, jaw clenching as he groans, "Cum on me, Bay, I want to feel it, give it to me."

A few more thrusts and I'm done. I arch my back as cum shoots across his stomach and chest.

"Fuck," he moans, letting me slide my softening cock out from his fist. He strokes himself a couple more times and then his whole body shudders, ropes of cum shooting up his body, mixing with mine. He barely has time to catch his breath as I lean down to kiss him, trapping his bottom lip between my teeth. My mind is blissfully empty—it's just him and me. No one can separate us again.

Once we've calmed down, we take turns in the shower and get dressed. I put on his tracksuit bottoms and hoodie again because even though I have my own clothes here, I like the way his are slightly too big. His smell is so deeply ingrained in the fabric, it feels like he's holding me.

He lifts the lid of the cedarwood chest at the end of his bed and starts rooting around inside. He used to have one when he lived in Surrey, too. "She's still knitting you jumpers?"

"Yeah, every birthday. Pretty sure I have thirty. Ma kept all the ones Gran made when I was a baby, and I haven't got rid of any since I moved back to Skye, so there are thirteen in here." Pausing, he squints at me. "Actually, there are twelve. My ex-boyfriend ran off with the one I got for my eighteenth birthday."

I feel hot all of a sudden, remembering I'd picked it up from the bed as I packed my things the day I dumped him. He'd worn it a couple of days in a row, and it smelled of him. "That's not funny," I mutter, my throat tightening at the memory. "I still have it."

He finally pulls out a dark green cable-knit. "You do?"

"Yeah. I can send it back to you when I get home," I say, trying to ignore the pain I feel at the thought of leaving him.

"You can keep it ... but maybe the next time I see you, you should wear it."

The next time ... I swallow, not wanting to hope for that. This is already more than I could have ever hoped for—finding him again, fixing things between us and having a few days alone together. I'm not sure how things would even work once our lives settle back into their normal routines, or whether I'm getting ahead of myself thinking Teddy would even want more.

"I want to take you out for the day," he says, cutting through my thoughts. "Some fresh air might do us good."

I side-eye him. "I'm not climbing trees."

"Why would we—" He groans, rolling his eyes. "It was *one* time."

"You almost killed yourself."

He scoffs. "I did not almost kill myself."

"Looked like it from where I was standing," I say, grinning.

"From what I recall, that day ended pretty well for both of us." He smirks, grabbing my waist, pulling me in for a kiss. It's short and sweet, with an ease so familiar it steals my breath away.

"Come on, we're going to the Fairy Pools."

WE TRAVERSE STEPPING stones and planks as we follow the trail along the stream. There's a slight chill on the breeze today, and by the look of the grey skies, the weather might be on the turn. I'm so busy concentrating on where I'm treading that I jump when Teddy slips his warm hand into mine. There are groups of people walking all around us, but when I look at Teddy, he doesn't seem bothered by the public display of affection.

"Are you out?" I ask cautiously. When we went to the pub, Isla and Robbie didn't know that Teddy was queer, yet out here he doesn't seem to care that everyone can see us.

He frowns at me, then looks down at our hands. "I haven't exactly *come out* to anyone other than my parents, but it's not because I'm closeted; I just don't date men."

"Oh?"

"I don't really date anyone, actually. I've tried over the years, but it never works out." He pulls me to the side to let two kids run past. "I dated one woman for a year when I was twenty-five, but we both agreed it wasn't working and split up amicably. The other women I dated, it either didn't work out, or they didn't like to wait."

"Wait for what?" I ask as I continue to walk, jumping unsteadily from one stone to another to avoid a large puddle, gripping Teddy's hand for stability.

"It takes me a while to feel comfortable enough to be intimate," he says, cheeks tinged pink.

"You like to wait before having sex?"

"Kind of. If I don't have strong feelings for them, then I can't." He stares straight ahead, refusing to look at me. "I've forced myself before, but I don't like it."

"How come you haven't dated men since, you know ..." I trail off, not wanting to mention our breakup again. "Would it make a difference?"

"No. I tried once and it was a shit show. I freaked out on him when he tried to kiss me goodnight, and then he called me frigid, got in his car and drove off." He shrugs it off, like it wasn't a dick move. "After what happened in Surrey, I didn't feel safe being alone with men anyway, so after that, I didn't try again."

My mind paints a vivid picture of Teddy tied up in that shed, with Shane holding a knife to his throat. I see red, hating that my brother affected him so badly. I squeeze Teddy's hand tight, and he winces.

"It's fine, Bay. I liked being on my own. Pretty sure I have the world's lowest sex drive, anyway."

"What? You absolutely do not have a low sex drive," I scoff. Back when we started dating, as soon as he discovered the wonders of a blowjob, he was insatiable. And over the past two days, he's initiated everything without hesitation. None of it felt *forced*. All of this reminds me of something Noah mentioned once. "Have you heard of the term demisexual before?"

He shakes his head. "No."

"It means that you need to be emotionally close to someone before you start to feel sexual attraction for them. If you don't trust the person you're dating, then it makes sense you wouldn't feel any desire to take things further."

I'm pulled to a stop, and when I turn, Teddy's standing there, looking perplexed.

"That makes sense, I guess," he says. "I didn't know there was a word for it."

"I think the fact people are being more open about their sexuality now is helping them realise they're not alone in how they feel. It definitely wasn't talked about when we were kids."

"No. Even back then, I wondered why Robbie was running around like a rampant rabbit, and I was happy to just be by myself." He tugs on my arm, pulling me close. "Until you, of course. It's always easy with you."

My stomach flutters as I look into his eyes and realise the implication of the last few days—he trusts me again.

"What about you, anyway?" Teddy asks, brushing a stray curl behind my ear. "Did you date much?"

There's really not much to say about that. Living twenty years thinking you could suddenly black out and hurt someone, or worse, is enough to dampen any sexual appetite I may have had. I'd never taken a risk like I had with Teddy again. "Not dating ... um, a few hookups." I swallow, feeling embarrassed all of a sudden. "When I started therapy they put me on antidepressants, and it messed with everything. I either couldn't get it up, or couldn't finish when I did, so I've been single for a while. Came off the pills a couple of years ago, but I felt a little out of the game by that point."

Teddy leans in, breath tickling my ear as he says, "I don't think that's an issue anymore."

"Apparently not," I mutter, as my stomach tightens.

His phone dings, startling us both. He pulls away to check it, and I watch as his eyes widen. "What is it?"

He turns the phone around to show me a picture of us on the dance floor; Teddy crowding over me, my back bending slightly as he cups my face. "Who ...? Why would they upload that?" I splutter.

Pulling the phone back, he looks again and says, "One of Isla's friends uploaded it and tagged me. I may have taken her on a date a few months ago, and not called her back for a second."

"That's not okay, Teddy," I huff.

"She didn't like shellfish! I'm a *scallop* diver," he says defensively.

"Not you, *her*. She doesn't know if you're out or not. She can't just upload shit like that on the internet." I'm so caught up in the fact that this woman is outing Teddy to the whole world that it takes me a moment to realise *I'm* in the photo too. "You need to message her. I-I can't have my picture on there," I say, feeling too warm.

"It's fine, Bay, I don't mind. Let everyone see, I have nothing to hide."

"I do!" I shout, hands going to my hair and gripping on tight. "I don't have social media. I can't have my family knowing where I am. Please, ask her to take it off."

"Shit, okay." He types out a message, and I hear the whoosh as it sends, then he pulls me against his chest. "You're fine. No one's going to find you here."

"Sorry," I mumble into his jumper.

"For what? You're allowed to have boundaries, Bay. I've only met her a couple of times, so I'm not sure why she took that photo, anyway."

I hate how fast my body reacts to danger—I'm fine one minute, and the next it feels like the world is closing in on me, as if I'm about to slip off a ledge and fall for eternity. I feel the coarse wool of Teddy's jumper between my fingers and hear the rushing water as it runs along giant boulders down the hill.

The mixture of the ocean on Teddy's clothes and the earthy smell of mud and moss from the trail fills my nose.

Another message dings.

"It's gone," he says softly, kissing my forehead. "Want to keep going? I think it's only a few more minutes until we reach the waterfall."

"Yeah." I pull away and let him take my hand again as we carry on. Teddy's talking, but I have no idea what he's saying as I'm busy trying to calm myself down.

They can't find me here. I'm safe. I have Teddy, Noah, and Jake. They won't let anything happen to me.

"Here," Teddy says a few minutes later. I shake my head, realising I wasn't even watching where I was walking. We're standing in front of a semicircle of rock face. Small waterfalls cascade over the ledge and splash into a crystal clear pool. Mountains dominate the landscape behind it. "It's beautiful," I murmur.

"Sure is," Teddy says. When I turn my head, he's looking right at me.

"Shut up." I smack his chest, and laughter bubbles up, bursting free. I forget for a moment that this is temporary.

"What are we doing?" I ask.

He rubs the back of his neck and hums. "I get that maybe we're rushing things, but—"

"I'm going back to Cumbria," I say, cutting him off.

He frowns. "I know that. You have a life there, and I have a life here. It doesn't matter to me. We were never finished, Bay." He steps into me, cupping my face, forcing me to look up into his dark eyes. "You ended things between us because Shane forced you to, not because you didn't love me anymore."

I nod without thinking.

"And I ran away from you because I was scared, not because I didn't love *you* anymore," he says with sincerity.

My heart pounds in my chest as I cling to every word that comes out of his mouth.

"Did it ever really stop for you?" he asks, eyes flicking between mine as he holds me prisoner between the palms of his hands.

"No," I breathe out. I can't look at him without my chest swelling with want. The thought of actually leaving him, of having to say goodbye when we head back south ... It makes me feel sick. I'm certain I still love him. There's a familiar prickling behind my eyes, and I blink rapidly to try and hold back the tears. "I wanted to look for you, but I-I couldn't. I needed to set you free because I didn't think I was good for you," I choke out.

Teddy swipes a thumb across my cheek. He doesn't look sad at all; he's got a massive grin on his face that makes me want to smack him. "But you found me anyway. It took a long time, but you found me, and I never needed to be free of you. I don't *want* to be free of you, ever. You're good for me, Bay. So good."

I shake my head. I'm not.

You're never good, Bailey. Never.

"Yes, you are, you're good, and you're home," Teddy says unwaveringly. "Your home is with me. It has been from the moment I met you, and I never should have let you go."

I try to look away, but he lifts my chin. "Hey ..."

"What?"

"Would you do it again?"

I almost laugh, remembering our first kiss in the woods. I cough to clear my scratchy throat. "Would you?" I say with more confidence than I feel.

His lips curl into a beaming smile, and he leans in until I feel just the ghost of his lips against mine as he says, "Always." Then he kisses me with such force, I stumble backwards slightly. There's a finality in his kiss, a promise that this time, it will be different.

BAILEY

Drops of water hit my nose, and I jerk away from Teddy, looking up at the darkened sky. He grabs my hand and we run all the way back down the hill just as the rain gets heavier. We make it back to his car soaked through. I take my shoes off and sit in the passenger seat, shivering. Teddy slams the driver's door, turns the heat on high, and starts the engine.

When we get back, the cottage is silent except for the sound of our bare feet slapping on the hardwood floors as we rush upstairs to the bathroom. Teddy switches on the shower and strips out of his wet clothes before turning to me. "Arms up." He grabs the hem of my shirt, and I lift my arms above my head as he peels it off. I feel his fingers brush against the scar on my ribs, and I freeze.

"This doesn't look like the rest of them ..." he mutters.

I catch my reflection in the mirror. It's barely visible now. Something so small should be forgettable, but I can still make out the jagged lines of the 'S', recalling the way the knife pierced my skin.

"When I stayed away from you for a month," I say, mouth

drying as the memory hits me vividly. "Shane, h-he gave me an extra punishment because I ran away to live with you."

"What did he do?" Teddy asks through clenched jaws.

"He carved an 'S' into me with a knife. Said it would remind me of him, because when everyone leaves me, he'd still be there. After he did that, I think I started to realise it wasn't just about helping me. It felt like ownership, and I—I just wanted to leave the next day and come home to you, but I didn't want you to see the burns."

Teddy is silent as he strokes the scar gently. "You don't belong to *anyone*, Bay."

I'm shivering again. My lip wobbles and I clasp it between my teeth, not wanting to ruin the day by thinking about Shane. Teddy bends down, kissing the puckered skin on my ribs, then around my hip to my back. "Fuck them," he says, standing back up. "You're home now, that's all that matters. I'm not willing to let you go so easily again." He nudges me into the shower and steps in behind me, quickly closing the distance, pressing his naked body against mine.

The hot water warms me until the shivering stops and any thoughts of the past wash away. Teddy leans around me, picking up a bottle of body wash, then pulls my arm to the side, running his soaped up hands from my wrist to my shoulder, curling around my neck. He slowly cleans every inch of me as I stand there, barely able to hold myself upright.

I gasp as his hand strokes down my stomach and wraps around my cock. "You're so hard already, mo leannan," he murmurs against my ear before nibbling on the lobe. Goosebumps break out all over my skin, and I start to feel overstimulated from the feel of his body and the heat of the water. He spins me around, palming my arse, fingers casually slip between my crease. I grab his shoulders, nails digging in as I use him to hold myself up.

"You okay?" he asks, hands pausing their motion. I nod,

and when I look at his face, his pupils are blown wide. He lifts my chin, lips touching mine, soft and gentle as he holds me against his chest.

When he pulls away, he sweeps my hair back and nudges me further under the water. I close my eyes and hear the click of a bottle opening, then Teddy's fingers are raking across my scalp, his nails digging in just the right amount to make my legs go weak. He swaps our positions and pours some shampoo into my hand. I run my fingers through his dark curls, taking my time massaging it in as he reaches back, stroking my hip, pulling me tight against his back. It all feels too good.

You can never have this.

You'll hurt him.

You'll always be bad, little mouse.

Hot.

Fuck, it's too hot.

My hands seek the cool tiles, and I lean against them, pushing my cheek against the ceramic, trying to cool myself down as quickly as possible.

"Bay?" I feel Teddy's hands on my shoulders. "Hold on," I think he says, but my ears are ringing with a high-pitched squeal, making it sound like I'm underwater. I'm lifted into the air just as everything goes black.

My vision is blurry, and static crackles in my ears. I feel Teddy's arms around me, and try to move my head off his shoulder but it feels like a lead weight. He hoists me up higher in his arms and steps out of the shower, walking through to the bedroom where he places me on the bed.

"What happened?" he asks.

I cover my eyes with my arm as the light burns my retinas. I hear the question, but it takes a while before I can answer. "Panic," I breathe out. "It happens sometimes when I panic. I'm fine, I just need my anxiety meds." I reach over the side of the bed for my suitcase, and fumble around for them. Teddy disappears and comes back with a glass of water.

"Stop saying you're fine," he grumbles, grabbing a small towel to rub my hair dry. I lean into the touch, exhaustion dragging me under, until he makes me jump, saying, "Let's go downstairs. I'll make tea and put the fire on."

I settle onto the sofa and take a sip of my tea as I watch Teddy poke around in the fireplace. It snaps and crackles to life, and the smell of woodsmoke fills the cottage. He slumps down next to me, pulling my feet into his lap. "What did you panic about?"

I look away from him, staring into the fireplace for a moment, before deciding to go with the truth. "I still feel like I'm going to hurt you." I close my eyes tight. "I hear his voice in my head, telling me I'm bad and that I don't deserve you."

Teddy digs his thumbs into my instep as he massages my foot, and I melt into the cushions. "Do you believe me when I say it was Shane who hurt me?"

"Yes," I snap, clenching my jaw tight. "But I can't help doubting myself. I've questioned everything for *years*. Once I moved in with you, I started to see things a little clearer, and when my mum found animals in the treehouse, I *knew* I hadn't done it. But I've never been able to trust myself, not when Shane was always so quick to defend me, or tell me he was hurting me for my own good." My body stiffens, angry. "There's always been a 'what if' in the back of my mind, and it's not going away. I still don't know what happened the day my dad died. I genuinely have no memory of it—only Shane does. So what if it was me? What if it's both of us?" Words are coming out so fast that my body is trying to hyperventilate again. "What if I'm just as fucked up as he is?"

Teddy leans forwards and grabs my hands, pulling me onto his lap. He looks up at me softly. "Want to know what my understanding of a psychopath is?"

"W-what?"

"Lack of guilt," he says as he leans forward and kisses my forehead. "Lack of empathy." He kisses the tip of my nose. "A manipulative, self-important liar." He catches my bottom lip between his teeth and sucks on it a little, making it throb. He releases me and asks, "Have you ever lied to me, Bay?"

The tears I was holding back come hot and fresh now. "Y-yes."

"When?"

"When I told you I—I didn't want to go with you to Scotland. And when I told you I didn't love you," I choke out, wiping the tears from my eyes.

Teddy strokes his hands up and down my bare ribs, eyes never leaving mine. "Did you ever manipulate me?"

"No!"

"Did you feel guilty when you thought you'd hurt those animals?"

"Yes." I close my eyes. I felt guilty about it all.

Teddy's mouth curves up on one side, "Who lied, Bay?"

"Shane," I say immediately.

"Who never felt guilty for hurting you?"

"Shane ..." I whisper. He never once apologised for hurting me.

"Who manipulated you for *years*?"

My childhood flashes through my mind like a horror reel. Cowering in the corner of a room, clinging to the bedsheets as I'm held down, submitting to punishments for things I never did.

I stare at Teddy and realise something I'd never given

much thought: even when I couldn't trust myself, I'd always trusted him. I grab his chin and tilt his head up, his beard soft against my fingers as I stroke along his jaw. I'm not the same as Shane. There were never any blackouts. He took my whole childhood from me. Took *Teddy* from me. I stare into whisky-brown eyes, my body vibrating with energy.

I want this.

I *deserve* it.

Teddy sucks in a breath when my lips crash against his. He opens his mouth to let me lead, moaning as my tongue brushes against his. I'm jerked backwards just as I feel his cock harden beneath me. "Should you be doing this?" He pants.

"I told you I'm fi—I'm good, Teddy, I promise."

His eyes darken and he grabs my neck, dragging me back into the kiss. Hands trail down my back, squeezing my arse so hard that I gasp. My cock thickens, pressing against his stomach as I grind my arse on his lap.

Teddy pulls away, then pushes me off his lap. He rushes out the room, coming back in less than a minute, raising an eyebrow in question as he holds up a condom and lube. I snatch the condom from his hand and grab the waistband of his boxers, pulling them down. Impatient, I shove him so he falls back onto the sofa, then I discard my own boxers before tearing open the wrapper and rolling the condom down the length of his cock. I hop back onto his lap, pressing my lips to his desperately. Teddy's slick finger strokes along my crease and pauses against my hole, waiting for permission. With neither of us willing to separate long enough to use words, I nod against his mouth and hum my agreement. He rubs circles over my rim, pushing gently on every pass until it softens enough for his finger to slip inside. We both groan into one another's mouths as he slowly drags his finger out, then back in. I run my hand through the back of his hair and grip it hard enough to draw a moan from him. The noises he's making are driving me insane. I need more. I pick up the discarded lube and squirt some over Teddy's cock, then reach behind and push his hand away, positioning his head to my hole. I lower myself slowly onto him and gasp at the sting.

Christ, it's so much bigger than I remember.

I push down with some force until the head pops through, then the rest of him slides in as I sink lower. Every inch ignites my insides until I'm fully seated. I tense, mapping out the length and girth of him inside me. It leaves me breathless, and I finally pull my mouth away from his.

Teddy's panting as he looks up at me. "Okay?" he asks.

"Yeah," I breathe, lifting myself off him experimentally. My balls tighten as his cock slowly drags out of me, then I sink back down, warmth washing over me. Using my knees to bounce, I start to ride him.

"Fuck," he moans, leaning back against the sofa, arms covering his eyes. He has one hand gripping the other wrist tightly, like he's not allowed to touch me. I place my palms on his pecs, feeling soft hair beneath my fingers, and his muscles as they jump with my every movement.

"Touch me, Teddy," I beg.

His arms drop from his face, and he gives me a look of pure heat as he sits up, grabbing my waist, pulling me against him so we're chest to chest. He drives up into me, the force of it making me choke. I bury my nose into his neck, breathing in the familiar scent of him before flicking my tongue out to taste the sweat that's built up there.

"You get me too close whenever you do that, Bay," he growls, gripping the back of my hair, tugging me backwards. I release his neck and reach back to rest my hands on his knees. Every time he pumps his cock into me, my own slaps against my stomach, pre-cum dripping down the foreskin. He wraps his hand around my dick, stroking me a couple of times. I'm so close to the edge, my balls ache with the need to cum.

Teddy suddenly stops moving, and my orgasm drifts away. "No," I whimper. What the hell is he doing?

He grins up at me. "I want you to say it again."

"Say what?" I huff, trying to take over, grinding my hips and gasping as his cock brushes over my prostate. He lets go of my hair and grips my hips, forcing me to sit still.

"Say you're good again." He starts stroking my cock, far too loosely to do anything except keep me on the edge.

"Why?"

"Because you deserve to believe it, *mo ghráidh*."

He thrusts up into me again and my mind stutters. We find a rhythm, and I've almost forgotten what he asked me. The climb to the peak is quicker this time. He loosens his grip on my hips, letting me meet his every thrust.

Just as I feel my stomach pull tight, he stops again, and I let out a cry as my release is snatched away from me for the second time. He traces my bottom lip with his fingertips then slips them into my mouth, brushing over my tongue, exploring then withdrawing, over and over until I'm sucking on them desperately. It distracts me a little from the orgasm that's sitting heavy in my balls, threatening to explode whether he moves or not.

"I can feel you throbbing around me, how much you're leaking on me." He swipes his thumb over my tip, then sucks it into his mouth. "If you can't say it, then I'll say it for you. I'll tell you every day how good you are."

Christ.

My eyes sting, and I feel as though I'm on a tripwire. Years of being told I'm sick, bad, *wrong*—so deeply ingrained within me. It lights up my whole body when he says those words.

"I'm good," I breathe out.

Teddy's brows raise slightly, like he's surprised I actually said it. "Say it again?" he asks as he thrusts into me again with no finesse, just pure determination.

"I'm good," I pant.

My orgasm, which had been held out of my reach, barrels through me. His arms wrap around me as we grind our hips in unison, and I finally let go. Hot cum smears between us, coating our stomachs as my cock throbs, trapped between our bodies. Teddy lets out a groan, biting down on my shoulder, his body shuddering as his cock pulses deep inside of me.

"Yes you are," he whispers.

BAILEY

Something soft brushes against my lips. I stir, but I don't want to wake up yet; my mind's still floaty, and I'm cocooned in Teddy's scent. I know as soon as I wake up, he's going to leave. A hand brushes my hair behind my ear, and I peel my sleep-heavy eyes open to find Teddy leaning over me. His dark curls are flopping over his eyes, and a smile dances on his lips. He looks so pretty. I reach out to grab his sleeve, wanting to drag him back into bed.

"I need to go to the docks, Bay. Go back to sleep, okay?" He kisses my forehead once more. "I'll be home around two."

"What time is it?" I groan, closing my eyes again.

"Four-thirty. Rob texted me last night. My trainee is off sick, and we've had a temp covering the numbers since I took time off last week. I need to get in early to get everything organised."

I'm barely listening, drifting back under already. I hear Teddy opening the bedroom door, whispering, "Sweet dreams, mo leannan." Then I'm out like a light.

"Morning, lad," Teddy's grandad greets me as I walk in through the back door.

I nod to him, feeling my cheeks heat. I realise that everyone knows now that Teddy and I have been holed up together all weekend. I avoid eye contact while I take my shoes off. "Hey, Malcolm."

"Parcel arrived for you early this morning," he says, pointing to the breakfast table. "Breakfast's on the hot plates. Take what you want. Noah's the only one who hasn't shown his face yet."

Of course Noah would be the last up. I check my phone and see it's eleven in the morning. "Thanks." I get my breakfast and sit down next to the small parcel.

"The boys might be coming in early," Malcolm mutters as he looks out of the kitchen window. I follow his gaze and see dark grey clouds. "Storm's coming. Can't have been in the forecast, or else they wouldn't have gone out." The deep frown on Malcolm's brow makes me a little uneasy. "I'll leave you to it, gotta go help clean up the barn." He sighs and heads out the back door.

My eyes drift to the parcel. I don't know who would have sent it to me. Everyone who knows I'm here is here also. Teddy could have left me something, I suppose, but then why would he leave it here and not at his house?

Deciding I can't finish my breakfast without looking, I take a deep breath and drag the parcel over. My name is written on the box in black marker pen, but there's no last name and no address. It must have been delivered in person, but I don't recognise the writing.

I rip off the brown tape sealing the box, and immediately

my stomach revolts. As I open it, the smell of sweet rust hits me like a punch in the gut. It takes me right back to when I was a kid, waking up covered in the blood of—

Not again.

Inside, there's a bundle of tartan fabric. With trembling fingers, I unwrap the cloth and shove my hand over my mouth to stop myself from crying out. A mouse lies unmoving, fresh blood smeared over its fur.

I jump off my stool and run out the back door, doubling over as my breakfast comes back up. I spit to clear the bile from my mouth, then lean against the wall, begging my heart to slow down.

He's found me.

How the hell has he found me…?

On shaky legs, I stumble back to the kitchen, not wanting anyone else to see what's in the parcel. I go to close it back up, but something catches my eye. Underneath the mouse, partially stained by blood, is a piece of paper. I pick it up by a dry corner and slide it out gently. My breath catches in my throat, and a sob threatens to come out. It's a screenshot of the picture from the wedding where Teddy's kissing me.

He knows where I am, and he knows I'm with Teddy. "Fuck!" I shout, slamming my hand on the counter. I turn the paper over and see scrawled writing that I finally recognise as my brother's.

Then my heart stops completely.

Found you, Little Mouse. You should have left him alone.

I throw it back into the box and seal everything up.

"What's that?" I jump at the sound of Noah's voice, not realising he'd come into the kitchen.

I tuck my hands behind my back, paranoid they might have blood on them, and mutter, "Nothing, it's just—it's just something from Teddy. I gotta go."

I've been staring at the parcel on the coffee table for so long I have no idea what time it is. Reality is crashing in on me hard and fast, and there's no escaping it anymore. There's no more hiding from Shane. He's going to take everything from me again—my job, my best friend, my family.

Teddy…

Any doubts I had about Shane being behind everything have been completely obliterated. The evidence is right in front of me, but I don't know what to do with it. I should call the police, but the thought of it spikes fear through me. I'll have to be interviewed and tell strangers about my life. They'll judge me and call me stupid because, 'How could you not have known?'

I head upstairs and take a shower to try to clear my mind. The hot water is close to scalding, and I scrub my skin until it's pink and raw, convinced the blood isn't coming off. The heat starts to make me feel dizzy, so I quickly turn the water cold and let it blast me until I'm shivering. When I can't stand it any longer, I switch the shower off and step out of the tub with stiff limbs, coming face to face with myself in the mirror. I stare for so long that it feels like Shane is looking back at me. That it's his eyes I see and not my own.

It's been years since I left. I changed my last name, kept away from social media. I *hid*. I didn't want to be fucking found.

After getting dressed, I storm back downstairs. Lifting the

lid of the parcel again, I stare at the note he left me. "You should have left him alone ..." I mutter to myself. A vice clamps around my heart, and a burst of fear rushes through me.

He's going to go after Teddy.

I find my phone and call him, but it goes straight to voice-mail. I try another three times before I give up and leave a message. "Teddy, please call me to let me know you're okay. I-I think Shane—just call me back when you get this!"

Staying here and waiting for a reply isn't going to help. I'm crawling out of my skin, needing to see him. He should still be at sea, and Shane can't get him there. But that isn't enough to stop me from grabbing my keys and running out of the house, towards the harbour.

THIRTY-FOUR

THEO

"The weather's turning," I tell Chris, pointing to the blackened clouds.

He looks up and squints. "The forecast says we have a few hours yet. We'll do one more dive, then head back."

I nod and start getting ready to go into the water for the second time.

The new temp, Dan, steps up to me, handing over the umbilical. "You're going in again?"

"Captain's orders," I say, checking my knife is secure and tightening the straps on my cylinders. I watch him as he makes sure the umbilical line is secure. "Remember all the signals?" I ask.

"Yeah, I worked for the coastguard when I was in my early twenties, hard to forget." He smiles kindly. He looks about fifty. I'm about to ask what else he's done since then, when Chris calls out to me to get into position.

I nod to Dan, grinning. "I'm trusting you to pull me back up if the weather turns to shit."

"Yes, sir," he salutes, and I move to sit on the edge of the boat. When Chris gives the go-ahead, I roll backwards into the frigid water and let my body adjust to the temperature.

The minutes go by quickly, and when I next check my watch, my half hour is almost done. I make sure everything is secure, and tug on the lifeline four times. A few seconds go by, but nothing happens. I count to sixty in my head and tug four times again. Still nothing.

Thinking maybe the line's caught on something, I follow it as I swim towards the surface, kicking my legs, fighting against the ache in my limbs that seems determined to drag me back down. As I get closer, I realise what the issue might be. It remains dark where I'd usually start to see the sunlight, and the water has taken on a frantic edge, pushing and pulling, demanding more from me than I have the energy for.

I'm almost at the surface when the slack in the lifeline suddenly goes taught, and I'm yanked to the side so suddenly, I choke on a breath. I pull the rope numerous times to let them know I've been under too long and I need help to get to the surface, but there's still no response.

I look up to gauge the distance to the surface, thinking I might just about make it if I push myself, but when I try to swim up again, another surge comes, dragging my body left and right, pulling me further down. I try to stay calm, but my heart is galloping and my head is pounding.

Making a last desperate attempt, I pull on the rope again. It gives completely, as though ...

Fuck.

Taking a deep breath just as the air supply cuts off, I swap to my pony cylinder, putting the mouthpiece in and biting down to hold it in place. The boat is still above me. Weighing my options, I realise I only have six minutes of air, and it'll take about four minutes to get to the surface unhindered, but if I swim too fast, I risk decompression sickness. There's no other option, though, so despite the risks, I push myself as hard as I can, reaching for the surface.

The sea becomes more tumultuous, throwing me around like a rag doll. My muscles burn as I try to push up against everything that's trying to hold me down. I finally break the surface and spit my mouthpiece out, gasping in the fresh air. It only lasts for a second before a wave hits me and I'm dragged back under, then up again. I try to orient myself by finding the boat, then make slow progress towards it, my body threatening to give out with every stroke.

Finally, I see the ladder at the back of the boat. I think one of the crew is standing there watching me, but he isn't moving. There's no life ring thrown to me, no rope ... he isn't even turning around to tell the rest of the crew that I'm here. I realise it's the temp, and call out to him, but another wave crashes into me and shoves me straight against the ladder. My head thwacks into the metal, and I blindly grab for the rungs to hold myself still. When I look back up, Dan's gone, and I wonder if I'd imagined him watching me.

I can't pull myself out of the water or call for help. My body gives out. A violent stabbing pain shoots through my head, and I sink back under.

BAILEY

I'M ABOUT HALFWAY TO THE HARBOUR WHEN THE breeze suddenly picks up, and a rhythmic, low whooshing fills the air. I stop running and look up just as a red and white helicopter flies over my head, low enough that I can make out 'HM COASTGUARD' written on the side. I stare as it heads for the harbour, and a lump forms in my throat. "Teddy?" I whisper, heart thumping in my chest. I'm frozen to the spot watching as the helicopter goes out to sea, and I just *know* it's him.

"TEDDY!" I yell, running again, as fast as I can to the harbour.

The sky has darkened considerably. Thunder rumbles in the distance, and it's hard to see through the driving rain. I get to the harbour soaked through, and every intake of breath feels like glass in my throat. There are people everywhere. A boat is tethered, and a Coastguard van with bright yellow letters saying 'SEARCH AND RESCUE' is parked up. My legs go weak as I search the crowd of people for Teddy, but I can't see him anywhere.

"What the hell is happening out there?" a deep voice

growls ahead of me. "Tell Chris to give a straight fucking answer! Why's he not saying whether he's conscious or not?" The crowd parts and I see Robbie standing close to Teddy's uncle Luke. He looks furious, baring his teeth, pointing at a radio Luke is holding, looking like he's one second away from grabbing the man and shaking him. He turns to look at me when I run up to him. "Shit," he mutters, grabbing my arm and pulling me away from everyone.

"W-where is Teddy?" I ask, unable to stop my lip wobbling. I already know it's him. Something's happened, and he's out there where I can't get to him.

"Their boat got caught in the storm. Theo was already diving when the order went out to return." He drags his hands over his face, wiping off the rain.

"What happened?"

"They went to pull him up, but the line snapped. They had to wait to see if he would surface on his own. He had an emergency air supply on him, so he should have been safe."

I turn away from him and start walking back to the jetty, for what, I don't know. I want someone to tell me Teddy's okay, or to take me on a fucking boat to get him myself because I would do anything right now to get to him.

"Hey, stop." Robbie grabs my arm, pulling me back. "If the helicopter was needed, then—then they'll take him to Broadford." He continues walking me until we get to a car. "Wait here, I just need to check something with Luke." He unlocks the car then walks towards Luke, throwing his hands in the air, pointing at him as they talk. I watch him until he comes back to me.

"Get in," he growls.

I jump in the car and buckle myself in as Robbie speeds out of the harbour, beeping for people to move out of the way. He taps on his display, and the sound of a phone ringing fills the car.

"What's up, Robbo?" Isla answers.

"There's been an accident. You need to get to Broadford Hospital."

"What? Who?"

"Theo. Pick up Noah on your way. I've got Bailey."

"Alright, see you there," Isla says, voice wobbling as she hangs up.

The drive to the hospital takes far too long. I feel like I'm vibrating out of my skin, thoughts racing. Not knowing what happened is making me think of the worst possible outcome. I want to see him. I want to touch him and for him to touch me back, so I know for sure he's still here with me.

My leg starts to bounce erratically as the hospital finally comes into view. I jump out of the car before Robbie pulls up the handbrake and run to the reception.

"Theodore MacLeod," I say to the receptionist, panting.

"One moment, please," she says, while tapping slowly on her keyboard. I take a step back and rake my fingers through my hair. *I can't shout at her. I can't shout at her.*

"Mr MacLeod has been taken to the ICU. Are you family?"

I look around as Robbie comes up behind me, and plead silently for him to say something, because I don't want to be told I'm not allowed to see Teddy. Robbie steps forward and points a finger at his chest. "Brother." Then points to me. "Boyfriend." Clearly he doesn't want to be told no, either. The receptionist doesn't question the lie as she gives us directions to the waiting room in the ICU.

Robbie takes a seat and rests his elbows on his knees, covering his face with his hands. It's stressing me out more to see him looking so upset, so I walk to the other side of the waiting room.

I'm not sure how much time passes, but when Teddy's

family comes through the door, I startle. Robbie sees Isla, and he's off his seat in a second, rushing over to her.

"Hey, he's okay. It's not the same as last time," she soothes, putting her hands on his cheeks so that he's forced to look at her. They walk off down a corridor, and I look at Noah. He just shakes his head, neither of us knowing what Isla's talking about.

"Lost his da at sea when he was fourteen," Teddy's dad says. "He came to live with us for a few years before he went off to university."

He died at sea? So Teddy really could have ... "Have you heard anything?" I ask.

John takes off his flat cap and scratches his head. "I spoke to the doctor before we came here; as far as I'm aware, he was hypothermic when he came in ... and unconscious. They've told us that they're running tests for decompression sickness and concussion, but so far, he just seems a bit banged up."

What the hell is decompression sickness? I pull out my phone to search it, but Noah quickly snatches it from my hand. When I glare at him, he just stares back, raising an eyebrow, daring me to challenge him.

"Stick to the facts. He's okay right now," Noah says calmly.

I hate when he's reasonable. Leaning back in my chair, clinging to the arm rests, I close my eyes. There's nothing to do but wait.

"Hey."

A hand shakes my shoulder and I jolt upright to find Isla hovering over me.

"He's asleep but stable. They said we have a few hours before visiting time's over. Do you want to go in first on your own?"

Surprised, I look around the waiting room and lock eyes with Teddy's mum. She nods and smiles reassuringly, but I still feel guilty. "I shouldn't. I ... family should go first."

"Go," Isla says sternly, pointing towards the corridor. The look on her face brooks no argument, so I pull myself up cautiously, coming eye to eye with her. Deciding today is not the day to argue with a six-foot red-headed woman, I edge around her and make my way down the corridor.

As I enter the room my heart leaps into my throat. I wasn't prepared to see him like this. I walk over on unsteady legs, taking in all the tubes and wires attached to him. His skin's no longer bronze, and his once blush lips have a tinge of blue to them. The only thing reassuring me he's alive is the steady beep of the heart rate monitor. I stare at his chest, watching as it moves up and down in shallow waves.

The ceiling feels too low, and the room too narrow. The clinical, bright-white lights stab my eyes and make my temples throb. My mind replays the same thought over and over—I could have lost him today.

I find a chair and drag it to the side of his bed, then take his hand in mine, holding on tightly. I take a deep breath to steady myself. "You can wake up now," I say weakly, searching his face for movement. My stomach turns over when I see gauze on the side of his head stained red from his blood. Carefully I stroke his hair from his face. "I'm here, Teddy."

When we were kids and I couldn't speak, Teddy would talk non-stop to fill the silence. His deep voice was enough to calm me and let me know everything would be okay. I try to do the same for him.

"The first time we met, I hadn't made it very far into the woods. It was dark, and I was getting paranoid that Shane was coming for me, or that there would be someone hiding behind a tree, ready to grab me. But then I saw you running. I don't know why I felt like I could trust you. We hadn't even spoken to one another, but I ran after you. Even knowing what I know now, I think if I were given a choice to do that again, I'd run after you every single time." My eyes scan his face, then his body, searching for any kind of response. Feeling hopeless, I try something else. "When you first told me you were Scottish, I was surprised because I'd thought you were Irish the whole time."

Nothing.

"Once, I bought you a big box of chocolates, but I ended up eating them all while you were at work. I didn't have enough money to replace them, so I bought you a twenty-pence candy necklace instead," I blurt out, biting my bottom lip.

"You're in big trouble if that's true." Teddy's hand twitches in mine, and his voice comes out deep and gruff.

I let out a startled chuckle. Then I laugh. I laugh until all my emotions get tangled up and they turn into heaving sobs.

"Stop it. I can't stay mad at you if you do that."

"I can't help it," I choke out.

Teddy groans as he tries to pull his body up, and I quickly find the controls to lift the bed into a sitting position.

"Are you okay?"

"No," is all he says, and he sounds pissed.

"Do you need me to get someone?" I stand and look at the door.

"No. I'm—fuck, my body feels like I've gone twelve rounds with Robbie."

I frown at him. "Twelve rounds of *what*?"

"Boxing …"

I raise an eyebrow at him.

"Robbie's a boxer. ... You know what—not important. My head is pounding."

"What happened out there?"

"The line broke somehow. I have no idea what was happening topside, but I can remember breaking the surface and there being no one there to pull me up." He frowns, then shakes his head.

"I'm staying with you until you're completely better," I say resolutely. "I'm not going back Friday."

"I'm fine, Bay. I just said, it's a few bumps and scrapes."

"I'm *not* going back." Not ever, if I can help it.

"Fine, of course I want you to stay." He pulls me until I'm forced to climb onto the bed. I settle alongside him, careful of the wires, and wrap my arm gently around his middle, resting my chin on his shoulder.

With the rush of everything that's happened, I forgot about Shane. Just as my nervous system starts to calm down, the memory of that box and the note comes front and centre, making my heart race all over again. I need to tell Teddy everything, but I don't want to do it here. I'll show him when we get home. ... He'll know what to do.

THEO

"Get off!" I slap Robbie's hand off of me.

Always with the fucking touching.

"I'm just trying to help," he pouts, letting go of my arm.

As soon as he does, I wobble, and Bailey quickly grabs me from the other side. I lean into him, letting him wrap an arm around my waist.

Ever since I was released from the hospital, Robbie's been attached to my hip; helping me into the car, driving me home, and now trying to come into my house. "You don't need to stay, Rob, I'm good," I say, hoping he'll get the hint and leave.

He stops in the doorway. Glaring, he points at Bailey. "You look after him."

Bailey's back straightens. "Of course I'll look after him."

"I don't need—"

Robbie shuts the front door before I can finish.

"I really don't need looking after," I say, but Bailey isn't listening to me either. He leads me into the living room and sits me down on the sofa, then picks up a parcel from the coffee table and stands in front of me.

"What's that?"

"Shane's here," Bailey says quietly, without looking at me.

My blood turns to ice in an instant.

"What?"

"He found me." Bailey opens the package, keeping it close to his chest so I can't see inside. "I think Shane got someone to deliver this to the farmhouse yesterday morning." He pulls out a piece of paper and hands it to me.

I feel light-headed. The paper is stained with something dark. I look back at the box. "What else is in there?"

"Just ... it doesn't matter. You can probably guess, you don't need to see it."

Shane is here. He's come for Bailey, and if I'm in the way again ... "Have you called the police?" I ask, handing it back to him. I ease myself off the sofa and go to the kitchen to wash my hands, trying to hide the way they shake at the thought of Shane laying hands on either of us again. He's just one man. He can't do anything.

"No."

"We need to call the police," I say, looking over at Bailey as he joins me at the sink. He squirts soap onto his hands, then spends way too long scrubbing them.

I lean around him and turn the water off, wrapping his hands in a towel. He sucks in a breath and squeezes his eyes shut. "I can't, Teddy."

"You've done nothing wrong, Bay."

"It doesn't matter! They'll ask questions, and I'll have to tell them everything; how I was so fucking stupid I didn't realise what he was doing to me. They'll ask why I didn't report him sooner, or why I didn't report Dean. Because that will come up too. They'll say I'm a liar." His breathing comes in short, sharp bursts, and he sways slightly.

"Alright ... alright," I soothe, pulling him against my chest and stroking his hair. "We can deal with this tomorrow, okay? Robbie will be over first thing anyway, and I'll lock everything up tonight." I get where he's coming from; I've done it myself, refused to speak up and report Shane. Now I'm hit with the guilt of knowing I could have. But then I remember, if I *had* reported it, it would have been Bailey, not Shane, who got arrested. "If he's trying to get to you, Bay, there's no other option, you know that?"

He nods against my chest. "Yeah. I just … not tonight, please."

"Okay, let's go to sleep, I'm exhausted anyway."

Once showered and in bed, I'm so focused on listening for any sounds downstairs that it takes a while to realise that Bailey's on the edge of the mattress, keeping his distance. I reach out for him, and he quickly presses up against me, like he was waiting for an invitation. He nestles under my chin, his breath hitting my neck in quick little puffs. I know he's scared, but I don't know how to reassure him, not when I'm barely holding myself together. In my head I know there's a fair chance I could fight Shane and come out on top, but my body still freezes at the memory of being tied up.

"Teddy," he murmurs, stroking the hair on my chest.

"Yeah, Bay?"

"I'm sorry for bringing him back to you."

I pull away from him a little too quickly, my head swimming. "How is that your fault? You tried your hardest to stay hidden from him. The photo was a screenshot from *my* social media. I don't know how long he's been keeping an eye on it, probably since the day I left, but he never would have found you if it wasn't for that." His nails dig into my chest as he clings to me. He stays silent, and I feel myself drifting off to sleep, exhaustion from the day's events crashing into me like a freight train.

The surface drifts further and further away. I try to swim up, but I can't get my body to move. I realise my wrists and ankles are bound, and I'm being dragged down into the depths of the sea. Bubbles explode from my mouth and nose, screaming until there's nothing left to give. Water floods my lungs, making me cough and breathe in sharply—but I don't drown. My body convulses as I take more and more of the sea into my lungs. Whatever is pulling me through the water gives a final tug, and I'm sucked right through the sea floor. There's suddenly oxygen again. I cough and gasp for breath as the salt from the sea burns my throat and stings my eyes. Someone grabs my chin and forces my head up. I lock onto ice-blue eyes, and freeze.

"I told you what would happen if I ever saw you again."

Pain sears through my stomach, and a yell breaks free from my lips. When I look down, there's a knife sticking out of me.

"Teddy, wake up!" a distant voice begs.

I'm back in the sea, drifting up to the surface. The pain in my stomach is now a dull, lingering ache, and the burn in my throat is fading. I choke on nothing. My eyes fly open, and I almost jump right out of bed when I find blue eyes staring back at me.

The split-second it takes to realise it's Bailey and not Shane hanging over me is enough for his face to crumple. "Bay," I plead.

He shakes his head furiously, tears gathering in his eyes as he scrambles off the bed and stands with his back against the wall. A sharp pain shoots through my head as I try to move after him.

"Bay, I'm not scared of you. Come back, please." He doesn't move, just stands there with his palms flat against the wall, chest heaving. "Jesus Christ, Bay, it was just a nightmare." I shake my head, trying to push away memories that keep popping up in fragments.

"About me?" he asks so quietly I almost miss it.

"No! Of course not about you. Just come here, please, *mo leannan.*" I hold my hand out rather than trying to chase him around the bedroom. He stares at it for a moment before taking hesitant steps towards me.

As soon as he's within reach, I grab his wrist and pull until he's forced to straddle my lap. I reach up and hold his jaw, stroking tears from his cheeks.

"I dreamt I was drowning, and my arms and legs were tied, so I couldn't swim up to the surface." Bailey's lip wobbles, so I pull him down to catch his lips between my own in a light kiss. "The dream shifted, and Shane was there. When I woke up, I saw you above me, and it scared me for a second." I purposefully leave out the stabbing, but Bailey still recoils from me. Grabbing his wrist, I say, "A *second*, Bay," through gritted teeth. "Then I looked into your eyes, and I was safe again. Do you get that? I was home. You and your brother are nothing alike, I promise." I tilt his chin so he's forced to hold eye contact. "Every time I look into your eyes, I remember."

There's a moment's silence. Then he whispers, "I love you." Wiping his eyes before he leans down and kisses the tip of my nose. "I've always loved you, Teddy. Even when I couldn't say it out loud."

"You never left my heart, mo ghráidh," I whisper back, stroking his jaw.

Bailey's mouth brushes against mine, tongue swiping along my bottom lip, seeking entrance. I open for him, and lift my arse when he grabs hold of my waistband. He pulls off my boxers and lowers himself on top of me, grinding his clothed cock against my bare one, making me hard in an instant. I slide my hands down his back, brushing the cotton of his underwear, but he pulls away from me.

"What are you doing?" I ask, sitting up to chase his lips. The head rush hits me as soon as I move, and I collapse back against my pillow.

"Are you okay?" Bailey asks, hovering above me.

"Yeah, just ... light-headed." I rub my face.

"Did the doctor say you have a concussion?"

"No, it's just from the pain. The stitches hurt like a bitch." I lean on my elbows so I can see him better.

"So take the pain relief," Bailey says, crossing his arms over his chest.

"I don't need tablets."

He scoffs at me. "Just lie still, then. Let me take care of you." He pushes a hand to my chest, forcing me to lie flat, then he slips down to the end of the bed, pushing my legs wide as he settles between them. By the time I realise what he's doing, he's already licking a stripe up the underside of my cock. I shiver and grab a pillow to prop myself up more so I can watch him. Bailey's eyes flick up and hold my gaze as his fingers dig into my thigh. He closes his mouth around the head of my cock, and a low moan slips out of me. He's barely started, but the sight of him between my thighs already has me leaking.

Bailey pulls back, and his tongue darts out, tasting my pre-cum. "You taste so good, Teddy," he says as he leans forward, taking me as deep as he can, humming his approval as he moves over my length. My fingers twitch with the need to touch him. I want to grab him by his thick waves and thrust into his mouth over and over. Take him by the hips and demand he ride me until he makes himself cum.

"Can you roll over?" Bailey asks, popping off of me.

"Why roll over?" I ask cautiously. It's been years since we discussed it, but he knows I was always hesitant to …

"Do you trust me?" His hands rest on my thighs, stroking them.

I nod, shuffling awkwardly until I'm lying on my stomach, resting my head on my crossed arms.

Bailey leans over me. Grabbing a spare pillow, he pulls my hips so that he can slide it under my body. Then he pushes my thighs wide and settles between them again. My cock rubs against the pillow, sending a wave of pleasure through me.

"You're going to stay still so you don't hurt your head, okay?" Bailey orders.

"O-okay."

Bailey palms my cheeks, pushing them apart. I've never felt so exposed. He laughs when I tense, and I feel his hot breath puff out over my hole. "Relax, Teddy."

"How am I meant to relax when you're—*ah!*" I gasp as Bailey's tongue licks up a broad stroke from my balls to my crease, brushing over my hole. My whole body tenses when he kisses my taint, then he licks my hole again slowly, making circular motions as his hands run up the back of my thighs and over my arse, spreading my cheeks wider.

He pauses. "Okay?"

My mind's turned to mush, and my body sinks into the mattress, with no desire to ever leave.

"Very."

The moment the word passes my lips, Bailey's tongue moves with vigour, drawing sounds out of me that might have been embarrassing if he wasn't responding so viscerally; pushing me harder or drawing back depending on how close to the edge I get. I start grinding my hips into the pillow, needing more friction as he gets me higher and higher. He matches the pace with his tongue, swirling it around my hole. I feel my orgasm coming, and my hands fist the bedsheet.

"Fuck, I'm right there," I pant.

His tongue suddenly spears me, pushing deep into my hole, and my whole body convulses as I cum across the pillow.

"So hot, Teddy." Bailey sits up, and I look over my shoulder to see him pull himself free and tug once, twice, then I feel the heat of his cum as it hits my lower back and arse.

"Shit," I say, chuckling, melting into the bed, unable to move.

Bailey smacks my arse with a loud crack, then gets up and leaves the room. I'm almost asleep when I feel him wipe me clean with a warm flannel. He then removes the ruined pillow from under me and climbs back into bed. With great effort, I manage to get my boxers back on and roll onto my back again, and then I pull him against me tightly, ready for sleep again, praying the nightmares stay away.

SOMETHING BUMPS MY SHOULDER, and a yell tears me from a dreamless sleep.

"Bay?" I murmur, fighting to open my eyes as a heaviness blankets me, trying to pull me back under.

When I finally adjust to the darkness of the room, I find myself looking into the same ice-blue eyes that haunt my nightmares. There's no ring of gold in them. No warmth. No light. My heart speeds up as I try to get away from him, feeling across the bed for Bailey.

He's not there.

I look to the side, only to find an empty bed. As soon as I bare my neck to him, Shane sinks a syringe in. I have moments before my body shuts down. "Where is he?" I demand through gritted teeth.

Shane's lips curl into a saccharine smile. "Long time no see, Theo."

THEO

My body threatens to give out. I fall to the side, but something stops me, pulling tight across my chest. My eyes flash open; it's too dark to see much, though I quickly work out I'm in one of the sheds near the back of the estate from the smell of hay in the air. When I look down, I can just make out a thick rope tied around my middle and thighs. At my back, there's something rigid running up the entire length of my body, holding me fast. Pulling against the ropes does nothing, and when I try to wiggle my hands free, everything pulls tighter around my body.

My hand touches something cold and I jump. Fingers— long, slender, and calloused brush against mine. Grabbing hold of them tightly, my heart kicks in my chest. "Bay?" I whisper. There's no answer, and his hand is limp. I realise that we're both tied to a support beam, Bailey at my back. I turn my head left and right, but I can't see him at all. "Bailey." I shake his hand, but he still doesn't answer me.

I can't move.

Can't breathe.

I promised myself I'd never let this happen again, yet

within a few hours of finding out Shane is on the island, I'm right back where it all started—weak and useless. The beam at my back is unmoving, and the ropes ungiving. There's nothing I can do. "Bailey, please! I need to know you're okay," I beg, feeling my throat closing up.

There's a creak in the darkness, and light slices through a gap in the shed door as it opens. Someone walks in, but it's not Shane. The shape of him is all wrong—shorter, broader, older. When he gets close enough for me to make out his features, my brain stutters. Walking towards me is Dan, the temp we took on.

Hope ignites inside my chest, and I don't stop to question why he's here on my farm, or why he doesn't look surprised to see me. I just want to get free so I can get to Bailey. "Dan, untie me, please!" My voice is desperate, scratching my dry throat.

Dan stands in front of me, his face blank and controlled. Unease crawls all over my skin. Memories that have been a jumbled mess since my accident start piecing together. Something in the way he stands—unmoving, staring right through me—reminds me of the figure on the boat. I thought I'd imagined him, but now I put his face to the memory, and it clicks into place.

"You left me to drown," I snarl. "What the hell are you doing here?"

The door opens more, and light floods the room, burning my eyes. Shane storms over to me, and my breath hitches in my throat as he gets so close we're almost nose to nose. My grip on Bailey doesn't falter as I stare down his brother. "What do you want?"

"What do I want?" Shane grabs me by my throat. "I want my brother back."

Bailey's fingers twitch in mine, and my body relaxes a fraction.

"He followed you the night you left. He chose you over me, when all I ever did was look out for him."

I clench my jaw, feeling anger rip through me. My hand tightens on Bailey's, and I feel him squeeze back this time, weak as it is. "You're sick, Shane," I bite out. He squeezes my throat tighter, cutting off my air completely. In my panic, I accidentally let go of Bailey's hand.

"Hey, not yet." Dan mutters quietly. He grabs Shane's wrist, and the hand around my throat is suddenly ripped away, causing an argument as they walk away, voices hushed.

"T-Teddy," Bailey whispers.

Reaching for his hand again, I feel him squeeze it back with more force than before. "I'm here, mo leannan," I soothe.

"I can't be tied up," he cries. "I can't—get them off me!" he gasps, thrashing against his restraints.

My chest tightens when I realise the ropes are triggering him, and there's nothing I can fucking do. "Listen to me. I'm right here with you this time. Try to focus on me, okay? You're going to get through this. Shane isn't going to hurt you." I'm not sure if that's true, but I'm pretty sure I'm the problem here, not Bailey. Shane wants him back, so he should be safe for now—I hope.

Shane turns to look at us and grins. "Oh, good, look who's awake," he says as he walks around me. Bailey sucks in a sharp breath, and I feel him stop moving altogether.

BAILEY

I hear Shane's voice before I see him, and it turns my blood to ice. Each footstep matches the thumping of my heart until he's standing in front of me, grinning. I'm paralysed, unable to pull on my restraints or even breathe. The look in his eyes borders on manic as he touches my face, stroking it gently with the back of his hand.

"I'd almost given up looking for you, little mouse, but then I saw you were in a photo Theo was tagged in: on your knees in a barn, hammer in hand. Guess it paid off keeping an eye on Theo for so many years." He pinches my chin so hard it hurts. "Why did it take you so long to get back to him?"

"Shit," Teddy mutters behind me.

My brain suddenly kicks into gear, and I pull against the ropes frantically, but they're too tight around my chest, making it impossible to move. The walls of the barn close in on me until nothing exists except for my brother, pressed to my front, and Teddy, pressed to my back.

"Let him go," I plead. "Let Teddy go, and I'll—I'll do whatever you want."

Shane chuckles, and Teddy squeezes my hand tighter.

"Shut up, Bay," he hisses. I hear a smack behind me, and a grunt from Teddy. His hand goes limp in mine, then silence ...

"Teddy?" I cry out. "Who else is here?" I shout at Shane, trying to turn my head. My jaw tightens, and I struggle with more force, needing to be free of the ropes. Heavy footsteps come from my left, and when I finally see who it is, a wretched sound rips from my throat. I shake my head, not wanting to believe that my stepfather is standing in front of me.

Shane hushes me, wiping away tears as they slip free. There's no comfort in it. My heart thumps so hard it makes my chest hurt. "Just let Teddy leave and I'll go home with you," I say weakly. There's no way I can get us both out of this, but I'd do anything for Teddy to be free.

"There's nothing to go home to, Bailey," Shane says.

My eyes dart from my brother to Dean, scared to look away from either for too long. I open my mouth to yell, but my throat closes up, cutting it off.

Fuck! Not now.

Growling to myself, I rock my head back, banging it on the wooden beam out of frustration. I just need to calm down, then maybe I can get control again. I start counting backwards from ten, focusing on the feel of Teddy's hand in mine.

Shane carries on talking, ignoring me completely. "How have you been getting on without your punishments?" he smirks as he strokes the scars on my bare hip. I want to tell him exactly what I think of him and his punishments. I've never wanted to hurt someone more than I do right now. He's ruined my life in the worst possible way—they both have. I want them to feel the pain I felt.

When I look at Dean again, he's scowling at Shane, jaw ticking.

"There was a house fire," Shane says, stepping away from me.

Memories of firemen wrapping me in a silver blanket, far

away from the smoke pluming out of our home, flash into my mind. A ten-year-old Shane sitting next to me, hugging me close as he whispers in my ear that I'd killed Daddy.

"Mum died quite a few years ago now. She fell asleep with a cigarette in her hand," he says indifferently. "The whole place went up in flames."

I take a deep breath, hit with conflicting emotions of anger and grief. It should hurt more than this, but I resent her. Out of everyone, she should have been able to see what Shane was doing. She was an adult, and we were only ten when it started. She ignored us both and drank because she was selfish. She created an environment where a psychopath had no consequences, and then she let a fucking paedophile into the home, too. If she ever loved me, I don't remember it, and I can't help but feel a weight lifted knowing she's gone.

My tears stay locked up, and I get my breathing somewhat under control. Teddy's fingers twitch as he starts to come around, and I breathe a little easier.

"Of course you're not sad about her death," Shane taunts. "The police believed it was an accident, of course. Just like they did when Dad died."

"You're a crazy fuck, Shane. Untie him!" Teddy shouts, making me jump. His hand clasps onto mine again, and I focus on the warmth of it.

"Me?" Shane asks, eyes wide with innocence.

"You," Teddy snaps. "Let us go and then leave. Fuck off back to England. We haven't told the police about the parcel you left Bailey. No one knows what you did to me. No one knows you abused your brother," he grits out. "And no one knows you killed your own father when you were ten years old," he says with a little less confidence.

The 'what if' that lingered in my mind, the not knowing whether I played a part in my dad's death dissipates as I watch Shane's nostrils flare and his jaw clench. He really did lie to me

—made me believe I was sick when all of it was him. Hot tears slip down my cheeks as I gasp for air.

"Deep breaths, mo leannan. I'll make sure you get out of this," Teddy whispers low enough that Shane and Dean don't seem to hear him.

Shane reaches behind his back and pulls a knife out. The metal glints in dim lighting, and I recoil as he stalks towards me, pressing as far back into the post as I can.

"What the hell are you doing?" Dean barks as he gets between the two of us. He pushes Shane back and pulls out a knife of his own. "I agreed to deal with the Scot, but Bailey's off-limits."

"Off-limits?" Shane asks calmly. "I suggest you get your filthy hands off me." The look in Shane's eyes is murderous as he looms over Dean.

Dean hesitates and lowers his knife. "You promised that once this was over, I'd get to—"

Shane grins. "I don't need you anymore. The police are looking for both of us because *you* fucked up. *You* got caught at work stealing the propofol. *You* didn't bury the last body well enough. Did you want to get caught, Dean? Did your conscience finally kick in? Tell me. What do you feel more guilty for, raping all those boys and men, or playing a part in their murder? You should be grateful I didn't leave you in that house to burn with my mother. It's more than you deserved."

"What I deserved?" Dean splutters, finally holding his ground.

"Yes, what you deserve! You fucked my brother."

Teddy jerks against the ropes behind me, and I hear a low growl in his throat. "Is that your fucking stepfather?"

Shane faces me and raises his voice. "Bailey is *mine*. He has been since the moment we shared a womb. Mine to play with, mine to fuck with, mine to break."

My jaw is clenched so tight that a sharp pain shoots

through my jaw. Shane's head whips back to Dean. "I don't like people touching my things, Dean. Do you really think I'd go through this much trouble to get my brother back just to—what? Hand him over to you and be on my way?" Shane gets closer and manages to spin Dean around. He pins him in place, pressing the knife to his neck.

Dean drops his own knife and struggles to get free until a drop of blood is drawn. He goes stock-still. "Shane ... he wanted me to do it. I-I wouldn't have—"

"I couldn't care less if he begged on his knees for you. You still did it, and you'd wanted to for a long time, hadn't you?" he snarls. "I knew what you were doing—fixing him up after I ruined him, letting your hands wander. I let you get away with it because you sped up his healing time, meaning more play-time for me. But the night I caught you fucking him, I wanted to kill you. I was going to. But then Bailey ran away, and I thought maybe, just maybe, you could be useful." Shane drags Dean back so that they're standing right in front of me.

"Well, now you're not, and you're shit out of luck."

"What's happening?" Teddy whispers.

I can't answer him. Dean's face has paled and his wide eyes are boring into mine. Teddy squeezes my hand, but I can't squeeze back. Shane talking about how Dean raped me like it was nothing, like I wanted it, makes my stomach roil. I swallow, trying to stop myself from throwing up.

"You really shouldn't have touched what's mine, Dean."

I close my eyes, refusing to look, but when I hear a choked gurgle, they open without my permission. There's a deep, jagged gash in Dean's neck, and blood spurts out, hitting my bare chest. I reel back, forgetting there's nowhere for me to go. I'm screaming in my head for someone to get the blood off of me; the heat of it feels like it's burning through my skin. It's worse than having him touch me again. It's never going to come off.

I'm vaguely aware of Teddy hushing me, trying to give me any comfort he can, but it's pointless. Shane drops Dean to the floor with a heavy thud, and it takes a monumental amount of effort to drag my eyes away from his twitching body. Blood pools beneath him, spreading outwards.

Shane grins, and a sob breaks free from me as he prowls forward. "Now you're going to do something for me, little mouse."

THEO

Blood spreads across the floor pooling around my bare feet. "Bailey!" I cry out, heart seizing in my chest. The choking sounds have died off, and he's still squeezing my hand. I'm pretty sure whatever happened didn't happen to him. Not being able to fucking see him, though, is going to give me a heart attack. There's nothing between him and Shane right now, and the fact that Bailey hasn't spoken in a while shoves my anxiety into overdrive.

"Now you're going to do something for me, little mouse." Shane's voice grates like nails on a chalkboard, and goosebumps break out along my arms. Bailey sobs behind me, and I squeeze my eyes shut. All I can do is hold on to him tightly. Bailey jostles against my back. Then suddenly, the warmth of him is being pulled away from me, and I shiver at the sudden chill on my bare skin. His hand clings to mine until my hold on him slips. There's some scuffing of feet and muttered curses, and then both brothers stand before me. Shane has his arms wrapped around Bailey's chest, holding him in place as he struggles to get free.

"I was never enough for you, was I?" Shane snarls in

Bailey's ear. "You kept running back to Theo. Why? I protected you from yourself, loved you when no one else would."

"Our families will notice we're missing and call the police. You can't go anywhere with him; they'll find you."

Shane glares at me. "I know that," he snaps. "Like I said, there's nothing to go home to. The police are already looking for me, but I'm not going anywhere until my little mouse gets his final punishment." I suck in a breath as Bailey is thrown forward. He crashes to his knees while Shane casually walks around him and stands behind me. I flinch when I feel cold steel biting at my ribs. My breathing picks up pace—it feels like the knife digs deeper with every ragged breath.

Bailey's eyes widen, and his mouth opens and closes a couple of times before he manages to choke out, "No!" Scrambling to his feet, he cries, "Shane, don't."

"Huh, so you *can* talk when you want to. How convenient." Shane chuckles in my ear. The ropes feel tighter. I can barely breathe. The reality of my situation hits me: I have a psychopath at my back, and I'm tied to a post with no way of getting free. I look around frantically, trying to find something —*anything*. The barn door is still ajar. Bailey can run. He *should* run, but he's just standing there. Before I can open my mouth, Shane starts up again.

"Grab that knife and come over here. I'm not doing this one for you, little mouse."

"No," Bailey whispers, hands balled into tight fists at his sides. "You have r-ruined *everything*, Shane. Is it not enough? W-what the fuck is wrong with you that you won't just stop!"

"You don't know the half of it," Shane snarls. "When you left me, I couldn't sleep knowing you weren't in the next room. Couldn't eat, not knowing where you were. I couldn't play my little games with you anymore, and it made me feel as if I were crawling out of my skin."

"Good," Bailey spits out, but Shane carries on.

"So I found replacements." I hear the smile in his voice, and it's as though icy fingers stroke down my spine, making my whole body tense up.

"Replacements for what?" Bailey asks, slowly making his way towards the knife that skidded across the floor when Dean fell.

"You. None of them quite compared, though. Hurting you felt like I was hurting a part of myself. Punishing you helped me to control some of my ... urges. For a while, at least," Shane says almost wistfully while holding the knife at my ribs steady. "I found boys and men who looked similar to us, but it never had the same effect. I felt nothing for them. They would scream and beg for their lives, but I felt little joy in hurting them. None of them were quite so well trained as you, little mouse, to stay so beautifully silent during your punishments."

Bailey nudges the knife with his foot, never taking his eyes off Shane's hand at my ribs. "What did you do to them?" he asks with a slight wobble in his voice.

"The only thing that gave me any semblance of joy was watching as the light went out in their eyes. Those final moments when their bodies convulsed and they couldn't scream or call for help. They were finally silent."

"Bailey, go. Please, just go. The door's open!" I beg as tears fill my eyes.

"Shut up," Shane hisses in my ear. "Pick up the fucking knife and come here," he snaps at Bailey. "You're finishing this."

Shane's knife digs deeper, and I suck in a breath from the pain of it, watching as Bailey bends down to pick up the other knife. He walks towards us, getting as close to me as he can. If he reached forwards, he could touch me, untie me, push Shane away.

"Good. Now, shove the knife into him and say goodbye." Shane lowers his voice with the command.

"No."

"What do you mean, no?"

"If the police are already after you, then what's the point of all this?" I interrupt.

"I'm not risking losing him again. If I get locked up, then he's coming with me. *You* are not getting in the way anymore. He needs to end this."

Bailey lunges past me towards Shane. The knife that was at my ribs is suddenly gone. Just as I breathe out in relief, there's a searing pain on the outside of my thigh. As quickly as it comes, it's gone again. It takes a moment to realise what happened as my body starts shaking. I feel blood running down my leg, and my stomach twists. I look to the side and see Shane and Bailey standing off with one another. Both have a knife in their hand, but only Shane's is dripping with blood.

"Bay," I try to call out, but it comes out as a whisper. I'm suddenly so tired. He turns to look at me, brows creased. His eyes flick down to my leg, then go wide as his mouth falls open. It looks like he's saying my name, but I can't hear him. The ringing in my ears is deafening. My vision swims, and I'm plunged into darkness.

FORTY

BAILEY

Teddy's head drops as blood runs down his leg, joining Dean's at it pools beneath his feet. I can't tell how much of the blood is his. "Teddy," I whimper, stepping towards him.

Shane slams into my back, and the knife slips from my hand. He grabs me, pinning me against his chest again, pressing an arm to my windpipe. I try to break his hold, shoving my elbow into his stomach, stomping on his feet, rearing my head back, doing anything to loosen his hold on me. I just need to get to Teddy, need to get him free of the ropes, and then ... and then, I don't know what; I don't even have my phone to call an ambulance.

When I look over at Teddy, he's still not moving. Blood isn't gushing out of the wound on his thigh, but that's far from reassuring. I swear he's getting paler by the second. Shane claws at my bare skin as he tries to keep a hold of me. I growl, grabbing his arm and bucking forward, forcing him over my shoulder. He lands on his back with a thud, writhing on the floor. I quickly pick up the knife again and start towards him as he scrambles to his feet.

"You're sick, Shane. For fucking years, you made me think it was me. Do you have any idea what it's like to think you're a psychopath when you constantly feel guilt? Having no memories of hurting anyone, but believing it must have been true because your own mother believed it. Because your brother would punish you for it. Did you want to make me just as crazy as you? Is that it?"

"Yes!" Shane shouts. "You were always so bloody *good*. You'd play quietly by yourself, ignoring me all day, and then when I'd take away your toy so that you'd pay attention to me, you'd get upset. And who would come to your rescue?"

Dad ...

"He'd shout at me and slap me for taking your things and making you upset. Then he'd give it back to you and tell us to stay away from each other for the rest of the day."

I can remember Dad telling Shane off for picking on me. I also remember him being spanked, but that was usually after he had pulled my hair or bitten me.

"I wanted to hurt you. I wanted to know what it would be like to make you bleed—see how far I could push you before you cried out. It got to a point where that need boiled over; I had to do something or I would have burst out of my own skin. Hurting you wasn't an option while Dad was around, so I snuck out into the fields behind the house."

My eyes dart across the room to Teddy again, and my knees feel weak all of a sudden. I tighten my grip on the knife.

How long has it been since he was stabbed?

When I look back at my brother, he's grinning at me.

"I found a little mouse," he continues. My breath catches in my throat. "Do you remember I brought it home to you?"

"No ..."

"You were in the living room, reading on the sofa. Mum had gone out, and Dad was working upstairs. I dropped it on your lap, thinking you would like it. But you opened your stupid mouth and screamed at the top of your lungs," he snarls. "I grabbed your arm to drag you outside so that Dad wouldn't hear. But you pulled out of my grip and fell backwards, hitting your head on the edge of the coffee table. You wouldn't wake up."

My free hand reaches for the back of my head, phantom pain making me flinch. I don't remember any of this.

"It all happened so quickly. I heard the door to Dad's office bang open, and he shouted my name. Then footsteps on the landing." Shane laughs. "The idiot tripped on the top step and fell down the stairs. I could hear him calling us for help."

"What the fuck did you do, Shane?"

"Mum had left a candle burning. All I did was accidentally nudge it until the flame jumped onto a curtain. Then I dragged your ungrateful arse outside and waited for Mum to come home while flames engulfed the house."

"You set the house on fire, knowing Dad couldn't get out?"

Shane's eyes widen in delight as he nods. "After that, I couldn't understand why you were feeling things I wasn't. I felt nothing when Mum told us Dad had died in the fire, but you cried for weeks afterwards. It was fucking annoying. You were scared of me, and you started to go long periods without talking. I wanted you to be more like me, so I spent years trying to make it so."

"You—you convinced me I was crazy to make you feel better about yourself?"

"You shouldn't have been different! I was alone in all of it."

"But you made me think I was alone in it, too. You made Mum think I was a psychopath to cover up all *your* crazy shit!"

Shane shrugs. "It was easier for me, having everyone's eyes on you."

"Fuck you, Shane," I spit.

"Drop your weapons!" A muffled voice shouts.

My head snaps to the shed door and I see a few police officers standing in the doorway, guns raised towards both of us. Immediately, I drop the knife, and throw my arms in the air. Shane's chuckling under his breath, but I'm too scared to take my eyes off the guns.

"Which one is it, sir?" one of the men asks.

"Eyes on both," the man at the front responds.

My heart gallops in my chest as simultaneous shouts of "Drop the knife" and "Get on the ground" ring out around us. I slowly drop to my knees and lie on my front, terrified that they'll shoot me. The shouting gets louder and I close my eyes, trying to fixate on the way the rough wooden floor scrapes my bare chest. Several guns are cocked, and Shane's laughter stops. There's a scuff of a shoe to my right, and I think he's moving closer to me. There's a single *bang,* and a heavy thud, then silence.

When I dare to open my eyes, I see my brother lying on the floor, staring back at me, a single bullet wound in the centre of his head and a trickle of blood dripping onto the ground. A sob breaks out of me, and I'm not sure if it's the shock of seeing Shane dead, or the relief of knowing he can no longer hurt me.

The officers rush in and go straight for Shane and Dean. I scramble to my feet and run to Teddy. My fingers are already in the knots of the ropes before the officers shout at me to get away from him.

"He's been stabbed!" I yell as the rope around his thighs drops to the ground. When I start on the rope around his chest, an officer rushes over and holds Teddy up. The second rope comes loose, and the officer lowers him onto his back. I drop to my knees by Teddy's side as the officer checks his pulse. He shakes his head and speaks into his radio: "Dispatch, this is PC Rivers, four nine zero three one. We have three people unresponsive and not breathing. Requesting ambulance urgently. Commencing CPR on one person."

Three not breathing? I look frantically from the officer to Teddy—his chest is too still.

I was too late...

It feels like vines have sprung from the ground and wrapped themselves around my legs, pinning me to the spot. I can't move—I can barely breathe. The officer leans over, putting his ear to Teddy's mouth. "You need to put pressure on the leg wound," he says, snapping me out of my daze.

"W-what?"

The man kneels, placing his clasped hands over Teddy's chest, pushing down in rapid movements. It's suddenly all too real—he's not breathing. I stare at Teddy's face, waiting for some sign, a flicker of his eyelids or something, but there's nothing. "Hey!" the officer shouts at me, making me jump. "In my kit, there's a bandage. Press it to the wound. The ambulance will be here in a few minutes, okay?"

I stare at the first aid kit sitting between us, frozen.

"Now!"

I flinch, ripping open the bag and grabbing a wad of bandages, pushing them against the wound. I lean on his leg, holding it steady as his body rocks from the CPR. PC Rivers tilts Teddy's head back, breathing into his mouth twice before carrying on with chest compressions. His arms strain, and sweat builds on his temples, brows furrowed as he tries to bring him back. I'm a mess of tears, with a lump in my throat that I can't swallow. I want to ask where the ambulance is— whether Teddy is going to be okay. My voice is free, but I'm terrified of the answers, so I stay silent.

After what feels like an eternity, a hand touches my shoulder. A woman in green asks me to move aside, but I shake my head. If I'm still putting pressure on his wound, that means he's still bleeding, and if he's still bleeding, then he's still alive.

"Sir, you need to move aside so we can get him into the ambulance," she says, voice calm and steady, hand never leaving my shoulder. Another hand grabs under my arm and gently pulls me to my feet. It's like I'm outside of my own body, looking at everything from above. One of the paramedics straps something to Teddy's thigh as another pushes their fingers to his throat.

"There's a pulse, let's go."

He's lifted onto a stretcher, and rushed out of the building. I follow on their heels, not letting him out of my sight. Everything's happening so fast. I can't focus on anything but getting into the ambulance with Teddy. Even when I hear someone calling my name, I don't look away. The officer who helped Teddy talks to the paramedics, pointing at me, then at the ambulance. He comes over and tells me it's okay to get in the back, and that he'll sit up front. I didn't need permission. They would have to drag me out if I wasn't allowed.

During the journey, I'm frantically trying to keep myself calm for him. But when the paramedics start rushing around, shouting things to one another, my heart thumps in my chest. I can't focus enough to understand what's happening. I take a deep, shuddering breath. "You need to wake up, Teddy. Okay?" I sniff and wipe my face with one hand while I touch his hair with the other. "You said you wouldn't leave me again." Leaning forward in my seat, I sweep his curls from his forehead, blocking out everything else. "You're not allowed to," I choke out. "I only just found you again."

Fuck, my chest hurts so much, I can't take proper breaths. My eyes flick to the paramedics; they're injecting something into the drip by Teddy's side, and one of them starts chest compressions again. I struggle to swallow as my heart drops out of my stomach. "Come on, Teddy." My voice cracks. "*Please*, I need you!"

BAILEY

"HE'S EXACTLY WHERE HE SHOULD BE," OFFICER Rivers tells me as he hands me a coffee. I take it on autopilot, feeling numb. Teddy's family haven't arrived yet, and I don't know how long I've been sitting in the waiting room.

I've been poked and prodded by half the hospital staff while Teddy was whisked off somewhere. PC Rivers has barely left my side, other than to get me coffee and a change of clothes—not that they've stopped me from shaking. He keeps talking to me, but it's just noise. The image of my brother staring back at me with blank eyes is still fresh in my mind—I can't shake it. I should be feeling sorrow or grief, but there's nothing. The hole in my chest is strictly reserved for the man I love. The only thing keeping me from breaking right now is knowing that Teddy was breathing again by the time we got here. My hand shakes, spilling coffee down my leg.

PC Rivers takes the coffee from me. "There's nothing you can do but wait. I know that's not reassuring or what you want to hear right now ..."

I nod, swallowing, finally taking my eyes off the corridor as I look over at the man. "Why are you still here?" I ask.

He shifts a little in his seat, averting his eyes. He looks young, and I wonder if it's the first time he's had to deal with something like this. "We require a witness statement if and when you're ready. I need to assess whether there are any further risks to yourself or Mr MacLeod."

"You don't ..." I look at the floor, prickles spreading across the back of my neck. "You don't think I'm responsible?"

"Ah, no. You had blood all over you and rope burns; the all clear was given once your brother was down. I can't say much, but it's public knowledge now that he was wanted on suspicion of numerous murders and arson in England," he says hesitantly.

I lean back and look up at the ceiling, blinking the tears from my eyes. "I know about my parents, and—and the others. He told me what he did before you turned up."

PC Rivers nods and passes my coffee back. I take it with a sturdier hand and sip the bitter liquid.

"Would you like me to take a statement now, while we wait? If you're feeling up to it, you can just tell me what happened tonight—how you ended up in that shed with your brother and ... friend?"

I scowl at him. "Boyfriend."

"Right, I didn't want to presume," he coughs and pulls out a little notepad.

Rubbing my eyes, I groan, hating that he's right. I have nothing to do but wait, and talking to him *is* distracting me from my thoughts of Teddy. "Fine," I murmur.

"Can I take your full name and date of birth?"

"Bailey Smith, previously Bailey Harrison Townsend. I changed my name by deed poll when I was eighteen. Date of birth is 14th April 1996."

"Okay, Bailey. In your own words, can you tell me what happened this morning?"

PC RIVERS GETS up to get more coffee. I've started crashing pretty hard. Recounting everything that happened in the past few hours has left my mind a mess.

"Bay!" a voice calls out.

I look over my shoulder, relieved to see Noah running down the corridor towards me. I stand up just as he barrels into my chest. I stay still as he clings to me, confused for a moment because Noah hates hugs. Tears start to stream down my cheeks again, and I wrap my arms around him. We stand there for a moment in silence, but when I look up, Robbie's glaring at me. He looks furious, dark brows furrowed, jaw ticking.

As soon as Noah steps away, Robbie pushes past him and grabs me by the shirt, forcing me onto my toes as he pulls me up against him. Shock keeps me immobile as I let him shake me about.

"What the fuck have you done?" Robbie growls. "They won't tell us anything. What did your psycho brother do to Theo?" My tongue's so tied I can't get anything out. Noah pulls on Robbie's arm, shouting something I can't hear through the ringing in my ears. He finally lets go when Noah barges a shoulder into him with some force, pushing him backwards.

"It's not his fucking fault!" Noah shouts.

Robbie growls and takes another step towards me, but Noah steps between us and shoves his chest.

"He never even told you that he *had* a twin brother, Noah. No one knew!"

I flinch at the truth in his words. I kept my whole childhood a secret. However much I trusted Noah, I could never tell him I was ... that I *thought* I was dangerous. I was too scared that he'd leave me like Teddy did, or that he'd report me to the police. It was stupid and selfish, but after a few years, I was *sure* I would never hurt Noah, so I stayed silent.

Years of guilt, and all for nothing ... just because Shane wanted a plaything.

I feel sick.

"Go for a walk," Noah orders, staring Robbie down until he relents.

"Fine. Theo's family will be coming soon. I'll be back when they get here." He storms off and I can breathe again, but only for a second—everyone's going to blame me for this, just like Robbie did.

"I shouldn't be here," I mutter.

"Why?" Noah asks.

"They're going to hate me." I start pacing, struggling to stand still.

"What happened? Why didn't you tell me about your brother?"

I run my fingers through my hair, gripping tightly, as I shake my head. I can't go through it all again. How many times am I going to have to tell the same story? Until it doesn't even feel like my life? Until I'm forced to separate myself from it or let it consume me?

"Okay, stop. You don't have to talk right now," Noah says, grabbing my arm and pushing me into a seat.

Eventually, Teddy's family arrive, and Robbie comes back, sticking to Isla's side. When I look over at him, he's glaring back at me, so I quickly avert my eyes.

I'm startled when everyone starts fussing over me, asking if I'm okay. Ellen pulls me into a warm hug, and I cling to her, telling her I'm sorry, over and over.

"Shush now, it's not your fault," she mutters, stroking my hair. I feel myself being passed into someone else's arms, and when I open my eyes, I see it's Jake. I instantly burst out crying, clinging to him like a child. So many secrets I kept from him, too. Now it's easier to see through all the lies my brother told me. I *know* Jake would have helped me if I'd told him what happened. He's the closest thing I've had to a parent since my dad died, and I'm so glad he's here. He holds onto me for a long time, and I notice Theo's uncle Luke hovering close by. He reaches out and strokes Jake's back, and I frown at the contact, curious.

After a couple more hours, the doctor finally steps into the waiting room. Just seeing him makes me sway. All I can hear is static. My body is about to give out when an arm wraps around my waist. I look up to see Robbie next to me, frown gone. His eyes are wet, but he's smiling.

"Doc said Theo's doing good. He's out of surgery and going to the ICU."

The pressure lifts off my chest, and despite Robbie's attempts at holding me up, I collapse to the floor anyway, chest heaving.

He's not leaving me.

THEO

THE KNIFE DRIVES INTO MY BODY IN SLOW MOTION. Skin piercing as cold metal slices into muscle. My mind plays it on a loop over and over until I gasp awake.

I open my eyes, expecting to see Shane, but it's so bright I have to squeeze them shut again. It takes me a moment to realise I'm no longer tied up. My back is no longer pushed up against an unforgiving wooden post—I'm lying on a firm mattress.

A hand slides into mine, warm and clammy. "Teddy?" Bailey's voice is small and uncertain. He squeezes my hand tighter, and my eyes land on his, the flash of gold in his irises makes me choke on a sob.

"Where's Shane?" I ask, voice croaking. I can't remember anything past the knife going into my leg. Lifting the blanket that's covering me, I see a large bandage covering my thigh.

"Gone," he says curtly. "After you passed out, Shane ... he told me what really happened with my dad, and why he had fucked with my head for years."

Wincing, I lean over and put my hand on his cheek, stroking my thumb along his jaw. He leans into it, kissing my palm. "I wanted to go for him, Teddy," he whispers. "If the police hadn't shown up, I think I would have. It would have finally given him what he wanted: for me to be just like him," he chokes out.

I shush him, cupping his jaw and forcing him to look at me. "You are *nothing* like your brother. Even if you had hurt him, Bay. He hurt you first—for *years*. Took your childhood and destroyed anyone who dared to love you. If I'd managed to get free of the ropes, I can promise you I would have done a lot more than hurt him."

"Really?" he whimpers.

I nod. "Yeah. For you and for me. The urge to hurt him— it wasn't a want, it was a need. You needed to get him away so that you could protect yourself."

"I didn't care about myself! I wanted to get you down off the post and call a fucking ambulance, but he wouldn't shut up."

"How did the police know where we were?"

"Robbie and Noah saw on the news that Shane was wanted for murder. They went around the farm checking all the buildings, just in case." He stares at my hand, tracing circles on the back of it. "The police searched the buildings that Robbie and Noah hadn't checked yet and found us at the far end of the estate."

"And what happened to Shane?"

"The police wanted us to drop our knives, Shane didn't. They ... Shane's dead, he isn't coming back," Bailey chokes out.

Lord help me, but those two words send relief flooding through my veins. I close my eyes and let my head fall back onto the pillow, grumbling, "Fuck, I'm tired."

"Me too. Unlike you, I haven't slept for the past sixteen hours," Bailey chuckles weakly. I watch as his face scrunches up and he struggles to draw breath.

"Don't cry. You're *here,* mo leannan. We're both still here." When he lifts his head and holds my gaze, tears cling to his lashes. Any anger that had built up softens. "I love you, Bay."

I watch his Adam's apple bob as he swallows and chokes out, "I love you too."

I SHOULD HAVE EXPECTED that everyone would follow me home. Bailey helps me out of Robbie's car with a hand under my elbow, and Noah hands me the crutches the hospital provided. I feel as though I've been in a train wreck. Just standing upright pulls on my aching muscles.

When I turn around, my grandparents, parents, and Isla are all getting out of their cars. My cottage is absolutely not big enough for this many people.

"Ma, I'm fine, go back to the farmhouse, please," I say as she follows on my heels through the front door.

"I want to make sure you're taken care of, Theo. I'll cook you some food so you can microwave it throughout the week."

"You don't need to do that, Bailey's staying here ..." I look at Bailey sharply. "You're staying here, yes? Or do you need to go back to Cumbria?"

Bailey looks nervously at Noah, "I need to talk to Jake, but I'm not going back to Cumbria yet."

"I already called Jake. He's not expecting you back anytime soon."

Bailey nods and looks back at me, "I'll stay with you until you get back on your feet, and then I'll—I'll figure out what to do after that."

"There, Ma, Bailey can cook and clean for me." I grin at him.

"Good luck. He's a terrible fucking cook." Noah laughs as Bailey shoots him a look.

Ma side-eyes Bailey like she's unsure whether she can trust him to feed me properly.

"It's no bother; we'll do some cooking back at the house. Ellen, let the boys get some rest." Gran nudges Ma with her elbow.

"We'll pop over in the morning. Come on, love." Da puts his arm over Ma's shoulder and leads her back to the car.

"You need to lie down," Bailey says, leading me further into the house.

"I'm not getting up those." I nod to the stairs. "You'll have to bring a mattress down or something."

Bailey takes a big step away from me, and I'm suddenly lifted off my feet.

"Jesus fuck! Robbie, put me down!"

He ignores me and heads up the stairs at an angle that keeps my leg from getting hurt, then puts me down gently on the bed.

I'm embarrassed and furious at him for lifting me so easily. "There is literally no bloody reason you'd need to carry me like that. Ever. And you've managed to do it *twice* in a month. Stop it!" I snap.

I'll never admit that I'm actually grateful to be in my own bed. The mattress is so much softer than the hospital's. It feels like it's trying to pull me under already. I blink, and it takes a while for my eyes to open again.

Isla leans over the bed and kisses me on the cheek.

"What's that for?"

"Shut up. We could have lost you twice in forty-eight hours. I was fucking scared, okay?"

"Okay ..."

Robbie goes in for a kiss also, and I flinch backwards. "Not you—ah fuck, my leg," I push my fingers into the muscle to try to alleviate the pain shooting through it.

"Fine, fine, we're leaving," Robbie sulks.

I'm already dozing off when the front door snicks closed, and the cottage falls silent, finally.

I FEEL as though I've barely slept. I stretch the best I can, trying not to pull on my thigh muscle, wincing as it twinges anyway. I reach to my side, but the bed is cold. The alarm clock on the bedside table shows it's only four in the morning "Bay?" I call out, uncertain. Christ, my mouth is so dry, and I really need to pee. I sit up, forcing my heavy limbs to move.

There's a bang in the room next to mine and the sound of a door opening. Bailey appears in my doorway, dishevelled. "What happened? Are you okay?" he rushes out, coming over and moving the duvet off my leg to check the bandage.

"I'm fine—stop that." I slap his hand away.

"Then what are you waking me up for?" He folds his arms across his chest.

I point at the space next to me. "Why aren't you here?"

Bailey rubs the back of his neck.

"I didn't want to hurt your leg, so I slept in the spare room."

"Okay. I really need to piss, and to drink something, but after that I'm going to tell you off." I wriggle to the edge of the bed and slide my legs off. "Can you help me first, please?"

Bailey helps me up, and I lean on his shoulder as we hobble to the bathroom.

"You're heavy," Bailey mutters under his breath.

I glare at him, then put a hand on the wall beside the toilet to hold myself up, groaning in relief.

Bailey disappears and comes back with two cups of water. I finish mine quickly—the liquid agitating my sore throat on its way down. He passes me his as well, then goes to get himself another.

"In." I point to the bed when he comes back, refusing to hear any argument on the matter. He'll be lucky if I ever let him leave my side again, let alone go back to Cumbria. "Don't roll your eyes at me, Bailey."

He huffs and gets into the bed, trying to keep distance between us. I stare at him in the dusky light of the room.

"What?" he asks.

"Move closer, unless you want me to come over there. And if I do, it's going to hurt my leg, so you should probably do as you're told." He doesn't move. "What's wrong?"

"He killed you." Bailey lets out a shuddering breath. "You died, Teddy, *twice*. If the ambulance hadn't arrived so quickly, you wouldn't be here."

"There's no point thinking about what could have happened when it didn't."

Bailey sits up and turns to face me. "How can you look at me? I look so much like him that it's going to haunt me every time I look in a mirror. But you have to see me all the time. A constant reminder that I wear the same face as the man who killed you. It's not healthy, Teddy!" he chokes.

Despite the throbbing pain in my leg, I drag my body upright so that I can look him in the eye. "You're nothing alike to me, Bay. My biggest regret is mistaking him for you. I'll have to live with that for the rest of my life. We've missed so many years because of it." I slide my hand behind his neck and pull him towards me so his forehead rests against mine. "*This* is not the face of my killer. This is the face of the boy I left behind.

The boy I loved, and the man I want to spend the rest of my life with. There's nothing of Shane in you, Bay."

A strangled noise comes from him as he shakes his head.

"Yes." I run my thumb over his bottom lip, wet from both our tears. "Stay with me, mo ghráidh. I'll show you every day who you are."

He kisses me gently and breathes against my lips for a moment before he whispers, "I never want to leave."

FORTY-THREE

BAILEY - ONE WEEK LATER

"So you're both going back tomorrow?" I ask, looking between Jake and Noah.

"Yeah, it's been far too long since I've been in the office. Don't want everyone thinking they can slack off," Jake says, downing the rest of his pint. He smirks at me.

"What?"

"You don't want to leave, do you?"

"No," I mutter, picking at the chipped wood on the pub table.

"What if you didn't have to?"

I peek up at him to see his green eyes glint in the firelight. "What do you mean?"

"I've been wanting to expand the company for a while now. I have some money saved up that would allow me to set up in the Highlands and Islands region. Specifically, one island."

"What are you saying, Jake?"

"I'm going to set up a branch here on Skye, but I'll need someone to run it, seeing as I'll be down in Cumbria."

"Seriously? Shit…" My voice wobbles. "I can stay?" I whisper.

Jake chuckles. "Yeah, kid, you can stay."

I'm almost bouncing in my seat. I want to go home to tell Teddy, but he's supposed to be sleeping, and I don't want to wake him up.

I jump as someone coughs behind me. When I turn around, my eyes go straight to a pair of heavily tattooed arms crossed over a broad chest, then up to a thick ginger beard and blue eyes.

"What's up, Luke?" Jake asks.

"I, ah, I need to talk before you leave," he mutters in his deep Scottish burr.

Jake's fingers go straight to his septum piercing, fiddling with it like he does when he's nervous, then he looks at me. "Bailey, I'll talk to you later about the details of everything, but for now concentrate on you and Theo, alright? You'll still be paid while we set the business up."

"Alright," I say, smiling at him. "Thanks, Jake."

He stands up and tucks his chair under the table, then follows Luke out of the pub.

"What about you? Are you still going?" I ask Noah.

He stirs his gin and tonic with the straw, frowning. "Yeah, I'm going back with Jake tomorrow."

"Will you be alright? You know, without—"

"I'll be fine," he says quickly, cutting me off before I can mention his sleeping habits. It's going to be weird not having him crawl into my bed every night, and I'm worried about how he'll get on without me. He really doesn't do well when he's on his own.

"If Jake is setting up an office here, why don't you just stay too?"

"Why would I stay?"

I frown at him. "You've been sleeping at Robbie's for the past few weeks, I assumed—"

"Nothing happened," he snaps. "He let me sleep in his bed, and that was it."

"Oh."

"I'll come up to see you in a couple of weeks. See how you're getting on with all the police bollocks."

I groan at the thought of it. They've left me alone for the past week, but I know it's all coming. There's the small relief of not having to go to court, but I'll still have to do interviews, and I'm not sure if they'll let me bring Teddy with me ...

"I'm glad you're staying," Noah says. "I think you're good for each other."

"You feeling okay? Was that something nice that just came out of your mouth?" I tease.

"Alright, I'm glad Teddy showed up because I was worried for a minute that you'd be perpetually single," he smirks. "Better?"

"Much," I say dryly. "Alright, I gotta go. I'll see you in a couple of weeks."

He salutes me, and I head out the pub, eager to tell Teddy the news.

When I get back, I can't control the grin that spreads across my face as I run into the cottage and upstairs to the bedroom. He's already awake, thankfully, so I jump on the bed, avoiding his leg, crashing my lips against his.

"What the hell?" he sputters into my mouth.

"I'm staying," I murmur against his lips.

He grabs my shoulders and pushes me away forcefully, frowning. "What do you mean you're staying?"

"Jake said he's going to set up shop here on Skye and he wants me to manage it," I grin, watching his eyes search my face.

"Really?" he asks, breath puffing out of him like a weight's been lifted from his chest.

"Really."

Teddy grabs my collar and drags me back into the kiss, and I melt against his side. All my anxiety drifts away, and I realise that Teddy was right. My home has always been with him.

FORTY -FOUR

"How's the office coming along?" Teddy asks as he prepares some sandwiches. The last month has been spent getting everything set up at the new office, and there's been a lot of driving back and forth between Skye and Cumbria. Much to my annoyance. I don't like leaving Teddy for long, and every time I go, I feel sick, like I'm never going to see him again.

"It's coming ..." I mutter, walking over to him and giving him a kiss.

"Do you need to go back again soon?"

"No, that should be it. If there's anything left, then Noah can bring it up when he visits next."

Teddy stops making his sandwich and grabs me around the waist before I can walk away, pulling me back against him, my hand getting trapped between us. "Good, I miss you when you're gone."

The tips of my ears heat up as I feel his voice rumble in his chest. "Yeah?"

"Yeah." He grins at me, hands slipping down to my arse, squeezing. I push him away and run, adrenaline coursing through my veins as he chases me up the stairs. We stumble into the bedroom, pulling at one another's clothes as we go. Teddy's mouth is everywhere: biting at my lips, sucking at my neck, working his way down my body until he gets to my hips. He drags my briefs down, kissing the tip of my hard cock softly as his hands stroke over my scars. My knees buckle and I go limp, gripping onto his shoulders to hold myself up.

He sucks me into the heat of his mouth, and my toes curl at how tight it is. "Fuck, Teddy," I moan as he bobs up and down along my length, over and over, until he pulls off to suck my balls into his mouth, one after the other, making my stomach tighten and my thighs tense from trying to control myself.

When he comes back up, we're chest-to-chest, and I can feel his heart thumping just as erratically as mine. I grab his hand and walk backwards towards the bed until my legs brush against it. I take a deep breath, making a decision—one I've thought about a lot recently. I slide backwards, pulling Teddy with me. His brow furrows, but he puts a knee up on the bed anyway, climbing on with me. I pull him until he's pressing his weight down on top of me.

Teddy's legs weave between mine, and his cock presses against my hip as he rests some of his weight on one elbow. I hold my breath, waiting to see if I'll panic from being caged in. I never take my eyes off his, feeling the length of his body— how it fits against mine.

I'm safe here.

It's just Teddy.

He won't hurt me.

"Like this," I say quietly, spreading my legs so that he can move between them.

"Yeah?" he asks, eyes slightly wide.

"Yeah."

Teddy leans down and presses his lips to mine, running his

tongue along my bottom lip, teasing the entrance before slipping it inside to tangle with mine. My cock throbs, pushing against his in response. He pulls away, reaching into the bedside drawer to grab the lube, then squirts some on his fingers.

I suck in a breath when he pushes against my hole, rubbing circles until it gives. He works me open while kissing my neck, and I writhe on the bed, relief washing over me—I don't feel trapped this time. I can lie here and let him take care of me, just like he used to.

Teddy sits back on his knees, lining himself up. "Still okay?" he asks, brow creased in concern.

"I'm good," I say, voice coming out husky. He goes to push forward, but I quickly sit up and put a hand on his chest. "Wait—your leg. Can you ... are you okay to?"

"I've been cleared for exercise. I'm fine, Bay."

I lie back down, and he slowly pushes inside me, lighting up my nerves as he bottoms out. I squeeze his forearms and hold on as he pulls out of me again, then back in. He does it again, and everything is so slow and controlled—I can't stand it.

"Teddy," I whine.

"What's wrong, mo leannan?" he asks, barely hiding the laughter in his voice.

"Please." I grip his arse, pulling him into me again, making my whole body light up.

"You like the feel of my cock buried deep inside you, Bay?"

I nod repeatedly as he picks up speed.

He hooks his elbows under my knees and leans over me, whispering in my ear. "Want me to fuck you hard?"

"Y-yes."

He pulls back then slams back into me, and my back arches as I cry out. He does it again and again, deliberately controlled yet forceful, hitting my prostate every time. His mouth latches onto my neck and sucks there, teeth nipping until pain mixes with pleasure.

I'm getting close. Every time he moves his stomach rubs against my cock. All I can do is lie here, body loose, mind gone as he drags me closer to the edge.

"Think you can cum for me? I'm barely holding on here," he chuckles, nipping my bottom lip.

"Faster," I say, putting my hands under my lower back to tilt my arse up. He slides in deeper, and I pant as he speeds up. "I'm close, Teddy; I want to feel you cum in me," I plead. He grunts against my mouth as his cock pulses inside me. His orgasm sets me off, and I feel my cum flood between us as our chests glide against one another. He continues to move slowly in and out as he softens, tongue languidly exploring my mouth.

When he finally pulls out, he goes to stand up, but loses his balance. I scramble out of the bed and force him to lie down. "What are you doing?"

"I was getting something to clean you up," he says quietly, rubbing around his scar.

"I can do that," I huff, going to the bathroom to grab a flannel. "You overdid it, didn't you?" I ask as I throw it to him.

"No," he says, avoiding looking at me.

"Are you lying to me?"

He peeks up at me through his dark curls. "Yes ..."

"You need to rest."

"But I want my sandwich," he says, trying to get off the bed again.

"I'll get the bloody sandwich, just stay still." I shove him back and head to the kitchen. I'm surprised he's got as much mobility back as he has. Trying to force the man to rest has been a nightmare over the past few months. There have been mood swings and arguments in between all the soft moments, and yet I'll happily put up with his grumpy arse for the rest of my life now that he's mine again.

"TEDDY?" I call out, looking in the living room for him. I slept like a log and didn't notice him get out of bed, but now I can't find him anywhere in the house. My palms sweat, and prickles go up my spine as I open the back door. "Teddy?" I shout.

I try to stay calm, banging the Wellington boots upside down against the wall before sliding them on and grabbing my coat. It's four in the morning, and the air is frigid as I step outside. I make my way across the fields, hopping over stiles and avoiding sheep as I go, until I finally get to the back field where I spot Heather and Rosie lounging about. As I get closer, I find Teddy wedged between the two of them, fast asleep. "Teddy, get up." I shake his shoulder. He groans, batting my hand away. "Come on, it's not warm enough to sleep out here."

His eyes flutter open, and he rubs his face. "Sorry, I had a nightmare."

I hold my hand out to help him up. "You should have woke me up."

"It's fine. I'm used to them. I like to come down to see the girls anyway," he says, stroking Heather's nose.

I don't know why it didn't click last time, maybe because I was in a spiral of my own, but now I realise why he said they calm him. "You ground yourself," I mutter.

"I what?"

"You use the cows to ground yourself. They break the cycle of anxiety, which helps you to calm down."

"I haven't heard of that before."

I've been thinking for a while now that I should bring this up with him. We talk about how we're feeling and about what happened with Shane quite a lot. Neither of us wants to keep things locked up inside again, but I know that's not enough. "Have you been to therapy at all?" I ask carefully.

"No. I didn't need therapy. I *don't* need therapy. It was all getting better. Just ... these past few months, it's like I'm right back where I started."

"Everything's heightened again? The nightmares, the mood swings ... flashbacks?"

"Yes."

"Noah made me start therapy when I was twenty-five because I was yelling out in my sleep and would keep him up all night. It took a lot of persuading, but I did it. I told her about my relationship with my mum, and about what Dean did to me, but I was too scared to tell her anything about Shane because I thought I'd get in trouble." I reach out to stroke Heather, flexing my fingers in her undercoat. "Even without telling her about Shane, I was told I had complex post-traumatic stress disorder."

"PTSD?" Teddy asks quietly.

"Yeah, but as it was going on for years, it became a little more complicated. Both are the result of trauma, and Teddy, what Shane did to you was traumatic, even before he stabbed you. You get that, right?" The expression on his face cuts right through me. He still hasn't told his family about what happened to him in Surrey. Kept it all inside for years, and now he's realising that what I'm saying is making sense. I've been there too. I didn't understand how everything that happened in my childhood was leaving more than physical scars, and I didn't want to admit that even when I was free of my family, my body still didn't register that I was safe.

"It's nothing like what he did to you, though. He was just trying to scare me."

"No, Teddy. He was trying to kill you," I say sternly, because I think he's still not realising the severity of it all. I step close to him and cup his face. "Now I'm here for good, I want to try and find a therapist in Portree. Maybe ... maybe you'd want to come with me to check it out?"

He blinks slowly, then bends down to kiss me gently. "I can try."

EPILOGUE

SIX MONTHS LATER

"Two cappuccinos for Bailey," the server calls.

I rush over to the counter to collect my order, then head down the street to meet Teddy. He's just coming out the door when I get to our therapist's office, his mouth splitting into a wide grin when he sees me.

"Everything go okay?" I ask, thrusting the coffee into his hand.

He nods, taking a sip. "Today was less heavy. He told me how to calm myself down from panic attacks—which I didn't realise I've been partly doing instinctively, anyway. But there were some new things to try. Different ways to ground myself."

"Using the senses?"

"Yeah, and a thing called a butterfly hug ... have you done that?" He side-eyes me, looking a little self-conscious.

"I've tried everything I could in the past five years, honestly." I've heard this all before from my own sessions, but I listen to every word. Proud of him for agreeing to go to therapy after I suggested it might help him. He didn't even argue; it took a few months to find the courage, but after coming with me, he booked his first session straight away. I think he just needed someone to tell him it was okay to go. That what happened to him shouldn't be compared to anyone else's trauma.

Teddy takes my hand as we walk down the street, and it's so ... normal. It catches me off guard. I realise that even if Teddy and I *had* left together twelve years ago, we would still be in the same place we are now. Holding hands as we walk through Portree, with two cappuccinos.

Both in therapy.

Both survivors.

My chest feels tight, and I squeeze Teddy's hand a little harder. I'm angry about the years we lost, but nothing could have kept us apart. I smile at that and lean over to kiss his cheek, his beard tickling my lips.

He looks at me and mischief sparkles in his eyes. "Wanna know what else he said?"

"What?"

"I should spend time with nature and take note of the details within the natural world," he says, mimicking his therapist's thicker accent.

I look up.

And up.

And up a bit more.

"No," I say.

"Come on! The therapist said it was good for me, I'm sure it wouldn't do you any harm either," Teddy whines.

I glare at him. "If you think climbing a bloody tree won't do me any harm, or you, for that matter, then you should go right back to your therapist and tell him you're delusional, too."

Teddy laughs, then quickly schools his face to glare back at me. "Climb the tree, Bay."

"No."

He stalks towards me, and I retreat, fully prepared to run.

"Come on, I'll give you a boost." He sticks out his bottom lip, and those brown eyes go wide like a puppy's.

Fuck him. He knows that works on me. I stomp over to the trunk where there's a lower-hanging branch and cross my arms over my chest. "Fine."

Teddy beams as he jogs over and bends down, cupping his hands. I place my foot on them, wondering why I'm doing this. He pushes me up, and I manage to pull myself onto the branch.

"Happy?" I ask.

He scrambles up after me, then sits, huffing and puffing. "That wasn't as easy as the last time."

"You did it topless last time, maybe your clothes made it more difficult," I say sarcastically.

He shoves me, making me wobble. My fingernails dig into the bark on the branch, and I look daggers at him. "Okay, I've touched enough nature. I want to go down now," I say.

Teddy groans, but jumps down from the branch, turning to hold his arms up to me. "Come on, then."

Feeling a little stupid, but not trusting my coordination enough to turn down his offer of help, I shift as far forward as I can, then drop into his open arms.

"Oof," Teddy wheezes out. His legs give out instantly, and we collapse to the floor.

Lucky for me, he softened the fall. "Thought you said it wouldn't do any harm," I say, laughing at his scrunched up face. I push myself off of him, but he wraps his arms around me and flips us over. He kisses up my neck and along my jaw, capturing my lips before pulling away again.

"Would you do it again?" he asks, brushing his thumb against my bottom lip.

I don't have to think twice. Nodding, I ask, "Would you?"

"Always," he whispers.

The End.

About the Author

Jordan Victoria lives in the suburbs south of London with her partner and two guinea pigs, Merry and Pippin.

Diagnosed with ADHD at eight years old, she didn't realise until her thirties that her many hobbies were just a rotation of hyper fixations. Writing had been one of those passions that came and went throughout her life, too quickly to ever finish a manuscript.

Finally she has managed to focus long enough to complete a whole novel.

And if she's reading this in a few years time, feeling lost, she needs to remember that she did it once, and she can do it again.

Acknowledgments

Firstly, I would like to thank one of my best friends, Lore, my editor Kevin, and one of my favourite authors, Marra Moore.

When I finally got the courage to try writing again after years of picking it up and dropping it, I sent these three some of the first chapters I wrote for TFOMK, and their feedback and encouragement was paramount in giving me the confidence to carry on. Since then, all three have been by my side throughout the making of this book.

Secondly, through Marra I met some incredible people who eventually became both my friends and my beta team. So I'd like to thank J.E. Ridge (Jen), Risa Cruise, Lizzy, Kat, and of course Marra for going through my second draft, and helping me see the potential of a rewrite. It was both daunting and exhilarating seeing how I could chop and change my work around to make it the best I possibly can. An extra thank you to Jen for reading through my third draft after the rewrite! Your comments really settled my anxiety and reassured me that I hadn't ruined the whole thing. And to Kat who offered to proofread TFOMK so that it was ready for publication. A lot of stress was alleviated through finding these friends in the MM book space, and I really don't think I would have got this far without them.

Thirdly to my editor Kevin, who I met on Reddit of all places, just to read my first chapter for feedback as an author to author favour. His editing journey coincided with my writing journey, and I honestly couldn't have wished for a better editor. He's done an excellent job.

Thank you to Lore and Terri, who also beta read for me, and to the readers who have joined me on my writing journey. My ARC team has shown incredible support for a debut indie author, and I appreciate every one of them who took a chance on me.

Additionally, I need to thank an incredible artist, Lea, who created the portraits for Teddy and Bailey, of which Bailey is now the most stunning cover model ever. My cover artist Katie, whose patience is ceaseless, and my sensitivity reader Aaron, whose research and knowledge on cPTSD and PTSD helped strengthen Bailey and Teddy's characters so much.

I struggle with anxiety, and over the past nine months it has fluctuated so much. I have two people who really helped me when I was spiraling, and needed a little grounding. So thank you to Lore and Theo (T. Rossmaur) for putting up with me having breakdowns in your DMs, and calming me.

Finally I'd like to thank my partner James, who has had to deal with me being a ghost of myself. When I hyperfixate on something, nothing else exists, so a lot of things get forgotten, or put off. His encouragement to finish the book helped to relieve some of the guilt when I felt like I'd really closed in on myself.